Georgia surrendered to the thundering hooves on the field.

Clueless as she was about the rules, and impossible as polo was to follow, she found herself completely absorbed. The game was thrilling and undeniably sexy. The players and ponies seem to merge together, storming down the field at top speed, fighting for the ball, blocking and marking each other mercilessly.

Alejandro was at the heart of it, the best of them all. He dove through the other players on a magnificent roan, man and horse, perfect specimens, fused as a team. It took tremendous skill to move as nimbly as he did. He was twisting and turning, wielding his mallet like the right hand of Thor. Over and over again, he made the crowd gasp, taking huge risks, riding within inches of the other ponies but always managing to pull back just in time.

All the pent-up energy that she'd noticed in the press tent suddenly made sense. This man was made to ride.

Nacho Figueras Presents:
High Season

NACHO FIGUERAS
PRESENTS:

High
Season

Jessica Whitman

Book One in The Polo Season Series

FOREVER

New York Boston

Copyright © 2016 by Ignacio Figueras
Excerpt from *Wild One* copyright © 2016 by Ignacio Figueras
Cover design by Elizabeth Turner
Cover illustration by Alan Ayers; author photo by Claudio Marinesco; horses photo by Ty Milford/Masterfile
Cover copyright © 2016 by Hachette Book Group, Inc.

Forever
Hachette Book Group
1290 Avenue of the Americas
New York, NY 10104
hachettebookgroup.com
twitter.com/foreverromance

Printed in the United States of America

OPM

First Edition: May 2016
10 9 8 7 6 5 4 3 2 1

Forever is an imprint of Grand Central Publishing.
The Forever name and logo are trademarks of Hachette Book Group, Inc.

The publisher is not responsible for websites (or their content) that are not owned by the publisher.

The Hachette Speakers Bureau provides a wide range of authors for speaking events. To find out more, go to www.hachettespeakersbureau.com or call (866) 376-6591.

ISBN 978-1-4555-6361-6 (trade paperback edition)
ISBN 978-1-4555-6364-7 (mass market edition)
ISBN 978-1-4555-6363-0 (ebook edition)

To my wonderful wife, Delfi—for giving me
Hilario, Aurora, Artemio, and Alba. You are
all the best things that ever happened to me.

Dear Reader,

I first learned to ride a horse when I was four years old, and I started playing the sport of polo by the time I was nine. Tango was the horse on which I learned to play, and she was my first love. I fell in love with the beauty of horses and idolized the strength and bravery of the best players. In my native Argentina, everyone has a chance to go to polo matches and see how thrilling they are. It has been my dream to share the game that I love, the game that has given me so much—as a person and an athlete—with the rest of the world.

I think polo is a very appealing thing. There's a reason Ralph Lauren chose it. There is something very sexy about a man and a horse and the speed and the adrenaline. It's very appealing to women. That's a fact.

It was at a polo match that I met my wife. I was in the stands and she was coming up the stairs, and I looked at her and she looked at me, and we looked at each other. I knew her cousin. I went to the cousin and said, "Can you introduce me?" The cousin tells me, "That's funny; she just asked me the same thing." So the cousin introduced us, and we talked for a little bit. It was the beginning of the summer, and we didn't see each other for two or three months. After the holiday, we saw each other and started dating, and we have been together ever since...

I am very excited to present the Polo Season series, which blends my favorite sport with a little bit of romance. Whether you're already a polo fan or completely new to the game, I hope you will enjoy these characters and their stories.

Nacho Figueras Presents:
High Season

Chapter One

No!" Georgia laughed. "I have exactly zero interest in polo."

"Only because you haven't seen it played," said Billy. "It's actually amazing. The way they fight it out on the field, all snarled together, slamming up against each other, a sweaty, dangerous tangle of heaving chests and pumping legs..."

Georgia shook her head at Billy's handsome, teasing face on the Skype screen. "I can't tell if you're describing the ponies or the players."

Billy quirked an eyebrow. "Well, both, actually. Anyway, Peaches, please. For me. One week in Wellington. It will be so much fun! We'll do it right. And, okay, full disclosure, I've met someone, and I desperately need your opinion."

"Of course you do," said Georgia. Ever since they met at Cornell, there had been a never-ending series of inappropriate men Billy desperately needed her opinion on. "What's his name?"

"Beau."

"No. Seriously?"

"I know. It's a Virginia thing. He rides to hounds. Don't you love how that sounds? I think he might be The One."

She laughed. "Because he rides to hounds?"

"No, because he's cute, and sweet, and a little bit rich, and he does this thing with his tongue that makes my—"

Georgia threw up her hands. "Okay, okay, spare me the details."

"Honest, Georgie, this is not just about me. You'd love this place. It's sunshine and high fashion, perfect beaches, gorgeous people, million-dollar ponies, oh, and the wildest and most decadent parties you can imagine!"

"Yes, well, I sunburn on sight," she said, "and as for fashion, I believe that you once told me that I dress like last season's bag lady. Even the idea of a Palm Beach party makes me break out in hives, and besides"—she glanced out the window at the snowy, moonlit, upstate New York farm—"I have horses that need me here."

Since graduating with her degree in veterinary medicine, Georgia had been helping her dad on the farm and assisting in the village animal hospital. It wasn't exactly a challenge—basically she was handing out tick medicine and checking for worms, with the occasional trip to a stable in the case of a colic false alarm—but she knew she was lucky to have found work that let her be where she was needed.

The farm consisted of a dilapidated stone cottage and a sagging barn set on ten acres of meadow at the edge of the Catskills. The place was so ancient that it was practically open to the elements, and cost a fortune to heat. Without her help, Georgia knew her dad would sell, and she couldn't stand the idea of losing their home.

There were definitely days when Georgia wondered if she'd parked all her ambition the moment she had arrived back home, but her father had gone into debt to finance her education, and helping him now was payback. If she sometimes found herself daydreaming about missed opportunities and other, perhaps bigger, lives, she quickly shook it off. She loved the farm and she loved her father, and they both needed her. That was enough.

Billy rolled his dark brown eyes in frustration, visibly filtering a retort about what he obviously considered to be Georgia's sad-ass life. "Georgia. All respect. But there are horses, and then there are *horses*. The team that Beau is down here with are, like, among the top ten polo players in the world."

"Are there even ten people who play?"

Billy sighed in exasperation. "There are tens of thousands, probably. And you are absolutely missing the point. It's a sexy, savage game, and I'm telling you, you will love it. Plus, it's totally trending."

"Right," Georgia said. "Among the one percent."

"Don't be snarky just because you're stuck in the snowy wasteland not getting any. Please, Peaches. I really like this guy. And I think he really likes me. But you know how bad I am at this. Every time I fall for someone, he ends up sleeping with my cousin, or emptying my bank account..."

"Or stealing your car," snorted Georgia.

"Oh God, I can't believe that actually happened twice," he groaned, "but you see! That's exactly what I'm talking about. I need your unbiased opinion. You're the only one I can trust."

"Billy, I'm sorry, I just can't."

"Georgia, who was there for you when you found out that skinny hipster you called a boyfriend was secretly banging that waitress with the uni-boob?"

Georgia rolled her eyes and sighed. "You were."

"And who sat up with you all night drinking cheap wine and watching *Downton Abbey* until you felt better?"

She shifted reluctantly in her seat. "You did."

"And so, who is going to get her narrow ass down to Florida and make sure her BFF isn't making another colossal romantic mistake?"

Georgia gave a groan of defeat. "All right," she said. "Four days. That's it."

"Yay!" Billy cheered. "You're going to love it! Cocktails. Scandal. Strappy dresses. Trust me. It will be everything you need. I'll text directions."

Georgia snapped her laptop shut and fed the woodstove. As she climbed the stairs to bed, her shadow was animated by the flare of the fire.

She undressed, shivering at the window, staring up at the milky indigo sky and full moon. Slipping under the covers, she wrapped her arms around herself as she waited for her bed to warm. She started thinking about all she'd need to do before she left, what she'd need to pack . . . It was one of the hard parts about traveling—the way it made her so restless. The minute a plan was in place, everywhere her mind fell, there was something that needed to be done.

She closed her eyes, trying not to think, willing herself to relax while wondering why this little trip felt like something so much bigger, a kind of seismic shift. The bed slowly warmed but she couldn't let go. She lay there in the dark, a thousand thoughts flickering through her mind like so many fireflies on an inky summer night, each one determined to keep her awake and unsettled.

Chapter Two

The horse let out a whinny, and Alejandro swore softly in Spanish. The last thing he wanted to do was wake the entire barn. He slipped a halter on MacKenzie, the favorite in his current string of ponies, and led her out of the stables. The moon was bright in the sky as he swung onto the pony's bare back. With a snort, she broke into a trot.

Approaching the gatehouse, Alejandro gave the guard a curt nod. He was determined not to seem furtive riding his own horse on his own time, but the guard's professional discretion didn't disguise his surprise that Alejandro was taking a pony out at night without a saddle. The Del Campo family team, La Victoria, had a match tomorrow, and with the odds already stacked against them, Alejandro knew he should be home in bed, not tiring out his best pony with a hard-riding midnight outing.

He couldn't sleep, though. Not yet. It was one of those nights when the darkness weighed down and his mind raced on. He felt particularly caged in Wellington. Every last inch of the landscape was tamed. For all its luxury, he felt trapped by the gated community—his guards and staff and fleets of grooms—when what he needed was a solitary ride in the wilderness. That's why he rode at night, willing to risk the hidden dangers on the dimly lit paths—the possibility of a shadowed dip in the earth where a hoof could catch, a nocturnal animal suddenly darting out in front of them and spooking his pony—in exchange for having the roads to himself. He needed to gallop, skin to skin, even if only for a short stretch, to lose himself in the strength and speed of his horse. To reach that soaring, unifying moment that felt less like riding and more like flying, when he and the horse joined together to become one seamless beast.

Alejandro turned onto the canal road, leaned forward, and tightened his thighs—clicking his tongue and murmuring in Spanish until the pony's gait smoothed out into a fluid gallop.

MacKenzie picked up speed, responding to his movements as if she could read his mind. Alejandro smiled. This pony loved to run. She was one of the few horses who could sustain this kind of pace and still be in world-class form the next morning. MacKenzie was such a fighter that she seemed to gain more fire, more heart, with every step she took. He'd find a role for her in the match tomorrow. She needed the game as much as he did.

He pressed his legs harder, driving the horse faster, determined to calm his buzzing mind and push his body until he could collapse, exhausted. It was practically the only way he could get any sleep these days.

It didn't use to be so hard, he thought, slowing to a canter. He'd always slept like a baby after they won a match, but Lord knows, those wins were few and far between these days. A few glasses of wine occasionally worked, but he'd stopped drinking as part of his training, knowing that even if the alcohol initially brought him relief, he'd be wide awake a few hours later, eyes on the ceiling, while ghosts and shadows chased through his brain...

He shook his head, wishing for other ways to exhaust himself.

A string of images flashed through his mind. The sweet, silken curve of an inner thigh. The beckoning swell between waist and hip. A flirtatious smile thrown over a naked shoulder, inviting him to take what he wanted...

He swore to himself and rode harder, violently shutting down this train of thought and replacing it with the simple conviction he had come to focus on since the death of his wife—he had to win. And in particular, he had to qualify for and win the biggest game of the season, the upcoming Carlos Del Campo Memorial Cup, named after his own late father.

In determined pursuit of this goal, Alejandro had turned to abstinence in this last year, in every sense of the word. He had given up most earthly pleasures—drinking, women, unnecessary socializing, anything that could distract him from the game—and channeled all his restless feelings of grief and anger directly into his training. Spending every spare moment in the saddle, mercilessly pushing his already hard and athletic body as close to perfection as he could get, riding until he could barely walk. And yet, despite his absolute focus on the field, La Victoria had already lost more games than they had won this season, making a mockery of their name.

Alejandro wanted to blame his other teammates. If only they would train harder, pay better attention, be willing to sacrifice more. His younger brother, Sebastian, for example, could barely bother to turn up for practice most days, much more interested in taking advantage of the endless parade of polo groupies that were at his beck and call. Rory, the other young pro on the field, was talented but suggestible, and only too eager to follow Seb's party-happy lead. Lord Henderson, the *patrón*, had once been a formidable athlete, but a lifetime of hard playing had taken its toll on the older man, and these days, like many *patróns*, it was more his ability to bankroll half of the team's expenses that secured his place on the field. Really, when Alejandro thought about it, it was a miracle they ever won a game.

Still, deep down, he knew that, as team captain, the responsibility for their losses ultimately lay upon his own shoulders. And that, despite his absolute personal focus and relentless pursuit of the cup, he was somehow failing them all.

Alejandro kicked his pony on, trying to shake loose his feelings of uncertainty and loss, to shed them like scales in his wake. The heavy sound of MacKenzie's hoofbeats, the dull thump of his own heart pounding, all resounded as one. Behind them, motes of sand kicked up by MacKenzie's hooves briefly danced in the moonlight and sparked a glimmering silver trail.

He rode until his body felt leaden, his muscles ached, and the sultry Florida air had soaked his shirt all the way through. Finally, turning for home, he felt the pull of his bed and knew that now he'd rest and get at least a few hours of sleep before he was up and ready to show the world his game face again.

Chapter Three

The moon had stayed bright all night, disturbing Georgia's every settled thought, until she finally fell into a shallow sleep. Too soon, she woke to the harsh scrape of the snow shovel and turned off the alarm before it rang.

Rolling out of bed in the dim gray light, she found she couldn't even put on her clothes without worrying what in hell she was going to wear in Wellington. Georgia believed she'd been born missing the fashionista gene and normally didn't care, but she knew, if she was to be seen with Billy, she'd have to raise her game. Her friend was always immaculately dressed and styled, and it wouldn't do for Georgia to look like an escapee from the Old Navy bargain bin.

She went downstairs, throwing a couple of logs on the glowing embers in the woodstove as she passed by. At the door, she shrugged on her coat, unballed a pair of gloves, and wedged her feet into her boots. Melvin, a sweet-eyed, elderly Australian shepherd, sighed in protest before he stiffly tottered out of his bed by the woodstove and followed her outside.

The clouds had swallowed the hills and turned the farm's

normally stunning view of the Catskills into a white blob. The snow shovel stood by the porch door, abandoned, and there was no sign of her dad. Georgia slipped and skidded across the drive, scattering salt as she went, and stepped into the warmer air of the barn, where she was welcomed with a low nicker from an old Mustang named Ben. She ran her hand along the length of his nose and cupped his velvet mouth while he chomped on an apple from the bin. She tightened his blankets and, having smashed the disk of ice that had formed in the barrel overnight, topped up his water. *Poor horses*, Georgia thought. Too bad she couldn't take them to Florida, too. They could all use some winter sun.

As she worked, Georgia considered the question of how to break Billy's plan to Dad. Looking around the barn, she saw a thousand places where she could be putting the cost of a trip to Florida. In the fifteen years since her mother had left, it was like the whole place had slowly run out of gas. There was a big blue tarp on the roof like a badge of shame, a pile of rotting lumber under Tyvek that was supposed to be the new shed, and icicles the length of ladders from the corner of every cracked gutter.

In some ways, Georgia thought, winter did the place a favor, landscaping the ragged yard in blinding white and making the little stone cottage look like a gingerbread house framed in icing. But if you took a second look, the cheerful front porch was starting to sag, the flaking paint on the carved trim looked gray against the snow, and Georgia knew, if they didn't get that woodwork touched up soon, it was going to start letting in the weather.

She started to clean out the stalls, shoveling muck into a wheelbarrow. Jenny, the one-eyed donkey, licked at her hair while a small parade of barn cats wound their way around her ankles, anxious to be fed.

She gently pressed back the cats with her leg while filling their bowls. She had never met a stray—dog, cat, horse, or otherwise—she could turn away, and after her mother left, her dad completely lost his ability to say no. Before they knew it, they had a ridiculously big menagerie of mouths to feed. Georgia was always amazed how love expanded to let every new animal in.

When her mother had been with them, the farm had supported itself; Susan Fellowes had family money, and savvy, and knew enough about breeding and training horses to keep things solvent. But as soon as she and her Thoroughbreds left, the cash slowed to a trickle and the family was never much more than poor. But Georgia's dad, Joe, had done a great job of keeping that to himself. She'd managed to spend her teens blissfully oblivious to their money issues. She'd felt so comfortable in their scruffy little house growing up, but once she went away to college, she could see her home more clearly when she came back, and she realized just how tight things had become.

As she finished shoveling out the stall, she thought about how great a little vacation would be, although the whole point of living at home was to give her father the relief he'd been needing for years. Georgia couldn't help feeling selfish for leaving him—even if it was only for four days.

She finished with Ben and the goats and chickens, grabbed an armful of logs for the stove and trudged back inside, Melvin at her heels. Her dad was on the phone about a job so she fed the stove and gestured with the kettle to ask if he wanted tea. He nodded yes.

Her phone chimed. There was a text from Billy about a

prepaid plane ticket. *Bring a bikini!* Just for a second, his un-expected generosity made tears smart in Georgia's eyes.

She handed her dad a cup of hot tea, tossed Melvin a bis-cuit, and then realizing her father wasn't going to be off the phone anytime soon, headed upstairs to unearth some clothes for the trip.

Chapter Four

Looking in her closet, Georgia ruefully concluded she had everything she could ever want to wear if she were painting a house. Most of her T-shirts were torn or stretched. All her favorite jeans were frayed at the heels. The sweaters had holes at the elbows. Practically everything was covered in horse-hair.

She pulled out a pale gold bias-cut thing she'd worn to graduation, where it had gotten a drink splashed on it. Holding the dress to the light, Georgia confirmed that the stains were still there but barely. She shrugged. It was the one dress she had. She laid it on the bed.

She dug out a worn pair of flip-flops and ragged cutoffs and paused to consider a vintage string bikini. The thought of exposing skin in January was seriously scary—she didn't even want to think how white she was under her long johns.

But screw it, along with the swimsuit, she retrieved tweezers, a razor, and an ancient bottle of nail polish from under the sink and flung them all onto the bed. Since she had to work the late shift at the rabies clinic tonight, Georgia figured she'd wait until she actually arrived in Florida before removing the layers and doing some damage control.

What to wear to watch polo? Georgia thought about *Pretty Woman* and all that fluttering silk while the crowd did whatever it was they did with divots at halftime. She shook her head. Was she remembering wrong or did Richard Gere actually deck Julia out in a hat and white gloves? What kind of weird throwback was that? Georgia felt herself getting annoyed. It was typical Billy, who always looked perfect in every way, to give her packing anxiety.

She looked skyward for inspiration and almost laughed when she actually found some. She remembered that the attic contained vacuum-packed plastic bags of her mom's old clothes.

Susan Fellowes had been beautiful. Probably still was. When Georgia was little, her mother had seemed impossibly glamorous, switching from one elegant and appropriate outfit to the next with the thoughtless ease most people spent brushing their teeth. It wasn't so much that everything was expensive (though it probably was, Georgia realized now), it was more that she somehow wore clothes better than other people. Georgia, on the other hand, was secretly grateful to have veterinarian scrubs as an alibi against what she thought of as her total lack of style.

As she headed up to the attic, it was hard not to be aware of the ways the house had deteriorated since her mother left. Old rain leaks stained the ceiling, damp had blistered the wallpaper, and the banisters had been patiently waiting to be fixed for years. Georgia pushed down a rising tide of anxiety, one that had fueled her through grad school. She had the education now, she reassured herself. She had the job. She had everything she needed now to give back to her dad and start getting the house and farm on track.

She picked through a dusty garment rack in the corner of

the attic, choosing a particularly plump and promising bag. She opened the seal and watched the plastic gradually un-crinkle and expand as if it were alive. There were dresses and slips and wide-legged pants. Georgia even found the garter her mother must have worn to her wedding. Shaking out a creased red sundress, she was suddenly hit with the memory of her mom in this—her smooth, tan shoulders, long neck, and chic cap of hair. Susan had paired the dress with strappy high heels and an armful of gold bangles that chimed like bells whenever she moved.

The dress still smelled faintly of her mother's scent, clove and roses, and the smell summoned an indelible memory of her mother's cool lips kissing her cheek. That would have been the day after Georgia's ninth birthday. Her mother was leaving again. That was when Georgia had realized birthday wishes don't always come true.

Her mom had lived for show jumping, and if she wasn't training, then she was leaving for a competitive circuit that seemed to expand to fill the year. She was always either about to leave or just back, looking exhilarated but talking about how exhausted she was. To her daughter, she had seemed like a glorious Thoroughbred on a lunge line, going in wider and wider circles until, one day shortly before Georgia turned fourteen, she disappeared from view for good.

Georgia tried to shake off the sadness and, summoning a defiant sense of entitlement, slipped the red dress on. She zipped it up and smoothed out her hair in front of the big mirror leaning against the attic wall. When people said that Georgia looked like her mother, it made her feel hot and claustrophobic. There was no denying some of the ingre-dients were the same—beach brown hair (though Georgia's was usually tied back or clipped up on her head in a tangled pile while Susan's was always blown out to perfection) and the same almond-shaped hazel eyes under dark winged brows. But Georgia had inherited her dad's pale skin and dusting of freckles, and absolutely none of her mother's effortless elegance, she thought ruefully. With her full breasts and curves—good child-bearing hips, an ex had once told her—Georgia felt like a sturdy little Shetland compared to the high-crested Arabian that her mother had been.

She tugged at the neckline, uncomfortable. She was like a little girl playing dress-up, she thought. And she'd never been that kind of little girl.

Georgia remembered one of her last moments with her mother, watching through the bars of the banister as Susan packed. Georgia hadn't known yet that her mother was leaving for good, but she never much liked watching her prepare to go, and she'd been looking resentful and accusatory probably—judging her mother the way only a daughter can. Her mom had gazed back at her, meeting her eyes.

"You're not so different from me, my girl. You'll see."

Her words felt like a curse to Georgia.

Still did.

She shook her head at her reflection—ready to put the haunted red dress away—when the scuff of a sole made her jump and she saw that her dad had appeared beside her in the mirror, staring at her wearing the red dress with a world of hurt in his eyes. Before Georgia could explain, he turned and trudged heavily downstairs.

Chapter Five

Georgia talked to her boss, Dr. Jackson, and arranged to work a double shift at the clinic to make up for the time she'd be taking in Florida. She scrubbed her hands for the last patient of the day, snapped on some latex gloves, and got to work checking an old pug's cataracts.

Georgia liked her job. And her colleagues and clients. Beyond being good at what she did, she was always willing to linger and hear the story that pet owners needed to tell. Which meant she was invariably running late, but promptness counted for much less than compassion in this world.

Georgia smiled at the little pop-eyed canine and scratched him behind his ear. "Looks like you're not blind yet, Franklin." The cataracts were not as advanced as she had first feared. A good case to end the day on—nothing like telling a pet owner that their beloved animal was in the clear.

That night, Georgia found her dad with his feet up reading the paper. She put the groceries away and began to put together some supper. It was funny—he'd held everything together for the two of them for so long, but since she'd come home, he'd been making it abundantly clear he was happy now for her to take over. As she set the table, he actually said how nice it was to have a woman's touch around the place. Then he sighed and said he knew it couldn't last forever.

"It's just four days," she said. "You're not going to lose me to Florida."

Her dad gave a skeptical grunt.

"You know I'm not interested in Palm Beach and that whole scene."

"How are you going to get there?" her father asked.

"Billy's paying," she said quickly.

"That's not what I meant," he said, raising a brow at her defensiveness.

"Oh. Sorry. I'm flying out of Newburgh tomorrow."

"So you'll need a ride?"

Her dad said he needed the car—the only one they had in action, a twenty-year-old Mercedes—to get to an interview about a renovation in the morning. He'd been out of work too long for him to miss a job possibility, but a cab would cost way more than Georgia wanted to spend.

"So let's ask Sam," he said. Georgia hesitated but her dad was already dialing.

Sam was Georgia's high school ex. They'd dated for three years, until she'd discovered a pair of another girl's underwear beneath his bed. It was sickening to realize he'd been fooling around, but she'd had to admit that there was some secret relief, too. She'd been preparing to leave for college, and the question of whether they'd try to keep things up long distance had been needling at her. Sam seemed to take it for granted that they would wait it out, but Georgia wasn't so sure. The infidelity had made it easy—no question about what to do at that point. But when she'd confronted him, Sam had been genuinely devastated, swearing it was a one-time thing, begging to let him make it up to her.

He had eventually accepted her decision—because he had no choice, really—but that had not kept him from faithfully calling and texting and sending care packages for all the years she had been away. And while she dated off and on, nobody had ever felt as serious, and Georgia had continued to feel tethered to her ex through the years.

Now Sam was doing almost embarrassingly well as a tax attorney in town and seemed determined to finally get her back for good since she'd returned from college. Local consensus was that the two of them getting back together was inevitable. Georgia's dad never tried to hide his opinion that she should forgive a few teenage indiscretions when the man was a catch by any sensible standard.

But every time Sam turned up, with his gentle smile and soft, questioning eyes, Georgia couldn't quite bring herself to open that particular door. She made excuses. She found reasons to be busy. She had so far been pretty successful in staying out of his way but it wasn't easy in the face of such romantic tenacity. Sometimes, it seemed that her surrender was only a matter of time.

Chapter Six

Alejandro impatiently raked back his hair, tilted his jaw to the mirror, and rasped the razor over his soaped face. A few silver strands had appeared above his ears in the last year. To his eye, he was aging rapidly. It might help, he thought wryly, if he could get more than two hours' sleep at a stretch.

The day's match had failed to go his way. His team had been all over the place—harmony and strategy conspicuous by their absence and the opposition had taken full advantage. The humiliation was grim, and after the game, all he'd wanted to do was come home and be left in peace, but there could be no sitting out the evening's dinner.

Social life in Wellington was a performance sport every bit as exacting as the competitive riding to which the town played host. The remainder of the season stretched ahead of Alejandro like an unending road—only one month in and the prospect of all the glad-handing and interminable dinners left to go already seemed exhausting. Alejandro splashed the last soap from his face, looked himself in the eye, and told himself to buck the fuck up.

Despite the previous night's ill-considered ride, MacKenzie had played like a dream, and Alejandro's own performance hadn't been criminal. In many ways, he knew he was a better and more fearless player than he'd ever been. All his energy these last years had gone into riding, and grief seemed to have diminished his sense of risk.

But one daredevil player didn't win a match, and Alejandro knew very well that he was not the leader his father Carlos had been. He would never have the hold over his little brother Sebastian that their father once had, and today his brilliant but dissolute *hermano* had been, at best, dialing it in. Plus Rory had seemed distracted by a pretty blonde in the stands, and though Lord Henderson had done his best, his best could not make up for the others.

Still La Victoria weren't yet out of the running for the Carlos Del Campo Cup, and if he was going to redeem the season, what Alejandro really needed to bring to the team was inspiration, discipline, and a deft and unexpected unifying strategy. Shave done, he slapped some Polo Red on his cheeks and pulled on a fresh shirt.

A rancher at heart, Alejandro always slightly resented the effort of dressing for dinner. He'd rather have his team around the kitchen table in Argentina, legs stretched under the long, scrubbed pine table, than meet under what felt like stage lighting in a Florida club. Still, dinner at the Player's Club had been his mother's initiative and canceling on Pilar was not an option. Certainly she had lost as much as he had over the years, if not even more, and she had never let her own grief be an excuse to dodge a single commitment, so he could hardly hold up one rather pathetic game as justification to check out. Buffeted by tragedy the last few years, the Del Campos would never welcome pity. He must show the world that the family were not just surviving, but thriving.

He left his dressing room and took the stairs two at a time

to his daughter, Valentina's room. She was lying on her bed, swathed in a velour sweatsuit, her glossy black hair covered up in huge headphones. She gave him only a cursory glance.

"Fifteen minutes, V," he said. "Go ahead and change. We don't want to keep your *abuela* waiting."

In fact, Pilar was already waiting in the huge front hall of their home, a long-suffering look on her face. She thumbed a magazine, sapphires flashing at her wrist and ears.

He kissed his mother's cheek. "*Cinco minutos, Mamá,*" he said. "I just have to check the barn."

He had a good loyal team that traveled with him from Argentina, and stable hands converged from all over North America in Florida each year. The relocation of his team and family and thirty ponies was a huge undertaking and needed almost as much of his time as playing did.

He took a quick tour of the barn to see that the tuck— the last check of the evening—was under way without event. Conversation ended abruptly as he entered. The atmosphere was muted, as it always was after a lost game.

In front of so many of his staff, Alejandro was acutely aware of their disappointment, and he knew he should offer his crew some apology. He realized what a boost it would have been for every one of his people had he managed to win today.

And yet, he suddenly felt himself tongue-tied, unable to make one more apology after a solid year of apologies. So he merely left his staff with a brisk good night and drove the car round to the front of the house for his mother and daughter.

Chapter Seven

Before Alejandro could take the ticket from the club's valet parking guy, Valentina, wearing a dress so short that Alejandro had to quell his urge to take off his jacket and wrap it around her waist, stalked ahead to the restaurant entrance.

Sometimes it was hard for him not to watch her with worry. Three years on and he could see that she was still in the teeth of the tragedy. He occasionally wondered whether she would ever be okay again, whether the damage was permanent. Thirteen was such a hard age to lose a mother. Just when she was turning into a woman, she had lost her most trusted guide. Now, at sixteen, she had grown into a tempestuous beauty who looked, and sometimes acted, much older than her age. She could easily pass for twenty. Alejandro could see the eyes of every man she passed appraise his gorgeous daughter, and he struggled to bite back his temper. They thought they were looking at a woman, but she was just a little girl.

Alejandro glanced at his mother. Her wide green eyes never missed a thing, and though her lips almost imperceptibly pursed at Valentina's rudeness, she didn't say a word.

Alejandro knew that Pilar adored her sons and granddaughter. She was careful always to let him lead, to make way for him as the new head of the family. But for all her tact, Alejandro had the constant feeling she was biting her tongue, restraining herself from saying something that might rock the already shaky foundations of the Del Campo clan.

They walked along the path of floodlit palms and were greeted by Rocky, the club's longtime doorman. He gave Alejandro a hint of a bow and held the door for Pilar. Inside, the place was packed with air-kissing, glass-clinking people who, Alejandro knew for a fact, loathed each other.

He smiled wryly. The Wellington scene made him think of wars past when combatants would dine together at the end of a day's battle.

As he passed the packed tables, heads turned and voices dropped. He thought he knew what they'd be saying. *Not the man his father was. Lost his nerve. Burned out. Peaked too soon. He'll never win in the wake of all that tragedy.* Alejandro kept his eyes straight ahead, jaw set.

They were shown to the central table, where Alejandro could see from his brother's flushed cheeks and predatory smile that he and Rory were well into a bottle of good Scotch already.

Lord Henderson stood to greet Alejandro warmly. Hendy, as they called him, was a rock. He came from a family as old as England and saw the world in strong and simple terms. He'd been a solid and loyal consigliere to Carlos Del Campo and offered not only his own fortune but a continuity and an affable stability to the team since.

Rory was busy ordering another drink, and Sebastian's eyes were unashamedly undressing the prettiest of the waitresses. And she wasn't making much secret of her appetite for him in turn.

Alejandro accepted a cranberry and soda and the menu. He loved his brother and sometimes envied the easy way he seemed to walk through life. Wellington was his element. Outside of polo, the majority of the men in the equestrian set were gay, so the heterosexual women outnumbered the straight men in Wellington by nearly two to one. The polo players could pretty much take their pick of willing sexual partners.

There was an undeniable draw about a man on a horse, and for polo players, "stick chick" opportunities were endless. Everywhere the brothers went, there were women angling for an invitation, and Sebastian had been taking full advantage since the age of fifteen.

Alejandro had always been content to let his brother claim that territory. Ever since Alejandro was a kid, polo had been his obsession, and any girl who was interested in him had to be willing to play second fiddle to the game. There had been a few women who were willing to tolerate his split affection, and they had all been perfectly lovely, bright young girls— but none of them had really managed to turn his head away from the ponies for long. And then, from the moment he'd been introduced to Olivia, his own path had been made clear.

The waiter arrived at the table to take their drink order. Valentina looked up from under long lashes and asked for a glass of champagne. The waiter looked like he was going to give it to her, too, until Alejandro growled, "She's sixteen. She'll have lemonade."

Ignoring his pretty daughter's protests and wondering when he got cast in the role of brooding, gloomy patriarch, Alejandro reflected that Olivia had only been two years older than Valentina was now when they'd first met.

He pulled himself up. His late wife was like a groove to

which his mind kept returning. *Let it go.* He was here at the start of a fresh new season. Today's result notwithstanding, anything was possible. He took a moment to enjoy his mother's imperious charm as she ordered. And smiled at his daughter bantering back and forth with Sebastian and Rory. For all the eyeliner and attitude, Valentina was still his little girl.

"Are you ready to order dinner, or waiting for one more?" the waiter asked, nodding at the empty chair.

Pilar met Alejandro's eyes. "I asked Cricket to join us."

On cue, there was a small commotion at the doorway and three men barked with laughter and parted to reveal Cricket—British show-jumping star and equestrian set pinup—making maximum impact on entrance as she did everywhere she went. Cricket had been given the nickname by her family when she and her first pony cleared parallel bars from a standing start. Since Cricket loathed her given name, Candida, and loved to jump, she'd made it her business to see the nickname stuck.

Rory stood prematurely to pull out a chair, and Cricket made her way slowly toward them, dipping her cheek to be kissed at tables along the way and glancing up coyly at Alejandro whenever her breasts were displayed to best advantage. With her platinum mop of hair and bee-stung lips, she always looked distractingly ready for bed.

She arrived in a soft cloud of some delicious Bond Street scent, waved kisses at them all, and slid into her seat with a quick look at the mirror behind the table. Apparently satisfied that she was perfect, she gave Alejandro a slow, entitled smile, which took in the entirety of their history.

There was an easy elegance about the way Cricket did everything, Alejandro thought as he watched her shake out her napkin and accept an air kiss from a passing publicist. Maybe because her family had been British horse royalty for generations, she made playing the Wellington scene seem like second nature. As Pilar repeatedly and pointedly said, Cricket was going to make some lucky someone a formidable wife.

She raised her champagne to Alejandro in a silent toast and brought the flute to her mouth, a gleam of speculation in her lovely, slanting eyes.

Chapter Eight

The morning of her flight, Georgia was up yawning before dawn to feed and say good-bye to the animals, the barn, the mountains, the land...The old stone cottage looked heart-stoppingly beautiful in the dawn light, the rising sun reflected off the snow in soft shades of rose and gold.

Get a grip, she thought. She was already nostalgic, and she hadn't even left.

Sam arrived early, and when he pulled up in his dark blue pickup truck, whether it was pre-trip jitters or not, Georgia's heart did skip a little. With his sandy hair and easy smile, there was no denying the guy's appeal. But once it was just the two of them in the truck, the intimacy felt like dangerous territory so Georgia stuck with thanks again for the ride and then gazed determinedly out the window, feigning fascination with the snow-weighted branches.

Sam didn't seem to mind the lack of repartee and comfortably went about filling in the silence. He told her how pleased his neighbor was with the way she'd looked after their dog's luxating patella. He didn't like to think what would have happened if she hadn't spotted the wobble in his walk. "The family thinks you're some kind of dog-whisperer now, Georgia. Kept telling me you saw the problem before it even was a problem."

Georgia shrugged him off, embarrassed. She did seem to have a knack for sometimes noticing things that other people might not, but she put that down to paying attention and a dose of beginner's luck. Taking it any more seriously might jinx things.

She politely asked about his work, and he chatted happily about tax season. Georgia tried to stay focused, but she couldn't help it—the minute Sam started talking about money, he always lost her.

After a few minutes, he seemed to realize she'd checked out and abruptly changed the course of the conversation by telling her that a space had come up for rent in the building he owned—right under his office—and how he always thought it would make a good place for a clinic.

He's right, Georgia thought. *It would.* And she was sure the rent would be cheap. She imagined what it would be like to have him just a stairwell away all day long and half smiled. Not a landlord you could complain about. But still, the complications felt infinite so she put him off, saying she was still learning so much at the animal hospital she wasn't ready to branch out on her own just yet.

He offered to park, but Georgia told him she'd be fine so they pulled up to the drop-off lane at the airport. While Georgia scrolled through her phone for her e-ticket, he jumped out and grabbed her bags. She awkwardly gave him a kiss on the cheek as a good-bye and said thanks again, but as she pulled away, he grasped her arm with one hand and produced a small, wrapped parcel in his other. For one breathless and irrational moment, she thought he might actually be about to propose.

"A late Christmas present," he said, smiling bashfully. "I've been carrying it around, hoping I'd get the chance to see you, but you've made yourself scarce."

It was a necklace. A contemporary silver pendant. Sleek and pretty, and so obviously expensive that, for a split second, Georgia could not help but imagine selling it to help with the cost of a new roof for the barn. She chased this ungrateful thought away, but paused before thanking him, not sure she was ready to accept all that this gift implied.

"Sam, I..."

He waved away her equivocation. "Please," he said as he lifted the chain, "just try it on." He clasped the necklace at the nape of her neck, and as his knuckles brushed against her skin, Georgia felt an involuntary shiver of pleasure. It had been a long time since any man had touched her—her dad's occasional absentminded pat on the top of her head most definitely did not count—and for a moment, she allowed herself to fantasize about being with Sam again, how easy it would be.

He stepped back. "It looks perfect on you."

She touched it, hesitant, and then relented. "Thank you. It's lovely."

Sam gazed at her intently. "Georgia, I know now's not the right time, but I do want to talk with you. When you're back? Can we have dinner?"

Georgia's smile faltered. But he'd been so decent, how could she say no? "Of course. I'd like that."

She walked away and then glanced back and saw Sam was still standing there, watching her go. He raised his hand and gave a sweet, easy, just slightly beseeching smile. Georgia firmly made herself smile back at him, waving with what she hoped looked like real enthusiasm.

She boarded, filing past the smug first-class passengers and into her seat. The cabin was cramped, she was sitting in the center, and the elderly man sitting next to her smelled distinctly of Bengay cream, but she suddenly realized that she was happier than she'd been in weeks. It was almost alarming, how excited she was to leave.

Checking messages before going into airplane mode, she found she had an e-mail from Billy with the title "Get the picture?"

There was a link to a piece in *Wellington Magazine* called "The Season's Most Sought-After Equestrian Accessories," flanked by ads for catering, cosmetic surgery, private jets, and multimillion-dollar realty.

Georgia swiped down to the photo of Billy's latest crush, Beau, proudly displaying on his arm one of the "beautiful bespoke saddles he makes for the world's most exacting polo players." He looked like the perfect Southern gentleman: strawberry blond, chiseled features, well bred, badly behaved. Exactly Billy's type.

The photo had him handing the saddle to a guy in his late twenties who looked like a rock star in polo gear. Brown, shoulder-length hair, caramel-colored skin, rakish eyebrows, and a mischievous smile. But it was the man next to him that really caught Georgia's attention. Has to be the older brother, she thought. Same hair, shorter cut. Tall, broad, maybe late thirties, but with a much wryer and more reluctant smile that didn't quite reach his ice blue eyes.

Georgia enlarged the caption:

Sebastian and Alejandro Del Campo, scions of the legendary polo dynasty. She looked at them a long beat, a little dazzled by all the beauty and privilege, before turning off her phone and worrying all over again about her wardrobe.

* * *

The plane banked as they readied for landing. Back home, the world had been snow white for so long that seeing the glorious colors—the turquoise sea against the white sand— was like some kind of retinal therapy—a color board of bliss.

Traveling was part of what she'd denied herself in what felt like forever. She was a little afraid now to find out how much she liked it. She had a sudden flashback to sitting at the kitchen counter as a little girl. Her mother spun a globe and trailed a long finger over all the places to which she'd already been and then all the places she still counted on seeing. "You'll see them, too, Georgie," her mother had said.

The plane bounced as it hit the tarmac, jolting her out of the unacceptable swell of emotion. Georgia brushed away a rogue tear. She hadn't counted on the possibility that coming to Florida—to her mother's old haunt—would affect her so deeply. She took a deep breath, determined not to let the old hurt ruin her long weekend.

Chapter Nine

Georgia was swept from the plane by a tide of money on the move. Exiting behind first class, she couldn't help noticing the ease with which the rich traveled. The loose white linen shirts on the men, beautifully cut white linen pants on the women. Monogrammed everything. And it was funny, since agreeing to help Billy grab his love in the land of polo, she was seeing the Ralph Lauren and US Polo Association logos everywhere. She had to wonder how many of the people walking around with ever-bigger insignias of the horse and player emblazoned on their chest had any idea how the game was actually played.

She found Billy waiting at the curb, leaning against a slate gray car as sleek and neat as he was. He flashed her his gorgeous smile, blinding white against his tan skin, slung her bags into the backseat, and then caught her in a warm hug. She always felt a bit unwieldy next to Billy, but it was far too good to see him to mind.

"Pretty," Georgia said of the little Porsche.

"Christmas," Billy said quickly, with the decency to look a little embarrassed. "I drove it down after the holidays." Billy's parents had made a fortune from some sort of powdered sports drink and seen to it their only son couldn't run through his trust fund if he tried. Which he did.

Though he didn't need the money, Billy did like to keep himself busy, always coming up with new business schemes. His latest venture was sourcing the world's most luxurious leathers to make artisan bags handcrafted at price-on-demand expense. Every few months, he copied Georgia on a press release to show they'd been featured in a *Vogue* somewhere around the globe, but as far as she could tell, he'd actually only sold one or two so far.

He put the roof down and tunes on, and before Georgia could put on her seatbelt, he lurched away from the curb with a reckless lack of clutch control. They sped out beneath the airport underpass and into the Florida sun.

Billy changed lanes without looking and chattered happily about everything he'd planned for the weekend. In classic Wayfarers, a sleek jersey tee, and spotless white jeans, he was, Georgia thought, a study in hip elegance. In her wrinkled pants and tank top, she felt horribly plain and frumpy.

They were cruising past some of the most immaculate landscaping she had ever seen. Manicured paddocks and pristine fencing, the edges of everything were impeccable. Vast barns were set back from the road, supersize houses looming behind. "This place is unreal," she said.

"Welcome to Welly World, Georgia Fellowes." Billy grinned. "You're going to love it, and I'm going to spoil you while I've got you. On today's schedule: manis, massages, margaritas—let the pampering begin! I owe you big time. But first, I'm afraid we need to make a quick pit stop at the polo grounds—"

Georgia groaned. "Already?"

"Sing for your supper, girl," he said. "But don't worry.

I'm not forcing you to watch any actual polo 'til tomorrow. Today's about scoping out Beau—while enjoying some generously sponsored drinking—before I whisk you off for a thorough spoiling."

He turned to her, his eyes sparkling. "Did you open that picture I sent? Was he not the cutest man you've ever seen?"

There was a tiny silence while Georgia thought about the brothers in the photo. Cute didn't quite cut it. In fact, magnificent was more like it.

"Beau," Billy pressed. "He's edible, right?"

"Oh. Yes. Beau." Georgia nodded quickly. "Super cute. And how perfect that he's in leather—"

"Right? He's in the business! I'm envisioning a dynasty built on love and rawhide. I mean, there are only so many six-figure purses I'm ever going to sell but these horsey types are made of money, and there's no portion control when it comes to their accessories. Beau has contacts up to his adorable little ears—"

"I bet," Georgia said.

"And you saw the Del Campo boys?" Billy said, adopting a terrible Spanish accent. "Del Campo...Don't you love how that sounds on your tongue? It's like the firm hand of fate on your lower back, like a deep clinch on a starry beach..." He groaned pornographically. "Oh, *Señor* Del Campo."

"Stop, you're ridiculous," Georgia said as Billy turned into a long private drive. "Anyway, they're probably gay."

"No, no," Billy said. "Maybe if they were show jumpers or dressage, but almost everyone's hetero on the polo field. Believe you me, I'd know."

She laughed to acknowledge that it was probably so. Then she rested her head back as they passed beneath towering palms, and she felt her muscles begin to unclench in the warm, lush breeze. It was surreal to Georgia to think it was January.

Passing a glossy red monogrammed horse trailer, she felt a swell of interest in seeing what were supposed to be some of the most impressive ponies in the world. She was surprised to find herself even a little disappointed she wouldn't see polo played right away.

"So, anyway," Billy said, "I think things are getting kind of serious with Beau. Last night—in the middle of what I will simply call a really good time so as not to offend your delicate sensibilities—he almost said the L word. And if he had, I swear to God, I would have said it right back. So you are here just in the nick of time, Peaches. If I'm missing the obvious and this guy is actually bad news, I need someone to tell me right now, before I'm in too deep."

Georgia shook her head. "I don't know why you think I have some sort of magical sixth sense for this kind of thing."

Billy swerved a little as he looked over at her. "Because you do. It's your gift. You can always read the vibes around someone—human or animal. It's what makes you such a good vet and a good friend. I mean, you called out every jerk I ever dated—right from the first day you met them—but it's just taken me this long to actually want to listen to you."

Georgia laughed. "I'll do what I can. But please don't blame me if I'm wrong."

"Oh, don't worry, I will," said Billy merrily. "Now, I happen to know that Beau's going to be trapped in the Maserati press tent right after the match, and so your job is to get trapped with him and chat the man up. Get a feel for him, find out his secrets, see if you think I should hide the keys to my car."

"Sounds easy enough," Georgia said distractedly as she

flipped down the visor to look in the mirror. Frowning at
the dark shadows under her hazel eyes, she made a face and
snapped it back up. "Shouldn't I change, though?" she said.
"I actually brought a dress—"

"You did?" Billy laughed. "Georgia Fellowes, I am astonished to learn that you're not immune to vanity after all." He
glanced at her. "No, you're perfect just as you are. There's no
hiding that body and that whole sexy librarian thing you've
got going is set to turn every head. You'll be a breath of fresh
air down here, Peaches. You just be you, and the men will
come running."

Georgia rolled her eyes. "I'm only here for four days. I'm
not looking to meet a man."

Billy raised an eyebrow. "Oh, darling, I'll make sure you
meet lots of men, and then you can simply take your pick. A
little flirtation to take the edge off your winter." He cocked
his head critically at Georgia a beat longer and reached behind him, swerving again as he did, to retrieve a gift bag
from the backseat. "You could use a hit of color, though.
See if there's something in yesterday's swag. Press tent goody
bag."

For a girl like Georgia with one wand of desiccated mascara and a smushed old lip gloss to her name, a bag full of
makeup freebies made her feel both giddy and intimidated.
She just never quite knew what to do with the stuff.

"Go easy," Billy said as she puckered up to consider a second coat of lipstick. "You want to work that whole 'I have
my mind on higher things' look."

A few minutes later, they were pulling in to the Ever-
glades Polo Club beneath a logo of crossed palms and mal-
lets. Billy tossed his keys to a parking valet with a wink.
Georgia smiled for a second to think how dismayed the poor

guy would be if she'd handed him the keys to her ancient Mercedes, scattered with old parking tickets and pistachio shells. But then again, she thought, as she saw the high-handed way some of the guests treated the valets, at least she'd be sure to give a big tip.

Chapter Ten

Inside the grounds, the air was festive with post-match revelry. Billy set the pace, scooping up their security passes without breaking stride. Looking longingly at the happy activity around the ranks of horse trailers, where ponies were being hosed and groomed and loaded back into their trailers by casually glamorous grooms, Georgia hurried to follow her friend.

Weaving through the many beautiful girls in Lilly Pulitzer prints and skimpy silk dresses fluttering like bunting in the sunshine, all Georgia's worries about being underdressed went out the window. With so many gorgeous sights to see, it was quite obvious that no one would look at her at all.

They passed vivid orange Veuve Clicquot tents; craft tents where little girls in smocked dresses painted wooden polo ponies; and a gaggle of women staggering by on six-inch heels that Georgia imagined they must be wishing they'd left at home.

She caught a glimpse of a red dress and felt her heart constrict in a sudden unreasonable flash of panic. Oh God, what if she ran into her mother here? She stopped for a moment and tried to shake off the silly fear. The last Georgia's dad had heard, she'd been in St. Moritz—a safe continent away.

Billy grasped her elbow and steered her through the crowd, giving his inimitable running commentary on the characters they passed. A literary celebrity in his trademark white suit, one of last season's *Real Housewives* in a ravishing backless sundress, a stunning transsexual actress recently seen on the cover of a magazine with cleavage as taut as rubber dinghies, actors, singers, bankers, dandies, barely dressed horsey groupies, and a theatrically busy club manager in a monogrammed blazer and orange suede loafers, conspicuously wielding a walkie-talkie. Between Billy's wry asides, Georgia caught snatches of passing conversations in a dozen foreign accents.

Nobody, Georgia saw, was trying to be subtle about their wealth here. Everything that could be had been dipped in diamanté: riding boots, saddles, wrists, ring fingers, and pinkies. It was as if all the money in the world had slid into the laps of people with horses.

They moved through something Billy called the tailgate section, but it was like no tailgate Georgia had ever seen. These tents were decorated in every conceivable theme, from Moroccan luxury desert dweller with Berber carpets and jewel-colored throw pillows to redneck hipster with pristine hay bales and ironic kerchiefs around the waitstaff necks.

Billy scanned the crowd with fierce determination and homed in on his target. "There he is." He smiled triumphantly. "With the team."

She followed the direction of his gaze and made out a distinctive profile, smooth gold skin, pale blue eyes, and a thick mop of red-blond hair. Beau was flanked by two tall, wide backs in tight La Victoria team T-shirts. Their sleek, dark heads ducked as one into the shade of the Maserati tent.

The tent perimeter was being policed by very pretty security—a girl with severely pulled back hair, bright red lips, and a look on her face that seemed to say she lived to turn people away.

"Oh God," Georgia said, frantically trying to brush the worst of the wrinkles from her travel-worn clothes. "I look like I just crawled out of bed. They'll stop me at the door."

But Billy flashed their laminated passes, and to the evident disappointment of the clipboard chick, they were in. As their eyes adjusted to the filtered light in the tent, Billy paused for a second to pat down his closely cropped curls and straighten his tee over his perfect abs, then scooped two plastic goblets of champagne, handed one to Georgia, and arranged himself behind Beau as if he'd been standing there all day.

Beau turned and smiled. "Hey, you," his voice a smooth Virginia drawl, "I was hoping you'd show up. Where you been all day?"

"Remember? I had to meet my best friend at the airport," Billy said. "This is Georgia. She's a veterinarian. Specialist in equine medicine."

Georgia raised an eyebrow. Given her recent responsibilities, that was a bit of a stretch, but she appreciated Billy trying to make her look good.

Beau tore his eyes away from Billy's to shake Georgia's hand with a warm smile. "I've heard a lot about you already, Georgia. So glad to finally meet you in person."

Georgia returned the smile. "Likewise," she said.

Georgia watched the way Beau moved closer to Billy, and she relaxed a bit. It was clear the guy was smitten. Which was no surprise really, since Billy was one of the most irresistible people she knew.

Beau briefed Billy on the honorable defeat of the Del Campo team, La Victoria, at the match they'd just missed, and Georgia resisted a retort about the irony of the team name. The two men talked animatedly about the party they'd attended last night, the tequila casualties and the overall extravagance, and as their voices rapidly rose and fell, Georgia felt her eyes wandering and her shoes sinking into the deep green grass. Finally, Billy looked over at her and gave her a little nod. "I'm going to go refresh our drinks. I'll be right back."

Beau watched Billy walk away and then turned to Georgia and grinned. "So, what do I have to do to pass the Best Friend Test?"

Georgia laughed, sheepish. "Oh, so you know?"

Beau shook his head, amused. "Billy is as transparent as a window. But that's one of the reasons I like him so much. The guy can't hide anything from anyone."

"That's true. He never could," said Georgia. She smiled at Beau. She had a good feeling about him.

Billy returned, and talk turned to the afternoon match and the saddles Beau made. Beau described them with lively eyes while never taking his hand off Billy's arm.

"Hey, Beau," came a low, laughing voice.

"Sebastian. You remember Billy. And this is Georgia."

She turned around to see Sebastian Del Campo—looking every bit as outlandishly handsome as he had in his photo. With him was a shorter, redheaded man with a dazzling smile, whom Beau introduced as Rory Weymouth.

The men shook her hand with old-world charm and slid into practiced repartee, taking turns asking where she was from and how long she'd be staying. Certainly their spirits didn't seem dimmed by recent defeat.

Georgia could tell that their disarmingly attentive double act was probably due to some running tally of conquests between the two. She had zero intention of being added to either of their lists, but she had to admit, it was fun to be flanked by two such good-looking and very friendly men.

"Georgia has horses, too," Billy said, apropos of nothing, and buried his nose back in his flute.

Sebastian looked interested. "What kind of stable do you have?"

Georgia shrugged, embarrassed. "Well, we don't have horses like you have horses. I mean, not ones you can actually ride these days. We have a sweet old mustang named Ben— you can't mount him, though, his last owner foundered him, and so his feet are too sore. And we have a one-eyed donkey named Jenny. You could ride her, I suppose—but she only goes in circles—you know, because of the one-eye thing."

Rory looked rather startled, but Sebastian threw back his head and laughed.

Chapter Eleven

Alejandro glanced across the room at the sound of his brother laughing and tried to see whomever he was talking to. He got a glimpse of a pretty, spirited face, animated by conversation, before Rory moved to loom over her and obscure the view.

He realized his audience was waiting for a reaction and smiled and nodded at the ring of people around him, trying to concentrate on the story that the socialite in the tight turquoise dress was telling and hoping he was hiding how claustrophobic he felt.

He hated these press events. Every which way he turned, someone waited to talk to him, touch him, demanding his attention. He knew it was part of the job—and he tried his best to satisfy—but the longer he stood, grinning like a fool and saying the same polite and predictable things over and over, the more horrifically restless he became. The mandatory mingling was bad enough when his team had won; but forced jollity after a loss like today's added serious insult to injury.

Sebastian laughed even louder, and Alejandro turned his head again. His brother and Rory were pulling out all the stops, competing over their afternoon target. They crowded in front of her, jostling for attention and blocking their poor prey from his sight. He saw Sebastian break away to get a refill on his drink. Fantastic—just what he needed—Sebastian on the rampage. He sure as hell didn't want a hangover handicap hurting their odds tomorrow on top of their dismal performance this afternoon.

The blonde finished her story finally, tossing off some dirty punch line about girth, which generated a round of guffawing laughter from her audience. Alejandro took that as his cue, quickly excusing himself before he was caught up in another round of unbearably inane conversation.

He wound his way through the crowd, past women sporting spray-on dresses and customer service smiles, and sought out his teammates.

He strode over toward his brother, laid one hand on his shoulder, and took the champagne from his hand. He spoke to him in quick, low Spanish. "*Che, hermano*, I thought we agreed not to drink during the season?"

Sebastian shrugged, then smiled and answered him in English. "I think maybe you agreed to that, Jandro. Not me. I'd never let free champagne go to waste." He plucked the drink back from Alejandro's hand and drained it.

Alejandro shook his head. Sebastian had more natural talent than any player he knew but sometimes seemed ready to piss it away with partying, and he was enabled by Rory, who never met a good time he didn't like. But after another defeat, with all eyes on them, someone had to set a standard.

Apparently Sebastian recognized the look in his brother's eyes and cut off the lecture before it began. "Before you start in on family honor, big brother, let me introduce you to some friends." Sebastian turned toward the group. "You know Beau, of course, and this is Billy."

Alejandro nodded as the sleek, dark-skinned man on Beau's arm shook his hand.

"And this is Billy's friend Georgia."

Alejandro felt his breath catch in his chest. The woman smiling up at him was not Sebastian or Rory's typical stick chick. In fact, Alejandro had never seen anyone like her in Wellington before. In a room full of women working their surgically enhanced assets to the max, she stood out in her simplicity. Tawny, golden brown hair was pinned up in messy curls; warm, hazel eyes met his with intelligent curiosity. Her luminous skin appeared to be free of makeup, except for a faint hint of red on her full lips. She wore a simple tank and wide-legged trousers that showed off the strong, clean lines of her generous curves. He almost smiled to see that, instead of expensive wedge sandals or designer riding boots, she wore a pair of little red sneakers on her feet.

He had a sudden unsummoned image of what it would be like to wake up next to her, the curls tumbling down her naked back, that beautiful, creamy skin bare from head to toe...

"Hello," she said, extending a hand. "Georgia Fellowes." Her voice was low and appealing.

"Pleased to meet you, *Ms. Fellowes*. I am Alejandro Del Campo." He took her small hand in his and felt his whole body tighten in response to her fingers' touch.

Her pale cheeks flushed a delicate, petal pink. He looked at her eyes, trying to decide if they were dark green or hazel. They seemed to change with the light.

"I know," she said, and blushed even deeper.

* * *

Ugh, thought Georgia as she snatched back her hand, rookie mistake. Could she be any more embarrassing—confusing celebrity for familiarity? Just because she knew who he was didn't mean she actually knew the man. She hoped he didn't think she was one of the countless polo groupies stalking the grounds.

God, he was good looking, though. Not in a flashy way like his brother. There was nothing flirty or boyish about him at all. He was entirely a man. He was taller and had broader shoulders than Sebastian. His skin was a slightly darker shade of gold. Sebastian was obviously athletic, but Alejandro moved with a deeply coiled strength and power, the muscles in his chest and arms straining against his form-fitting polo shirt. She couldn't help glancing down at his tight white jeans, at his long legs and taut thighs, his polished knee-high boots, the way the fabric stretched tantalizingly over the considerable bulge at his crotch. She blinked rapidly, willing herself to look back at his face. His mouth was not his brother's either, both more generous and yet more severe. But it was his eyes that were the most striking difference. While Sebastian's light green eyes were filled with rude mischief and the promise of fun, this man's ice blue gaze was unfathomable, almost haunted. He was definitely a man in some kind of pain, she thought as she studied his face.

Listen to yourself, she thought impatiently, *presuming all this understanding. He's probably pained by my inability to make conversation, more than anything. Get a grip, girl.*

Realizing that she'd done little but stare, and mortified by her awkward silence, Georgia opened her mouth to speak, but before she could get a word out, a polo groupie—who couldn't have been any more than sixteen—came crashing into the tent for an autograph. She sent Georgia's elbow flying, and her champagne nearly spilled onto the ground. In one deft move, Alejandro stepped up, grabbed her elbow, and steadied the glass.

Security arrived just after to lead the poor girl away, but Sebastian stopped them and signed the girl's napkin first, giving her a wink and a smile as well.

Alejandro stood beside Georgia, still gripping her arm. She could feel his warm breath against her temple.

Georgia swallowed nervously. "Nice reflexes." She showed Alejandro her still almost-full glass.

He raised an eyebrow and slowly released her arm, his fingers brushing against her skin. "I should hope so," he said dryly. "It's how I make a living."

"Well," she blurted out, "I hope to see you play," and cringed inwardly at how fantastically banal she could be.

He took a step closer. "And I hope you'll see us win. You'll be here tomorrow?"

"Of course she will," interjected Billy. "She's dying to see the ponies. She's a veterinarian, you know, specializing in equine medicine."

"Really?" Sebastian asked. "She seems unfairly attractive for a vet."

"Considerably easier on the eye than our Dr. Gustavo," Rory remarked.

"Speaking of which," said Sebastian, tipping his head meaningfully.

Alejandro glanced across the room and his face grew stony. He turned to his brother. "Why aren't those two checking the ponies?"

Georgia followed their gaze and saw, across the tent, a short, barrel-chested man jabbing a chinless Brooks Brothers type in the chest.

Sebastian nodded, amused. "Dr. Gustavo's too busy letting Dr. Evan know who's boss."

Alejandro made a low sound of exasperation. "Excuse me," he murmured, and brushed past Georgia to head for the unfortunate pair at the bar.

Chapter Twelve

Alejandro felt his annoyance grow as he glad-handed his way rapidly across the room. The first interesting face he'd seen since getting to Florida and immediately work intervened. He glanced back at Georgia, briefly pausing to watch the way she toyed with a stray caramel-colored curl at the base of her neck. For a moment, Alejandro was tempted to turn around and finish the conversation that had barely begun. But then he looked back at the bar and saw Dr. Gustavo, his face already flushed with drink, slam down a shot of something. Now was not the time to get distracted. There was the string to think of.

He threaded his way through the crowd, trying to ignore the fact that everyone he passed wanted his attention. Every interaction in these tents was a trap. All those bright, eager faces wanting something from him. He knew he should be grateful, these were his fans for the most part—people who only wished him well—but sometimes the unrelenting scrutiny could feel less like love and more like ownership. As if they were entitled to just about everything he had to give—not just an autograph or a quick selfie, but his heart, his soul, and when he was losing as he'd been lately, even a pound or two of his metaphorical flesh.

Alejandro could see that Gustavo was snapping his fingers at the barman for another drink. The vet's manner was really getting more and more insufferable.

The other vet, Dr. Evan, had been a problem since day one. Alejandro never should have let Gustavo make the pick. Worried that he was losing influence with the team, the older man made sure that the new vet was cringingly weak and totally biddable. And while the pathetic specimen he'd chosen did serve to make Dr. Gus look good in comparison, he did pretty much zero to benefit the team.

Alejandro gave the men a terse hello and suggested they might like to get back to the barns to check on the ponies. Gustavo colored and set down his drink as if he'd been slapped.

Alejandro resented the older man for forcing him into what had to sound like a reprimand and wished—not for the first time—that he had whatever quality would inspire his staff simply to do the right thing, sparing him the necessity of acting like an asshole.

Valentina appeared, wanting money for one of the thousands of overpriced trinkets on sale. The girl could run through cash like nothing Alejandro had ever known. Still irritated by the vets and his brother, he decided it would be easier to just give in. He reached in his pocket for a fifty. Valentina gave him a perfunctory kiss on the cheek and then folded and pocketed the crisp note and turned away. He was left with the uncomfortable feeling he'd just bought his way out of a scene. One more loss of unrecoverable control.

* * *

Georgia watched as Alejandro was kissed by a stunning girl with long, dark bangs wearing the latest everything. By contrast with the blushing wreck the man had made of her, this woman looked completely fearless in his presence, tugging on his shirt and speaking to Alejandro as if they were the only two in the room. He offered her something which she snatched from his hand before kissing him and then turning on her heel. Alejandro looked for a second like his heart might break.

Georgia tried to curb her stupid disappointment. Of course, she didn't know who the young woman was to Alejandro, but the interaction between them dripped with intimate familiarity. She smiled ruefully, thinking that she had, at last, disproven Billy's faith in her ability to take the measure of a man almost as soon as she met him, because she sure as heck hadn't pegged Alejandro as being the type who dated the barely legal.

A voice over the loudspeaker announced that the grounds would be closing in thirty minutes. Sebastian suggested Beau and Billy and Georgia meet them at the Player's Club after the match tomorrow evening. Rory gave Georgia a salacious wink as he left. Sebastian swooped in for two kisses, murmuring a very private "Lovely to meet you" in Georgia's ear as he slipped away.

Beau had to return to pack up his booth so he and Billy unpeeled their fingers with a lingering look of promise. As the tent crowd moved toward the exits, Billy looked to Georgia with barely contained hope in his coffee-colored eyes. "So?" he said. "What did you think?"

Georgia smiled at her friend. "Honestly? I thought he was great. But I'm not so sure that my judgment can be trusted at the moment."

Billy swept her up off the floor and into a bear hug. "Oh, I knew it! I knew you'd like him. He's just about perfect, right?"

Georgia laughed. "He seems to be a very nice man."

Billy put her down, but continued to beam at her. "And didn't you have fun?" he asked. "You were a hit with Sebastian. And Rory, too, from the looks of it."

Georgia waved that away, embarrassed. "Oh, come on. They were just being polite, is all."

They left the shade of the tent and headed for the car. Billy was chattering happily about the evening treatments he'd booked for them both at the spa.

Georgia waited until she trusted her voice to sound casual. "So, what's the older brother's story?"

"Alejandro? Oh, total bummer, right? His wife was in a coma forever after being injured in a show-jumping accident. His father passed only a little while before they turned off her life support." He glanced at Georgia and frowned. "Oh, wait. No. No. For God's sake, I present you with your choice of available heaven in Sebastian and Rory, and you're blowing them off for tall, dark, and gloomy? No way. He and his death wish are off-limits. What you need is fun."

"How long ago did his wife die?" Georgia persisted as she buckled up.

"Oh my God, Georgia." Billy laughed. "You're wondering if there's been a sufficient interval since he was widowed?"

"No!" Georgia protested hotly. "I was just curious."

Billy snorted. "You vets are worse than doctors. Extreme rescuers. But not this time. The Del Campo situation is tragic, but, like, not sexy, easy-fix tragic. Toxic, impossible tragic. Give it up."

Georgia shrugged, tuning him out as they merged into traffic and the stereo started to soar. She'd been right about the pain, then, losing his wife and his father in such a short amount of time. Still, she thought wryly, that raven-headed girlfriend might take the edge off his loss.

Chapter Thirteen

God, the equestrian set are sexy," Billy said as they settled onto the warm bleachers and gazed out at the field the next day. "Look at them with the kinky accessories—the whips and the reins. What's that thing?"

"A riding crop," Georgia said.

"Mmm, hot. This gear's all kinds of shades of gray. I can't believe it's taken me so long to realize this is the business my business should be in."

Georgia laughed. "Why do I feel like we have this same conversation every six months? Last time it was car interiors."

"You have to admit that the tight white jeans and tall, shiny boots are hot as all hell," he said. "And look"—he clutched his chest—"leather knee pads! Be still, my heart!"

Georgia shrugged. "They're okay, I guess."

Billy snorted and elbowed her in the ribs. "'They're okay, I guess,'" he imitated her teasingly. "Like you weren't checking out the goods."

Georgia laughed, caught. "Yeah, okay, maybe on the right guy they can be pretty spectacular."

Billy nodded his head, "Sing it, sister."

Soon, between the Bloody Marys they'd enjoyed at brunch and the pleasure of hanging out together, the pair were almost giddy with giggles. God, thought Georgia as she leaned against her friend, weak with laughter, she'd been holed up on the farm with her dad for so long that she'd practically forgotten what fun was.

She turned to Billy and kissed him on the cheek.

He touched his face, pleased and surprised. "What was that for?"

"That was for making me come down to visit," she said. "And for just being you."

Billy put his arm around her. "Aw, Peaches, it's been too long."

As the teams took their positions, Georgia was completely unprepared to feel so impressed. She'd seen some Thoroughbred animals, but never a collection like this. The ponies were groomed to superhuman perfection, but beyond the gleaming neatness, they seemed like a different species of horse than any she'd ever known. Their eyes glittered with intelligence and restless competitiveness. Their muscles twitched under gleaming flanks as they strained against their reins in excitement. She had never seen ponies look so alive.

Georgia suddenly had an epiphany. She got it—polo and every elite thing it stood for—it was the game that horses of this caliber deserved. These ponies were born and bred and trained every day for this release. It was in their blood. Clearly, they wanted nothing more than to race onto that field and play.

The horn was blown, and Georgia surrendered to the thundering hooves and the solid click of stick on ball. Clueless as she was about the rules, and impossible as it was to follow anything the commentator said except the name

"Del Campo," she found herself completely absorbed. She couldn't believe the speed with which the players rode, or the height the ball soared. Billy had been right—the game was thrilling and undeniably sexy. The players and ponies blocked and marked each other mercilessly, dancing around the ball to gain control before storming down the field at top speed, sparks seemed to fly from the ponies' feet as horseshoes caught the light.

Alejandro was at the heart of it, the best of them all. He dove through the other players on a magnificent gray, man and horse in perfect communion, fused as a team. He was twisting and turning, galloping face backward to follow the soaring trajectory of the ball, all the while wielding his mallet like the right hand of Thor. All the pent-up energy that she'd noticed in the press tent yesterday suddenly made sense. This man was made to ride.

It took tremendous skill to move as nimbly as he did. Over and over again, he made the crowd gasp, taking huge risks, riding within inches of the other ponies but always managing to pull back just in time. It was riveting.

"It's really dangerous, isn't it?" she murmured to Billy, never taking her eyes off the field. "I mean, the speed—they could get seriously hurt."

"Oh, polo players die on the field every year," he answered casually.

Georgia turned to him, surprised. "Die?"

"Sure. I told you. It looks friendly, but remember when the game got started, it was played with the heads of your enemy. Polo's savage as all hell."

There was a break as the players swapped out their mounts, and Georgia stood to applaud. Not only for the players, who were impressive, but for the brave-hearted ponies themselves. Georgia felt the animals were every bit the athletes their riders were.

The players leaped onto their fresh horses. As Rory swung onto his pony, something caught Georgia's eye, a sway in the gait of his incoming horse. She blinked, straining to see, but within seconds, they were moving so hard and fast it was difficult to be sure. Georgia glanced left and right, seeing if anyone else noticed anything off, but no one seemed to be concerned. Rory was quickly back out there, playing with giddy oblivion. While the rest of the crowd cheered another goal, Georgia craned forward as he and his pony raced past her. Her stomach clenched—there was that sway again.

Georgia looked to the sidelines, hoping to find one of the vets, but if they were in attendance, they couldn't be seen from where she sat.

Another goal was scored, and the players bunched in a shifting knot in the center of the field, fighting for control of the ball. "Do you see anything funny about the horse that Rory is riding?" she asked Billy.

Billy squinted at the field. "Looks fine to me. Should I?"

Georgia bit her lip. "I—I'm sure it's nothing."

Billy patted her arm. "Rory's a pro, G. They all are. Plus the price they pay for those ponies? They'd notice if something was wrong."

Georgia slowly nodded. Of course Billy was right. She was being ridiculous. These were among the finest players in the world. They knew their horses better than she did.

Still, she kept her eyes on Rory and his pony while Billy caught up with her New York life. Work, her dad, the animals. People often made the mistake of underestimating Billy. They saw his good looks and designer clothes and thought he was all flash. But he didn't miss a thing. He paid attention and remembered just about everything his friend had ever said.

"You haven't succumbed to that cheating, reheated suitor, have you? What's-his-name? Sam?"

"Yes, Sam. But no—"

"Ugh. I get bored just thinking about him."

"You've never even met him."

"Well, I know what you've told me—and he's all sorts of deadly."

Georgia shook her head, ready to argue, but just then, Rory's pony stumbled on a tight turn. The horse righted herself immediately, but that was enough for Georgia. She felt positive that something was wrong. She looked wildly about again. Hoping that someone would step up. "Billy, I have to go down to the field."

"What?"

"That pony—there's something wrong."

She was up and moving before Billy could stop her, pushing her way through a crowd of women in silly hats, heading for the umpire who stood on the sideline.

She leaned down over the wall that separated her from the field. "Excuse me," she shouted at the umpire, straining to be heard over the crowd. "Excuse me! There's something wrong with that horse!"

The umpire glanced over at her, an irritated look on his face. "Get back, lady," he yelled. "Are you crazy?"

Georgia leaned over even farther, feeling that she might topple onto the field at any moment. "The horse—that Player Number One is riding on the La Victoria team—something is very wrong with it."

The umpire shook his head, refusing to listen. Billy had

reached her by now and was pulling at her shoulder. "Georgia! What are you doing?"

Georgia shook him off. She felt sick. She knew she was making a spectacle of herself, but that insistent diagnostic voice in her gut persisted, the one so stubborn that, when it kicked in, Georgia knew that either she was going to be right or totally humiliated trying to prove that she was right.

"Hey, you!" she yelled. "Goddamn it! Listen to me!"

The umpire had obviously decided to ignore her. She looked out at Rory and his horse again—her heart thumped—there was nothing else to do.

She climbed up over the wall and dropped down onto the field, landing with a solid thwack onto her rear. The umpire turned to her, horrified. "Holy shit, lady, what the hell?"

Georgia looked up at him and took a deep breath. "You need to call a time-out. And help me up while you're at it."

Chapter Fourteen

Alejandro lifted his head, squinting to see what the commotion was on the other side of the field. The umpires, two on horseback and one on the ground, were huddled around something—no wait—*someone*. Someone was on the field.

"*Que mierda pasa!*" he swore, as he recognized the caramel curls and wildly waving arms of the woman standing on the green. "Time out!" he shouted. "Time out!"

The other players pulled up and looked at him in surprise. Players almost never called a time out—not unless there was a major injury or a necessary piece of equipment had broken.

He wheeled away from the others and galloped across the field.

"Stop being so idiotic and listen to me," Georgia was yelling at the umpires. "That horse is going to be permanently damaged if—" She broke off and looked up at Alejandro as he rode up. Relief flooded her face when she saw who he was.

"Oh, thank God, Alejandro! These asses won't listen to me! Rory's pony, there's something wrong. It's her spine—

maybe spondylomyelopathy. You need to get her off the field immediately."

Alejandro frowned and looked over at Rory and his horse. "MacKenzie?" he said. "No, you're mistaken. She's in perfect health."

Georgia stamped her foot in frustration. "No, she's not. She's got a sway in her gait, and if she keeps being ridden that way, she's going to have permanent damage. She's probably in terrible pain. She needs to be taken off the field and rushed to a hospital, right now!"

Alejandro stared at her for another moment. She looked up at him, her eyes imploring him to listen. "Please," she whispered.

He reared his horse around. "Rory!" he yelled, racing across the field. "Bring in MacKenzie!"

Rory waved and started riding toward them, but halfway across the field, the brave pony's knees buckled.

"Damn it," breathed Alejandro as he raced toward them. He sprang off his horse and grabbed MacKenzie's reins as the pony hit the ground.

"Find Gustavo," he spat at Rory. He held MacKenzie's head, stroking her face. "*Bueno, bueno, shhh, tranquila.* Just hang on."

Georgia ran up behind them and knelt at the pony's side, her fingers gently probing the pony's spine.

"I think she might need a fusion," Georgia said. "How quickly can we get her to an X-ray?"

"Minutes. They're calling for an ambulance now." He clenched his jaw as he saw the sweat foaming on the pony's neck.

"She's in pain. I should have acted sooner," muttered Georgia.

Rory ran onto the field, carrying Gustavo's medical bag, which he gave to Georgia. "I couldn't find Gus," he said to Alejandro.

Georgia tore the bag open and riffled through it, pulling a fresh pair of gloves from their packet. She loaded a syringe and looked up and met Alejandro's eyes. He looked back at her for a second, hoping to hell that he could trust this woman, and then gave a barely perceptible nod of permission, and she quickly found the vein.

Stress made the moment seem like forever but it was probably only seconds before the pony showed signs of some relief. As MacKenzie was being loaded onto the stretcher, Gustavo finally showed up. He strode over, Dr. Evan trailing unsteadily behind him.

"What the hell is going on?" Gustavo demanded.

Georgia briefed Gustavo quickly on her diagnosis and the dose of drug she'd given. Gustavo's face flooded puce. "You gave that horse a shot? Are you insane? Who told you to do that?"

Alejandro looked up at Gustavo. "I did," he said icily. "In the absence of any alternative."

"That's astoundingly irresponsible," sputtered Gustavo. "She might have done irreparable damage!"

"That pony was in agony," Georgia said in frustration. "I couldn't just stand by."

She peeled off her latex gloves and held out Gustavo's bag to him. In outrage, Gustavo looked to Alejandro. Alejandro coldly nodded at him to take the bag, and then turned to board the ambulance. Gustavo made to follow, but Alejandro stopped him before he got on.

"You reek of booze, *amigo*," he said quietly. "You're in no condition to take care of this animal." He looked at Georgia. "Will you come? I'd like for you to talk to the vet at the emergency clinic."

Georgia nodded mutely and climbed in beside him. The last thing Alejandro saw before the doors slammed shut was Gustavo's face, absolute rage in his eyes.

Chapter Fifteen

It was quiet in the waiting room. Georgia had briefed the emergency vets as soon as they had arrived, and Alejandro had filled out all the paperwork, telling the senior surgeon to do whatever was necessary to help his horse.

Alejandro leaned back and closed his eyes. The ambulance ride, the interminable wait, it all hurled him relentlessly back to the night of Olivia's accident. He remembered the medevac helicopter that had transferred him with his wife from the farm. Valentina's little face, her nanny's arms around her, as she looked up at the chopper in flight.

It had been a nightmarish ride, listening to the medics radio ahead about Olivia's condition. "Pupils fully dilated. Nonresponsive." He remembered willing his wife to make it, calling on every ancestor in memory and every last remnant of his childhood Catholic God, as the lights of the city finally came into view and they landed on the hospital roof. He'd climbed out of the cabin beneath the helicopter's whirring blades and followed his wife's gurney into the bright, cold light.

He opened his eyes and glanced over at Georgia. Her pretty face was pale, her shirt was torn at the shoulder, and there were grass stains all down the front of her pants. She smiled wearily at him. There were purple shadows under her hazel eyes. "I think she'll be all right," she said softly. "I think she'll compete again. We caught it in time."

He shook his head ruefully. "You caught it in time. Not me."

"Well, you were playing, so of course you couldn't see, and Rory—"

"Rory shouldn't have been riding her. She's my pony, but I loaned her to him. I thought that it might give him a little inspiration. I wanted the win. I should have been paying better attention."

Georgia frowned and looked as if she was going to say something else, but she was interrupted by one of the veterinary assistants, who emerged in scrubs to tell them that things were going fine, but that it was a bit more complicated than they first thought, and it would be several hours before the surgery was over.

Alejandro turned to Georgia. "You should go home. I'll call you a car."

"I'd rather wait, if you don't mind," said Georgia. "I want to make sure that the pony is all right."

Alejandro was surprised to feel relief. He realized that he actually wanted her to stay. She shivered, tucking her hands under her arms.

He shook his head. "I thought you said you were from New York? How can you be cold in Florida?"

"This air-conditioning's colder than snow, I think."

"At least let me get you something to eat and something

warmer to wear. We can't have you sitting here freezing to death."

She looked around the antiseptic waiting room and laughed. "How are you going to manage that?"

He smiled. "I know a place nearby."

Chapter Sixteen

What, exactly, was she doing? thought Georgia as she followed Alejandro onto the boat. No, not a boat—it was a yacht. It was much too big to be considered a plain old boat.

"*La Bonita Pilar*," she read out loud as they boarded. "And who's Pilar?"

"*Mi mamá*," said Alejandro. "My father bought this boat for her, but she hated it. She gets terribly seasick. So he mainly sailed alone."

"Big boat to sail alone," she said, impressed.

"Well, there's a crew, of course, when she's at sea." He opened a cabin door. "Give me one moment to get things in order."

As he ducked below deck, Georgia walked to the front of the boat, looking out at the view from the private dock. It was dark now, but the moon shone so bright that it eclipsed the stars. She could hear the waves softly lapping, smell the tang of salt on the velvety ocean breeze. It was unbelievable to imagine that she had been shivering in her cold upstate barn less than twenty-four hours before.

She took out her phone and sent Billy a quick text. *Um. I'm on a yacht with Alejandro Del Campo*, she wrote.

Her phone chimed an answer within seconds. *GET IT, GIRL*, she read. She smiled and rolled her eyes.

Suddenly she heard the snap and whir of a generator, and the boat lit up with soft, amber lights. Alejandro emerged, carrying a sweater, a tray of food, a bottle of wine tucked under one arm, and a bottle of San Pellegrino tucked under the other. "I thought we could sit up above," he said, and he motioned to a small set of stairs.

She followed him up, and they emerged onto a snug little balcony with a built-in table and bench. The view was even better from up there, an endless expanse of dark water and sky, broken only by the warm reflection of the lights on the boat and the silvery, wavering rays of the moon, which had just begun to wane. He handed her the sweater, dark green cashmere that was so light and soft it felt woven from silken cobwebs.

"Sorry if it's a little big," he said. "It's mine."

She slipped it over her head and rolled up the sleeves, happy to finally cover her torn tank top. It smelled of something warm and spicy—a cologne that she didn't recognize—and under that, a scent she'd know anywhere—the sweet smell of hay. "Thank you," she said.

"Please," he said, "sit down."

She sat on the cushioned bench, and he took the seat beside her. It was an intimate table built for two, so they were almost touching shoulder to shoulder. Georgia could feel the heat emanating from him. For a moment, she remembered the way he had stood so close to her in the tent, the way his breath was so warm on her neck. She shivered.

"Still cold?" he asked.

She shook her head. "No, no. I'm fine."

He offered her a plate, and she turned her attention to the

tray on the table. There were fat purple plums and a hunk of blue-veined cheese, a selection of crackers and rolls, some tiny dark green olives glistening with olive oil, and pale pink slices of prosciutto. She looked at him in wonder. "All this was just sitting there, below deck?"

He shrugged, opening the bottle of wine. "As I said, there's a crew. It's always kept ready, just in case. Wine?"

She nodded and watched as he poured a glass full of golden liquid and handed it to her. He filled another glass with sparkling water.

"You're not having any?"

He shook his head, "I don't drink when I'm in training."

She cocked her head at him. "I would think that you might make an exception, after the day you've had."

He leaned back and sighed. "You know what? You're right." He poured another glass of the wine, took a sip, and smiled. "Ah."

Georgia filled her plate, suddenly realizing that she hadn't eaten anything since brunch that morning. "I'm starving," she said to him as she took a big, juicy bite of a plum.

He laughed. "Apparently."

She swallowed. "So, what happens when the game ends halfway through like that? Will you play that team again?"

His face darkened. "No, we forfeit." He took another drink.

"Oh. I'm so sorry."

"For what?"

"Well, if I hadn't decided to flop down onto the field like that, I suppose you might have won."

"Don't be ridiculous." He turned toward her. "If you hadn't come onto the field, I would have lost my favorite pony." He put his hand on her wrist. "God, I haven't even thanked you yet. What you did was so brave, and I am so very grateful. I don't think I could have taken it if I'd lost MacKenzie."

His eyes were the truest blue she'd ever seen, thought Georgia as she looked into his face. Beautiful against the dark tan of his skin. His mouth was almost as ripe and inviting as the plum she was eating. And his hand on her arm was causing her heart to beat triple time. She was absurdly glad for the shadows, hoping that they hid the flush that she knew stained her cheeks.

"I just did what anyone would do," she said softly.

He squeezed her arm tighter. She caught her breath. "Not at all." His voice was hoarse. "You saw what no one else saw, and you acted. You saved a life."

She blinked. "No, really, I—"

And just like that, he leaned down, took her face in his hands, and kissed her.

Georgia had been kissed her fair share in life, but she had never been kissed like this before. This kiss was gentle and urgent, hard and soft at the same time. This kiss suffused her with warmth and sent crackling bolts of electricity all through her limbs. This kiss made her toes curl, and her breath catch in her throat. This kiss melted her to her very core and pulled her inexorably toward him. She reached one hand up and stroked his hair; it was like raw silk, slipping through her fingers. He made a low sound, almost a growl, and kissed her even deeper, parting her lips with a dart of his tongue and then entering to languorously explore. She tasted the wine he'd been drinking, and the salt on his lips. He pulled her closer, and she writhed up against him, locking her hands at the back of his head, pressing her breasts against his broad, hard chest. She could feel his heart beat, and it felt as wild as her own.

Suddenly, the image of the young, dark-haired woman she had seen him with earlier that day swam before her eyes. She wrenched herself away with a gasp. "I'm sorry," she said, "but this is a bad idea."

He looked at her face, his breath coming in short, hard pants. "No," he said roughly. "No, it's not." And he kissed her again. But this kiss was not gentle at all. This kiss was demanding and full of need, and she felt herself answer him, kissing him back with an urgency that untethered her. His hands slid through her hair and then roamed down her throat and it felt as if his fingers were trailing sparks wherever they touched her. He ran a finger over the bare skin at her chest, and then slipping his hands beneath the sweater, he cupped her breasts and gently rubbed her nipple with his thumb. A searing heat rocketed straight through her veins, making her arch and moan.

This time it was Alejandro who broke the kiss, taking her chin in his hand and looking into her face. His sky blue eyes were stormy now, his pupils dilated with desire. "Georgia," he breathed, "my God."

She wanted nothing so much as she wanted to kiss him again, to feel her body twined with his, to answer the raw need she saw in his face, but then she thought of the troubled way he had looked at the girl in the tent—his face so full of emotion—and she knew she didn't want to be some sort of fly-by-night substitute. She knew she better seize the moment and break away, that she was seconds from giving herself over completely and getting caught up in something all wrong. After all, she'd been cheated on before—she knew how terrible it felt—and she hated the idea of being complicit in some stranger's pain.

"I—I think we should get back to the clinic," she said shakily. "MacKenzie should be out of surgery."

He took a deep breath, took his hands off her, and sat back. His mouth tensed, and his eyes, which had been so alive with longing a moment before, slowly went cold, his professional mask descending again. "I'll call a car," he said politely and took out his phone.

Chapter Seventeen

As much as she enjoyed Billy's folks, Georgia had been more than a little relieved when, after another hour with MacKenzie in the recovery room, she had finally arrived at their beach house and found that they were skiing in Aspen and she and Billy had the place to themselves. She could not have imagined standing there in her grass-stained clothes, knees still weak from Alejandro's kisses, and having to make polite and intelligent adult conversation. It was sweet relief to have Billy take one look at her, arch a perfect eyebrow, hand her a cup of hot tea heavily laced with whiskey, and then tuck her into the soft and fluffy guest-room bed.

She sat up for a minute, wanting to tell him about her strange night, but he gently pushed her back down.

"Now, Peaches," he said as he smoothed back her hair, "you know I want to hear every little dirty detail of what happened, but you're so tired that I might as well be talking to your one-eyed donkey right now. So go ahead and sleep and you can tell me everything over mimosas in the morning."

She'd slept into the afternoon and awoke to Billy standing

by her bed, holding a cup of scorching hot coffee in each hand. "Scooch over," he said, and climbed into bed with her. "Now, start from the beginning, and don't leave anything out."

They had lingered in bed, laughing and talking, until they finished a whole pot of coffee and Billy had wrung almost every last detail out of her. Not wanting Billy to tease her about her excessive morality, she left out the part about ending the kiss because she thought Alejandro might have a girlfriend. Instead, she just said vaguely that things had "felt wrong somehow."

Finally, Georgia declared she was starving, and Billy had shown her the huge, light-filled kitchen and told her to help herself while he took a shower.

Georgia munched on a croissant and took herself on a tour of the premises. The beach house was predictably incredible in the late afternoon light, modern and open, with floor-to-ceiling glass and a beautiful gray slate pool too tempting for Georgia to ignore.

She stuck her head back in the house and yelled, "Billy? I'm going to swim, okay?"

"Go right ahead, darling," came the faint reply from upstairs as Georgia went to her room to dig out her suit.

* * *

After spending most of the night on a hard plastic chair at the emergency clinic, Alejandro made it back to the *hacienda* early that morning and had gone straight to bed, exhausted. He awoke hours later to a slight hangover and thoughts of Georgia. That woman exerted a terrible influence on him. An entire year of abstinence had been broken in one night.

He hadn't been able to help himself. He'd been so twisted up over MacKenzie and the terrible memories of Olivia's accident, and then so grateful for Georgia's sweet, steady company, that he'd become sloppy and careless. She'd talked him into wine, though he didn't need much convincing, and they'd been sitting so close that when she had turned her bright face up toward him like some night-blooming flower, the moonlight reflecting in her hazel eyes, her red lips parted just so . . . he'd been overtaken by an absolutely unstoppable need to find out what she tasted like.

He stretched in his bed, thinking about that kiss, and felt himself getting achingly aroused all over again. Perhaps it was the fact he hadn't touched a woman in such a long time, but from the second his lips met hers, his body had been throbbing with a strength that shook him still.

He groaned and rolled out of bed. He did not have time for this. They had forfeited the game yesterday, so they were that much farther from the Del Campo Cup. He had to get to practice. The last thing he needed right now was to lose his focus. Thank God, he told himself as he pulled on his riding gear, that she'd had a cooler head than his, that she'd stopped things before they'd gone too far. Their return to the clinic had been excruciatingly awkward but at least professionalism had been restored. He pulled on his shirt, and the memory of her hands on the base of his neck, pulling him into an ever deeper kiss, welled up again. He felt his entire body tense and go hard. He shook his head violently, attempting to dislodge the vision. Damn it. This would not do. He needed to ride.

* * *

Alejandro drove to the barn and put himself through the paces for a good four-hour stretch, until he was soaked in sweat and felt barely able to walk. Still, no matter how hard he pushed himself, every time he closed his eyes, Georgia appeared before him—her mouth, her curls, her eyes, the curve of her breasts, the swell of her hips, her hands, her smile—it was maddening.

He was relieved to have a real distraction when Hendy showed up, waving him over to the side of the field.

"We need to talk," said Hendy. Alejandro swung off his horse and started to lead the mare back to the stables. Hendy walked alongside him. "Considering what happened last night, I assume you have no objections to the fact that I fired Dr. Evan this morning, and I damn near fired Gustavo, too. They were both stinking drunk and totally incapacitated. It was a serious breach of their responsibilities."

Alejandro fought a wave of irritation. He'd been preparing to do the same thing, but he'd hoped to find another vet first. Dr. Gustavo followed them up from Argentina every year and did not have a license to practice in the United States, so they needed an American vet to prescribe medications.

"It's late in the season to find a replacement," said Alejandro.

"I know, but by God, we could hardly keep him on after we almost lost our best pony. We were just lucky that lady vet was there— what was her name again?"

"Georgia," said Alejandro. "Georgia Fellowes."

"Yes, that's right. A bit odd, eh? But obviously knows her stuff. You know anything else about her?"

I know that her mouth tastes like wine and plums. I know that when her skin touches mine, we burn together...

He shrugged. "I believe she's returning to New York in a few days."

Hendy nodded. "Ah, too bad. Well, we'll have to put the call out. I swear, it was only out of respect for your father that I kept Gustavo on, but damned if I'll let him choose the next vet. We need to find someone capable, and we need to find them fast, my friend."

"Agreed."

* * *

Georgia dove into the pool. She and Billy had laughed about her adventures that morning, but with every length she swam, things started to feel more serious. She relived all the events of the night before, starting with her insane decision to jump onto the polo field, to what felt like her even more insane decision to kiss Alejandro on the boat, and ending with the note of cold fury with which he'd wished her good night when, satisfied MacKenzie would be all right, she finally left the clinic. Georgia was always conscientious to a fault, raking over every professional decision at the end of the day to be sure she had no regrets. But yesterday's situation ate at her way beyond that. She felt so exposed somehow and couldn't help doubting everything that had happened, professional and personal.

She hoped MacKenzie really was all right. She'd already checked her phone, half expecting a morning update, but there had been nothing. The surgeon had said that she'd made the right call, but she couldn't help worrying. She had acted so impetuously, and Dr. Gustavo had looked so horrified at her conduct. What if she'd gotten things wrong? What if there had been complications after she left, and the beautiful horse was maimed, or worse yet, dead?

She pushed herself under the water again, willing away

the thought. *Enough.* She knew she'd been right. Her medical decisions were sound.

But the rest of it. Alejandro...

The man was ridiculously beautiful and the way he had kissed her—no wonder he got under her skin. He was also unforgivably presumptuous. No doubt he was used to any number of women simply throwing themselves at him. No doubt he assumed that she didn't know about his young girlfriend or that, even if she did, she wouldn't care. Well, fine. It was merely a kiss, after all. Well, a kiss or two. And, she told herself sternly, it had practically ended before it began.

She climbed out of the pool, and Billy called out from the kitchen that they would go out later tonight. A quick glimpse of her pale and hairy legs sent her straight to her glorious guest bathroom for some serious damage control. Half an hour later, legs smooth, razor blunted, she slipped into one of Billy's hotel-cozy robes and gladly accepted the mojito he handed her.

While Billy lounged by the pool, Georgia gave her dad a quick call. She'd sent him a text from the airport when she landed yesterday, but she knew he would be uneasy until he heard her voice.

Sam was with him. They were chatting about farm taxes, her dad said, but from the sound of his half-jocular, half-bellicose tone, it actually sounded to Georgia as if they were a good six-pack in. Georgia shook her head at her own hypocrisy. It was late in the afternoon, and here she was, after all, enjoying her own glass of rum and lime, but there was something about the forced mirth of her father when he was drinking that she found hard to take. Sam was talking over her dad, the two of them laughing and sharing inside jokes. Her dad always seemed to have more in common with Sam than she did. She tried to cut the conversation short with a breezy promise to call tomorrow.

"Just you hold on," her dad said. "Sam's got an idea. He wants to set you up in business in the space below his offices in town. You can work off the rent. Says he'd much rather have a tenant he likes. He wants to invest in you."

"I know," she said. "Sam and I talked about this earlier, but I'm not sure. I need to think about—"

"What's to think about?" her dad said, a little bit belligerent from the alcohol. "You'll be your own boss from the get-go, not saddled by an overhead over which you have no control."

"Yes, Dad, I'm sure you're right. But I don't know if—"

"It's a generous offer, Georgia. Don't disrespect it. Sam's a good man. It's what you don't do that you regret."

She bit her lip, wondering what it was they were really talking about here. She knew her father would like nothing better than to see her settled nearby and couldn't help being a bit dismayed that, despite full knowledge of Sam's betrayal, he still acted as if Sam were the best she'd ever do.

"We'll discuss it when I get home, okay?"

She eased off the phone and looked over at Billy, who was not even trying to pretend he hadn't heard the whole conversation.

"That sounded fun," he said.

She sighed and closed her eyes for a minute. "We're not going to talk about that. I'm right here, right now. So"—she opened her eyes brightly—"what's a girl to do in Wellington? Just keep me off the boats and well away from the elder Del Campo brother."

Billy laughed. "Not a problem. The man never goes out, from what I hear. He's basically a monk. Anyway, first, we need to get you dressed. And no offense, but I know you, Fellowes, and I happen to know that the only dress you own is probably that sad little polyester number you wore at graduation. So I pulled in a few samples. It may look like overkill. But the thing you have to know about Wellington is that every night's prom night..."

Thanks to the bounty of freebies from Billy's stylist friends, Georgia's bedroom was soon an explosion of tissue paper and sparkling sequins and strappy heels. The suitcase containing her stained gold dress sat ignored to one side while Billy plied her with Prosecco and an assortment of outfits with the price tags still attached.

She tried on a sweeping silk maxi-dress the bright green of a parrot's wing. Billy shook his head and called for more leg. "Why would you cover those gorgeous things up?"

She wiggled into a short black Versace dress and stepped into a pair of six-inch pumps. Billy whistled. "That's better. You look like a high-class hooker! And I mean that in an entirely good way!"

Georgia took that dress off quickly.

It was like a Hollywood movie montage. Georgia tried on dress after dress while Billy made her bandy about horse terminology to amuse him.

"Wait, so what part's the gaskin again?" He giggled. He managed to make everything sound dirty.

There was only so much looking in a mirror Georgia could stand so she finally settled on an inky blue Calvin Klein slip dress with silver sandals. ("Sexy but not slutty," pronounced Billy. "Not that there's anything wrong with slutty.") She considered putting on the pendant that Sam had given her, but then hesitated and decided to leave her neck bare.

Billy looked immaculate in his uniform of never-before-worn white V-neck tee, fitted gray Armani jacket, and perfectly cut jeans.

Another mojito while Georgia painted her toes, and they were good and ready to go.

Wellington was a scene. Sleek Italian cars cruised under a picture-perfect Florida sunset, every restaurant teeming with people spilling out onto the gorgeously landscaped streets. Women struck poses in heels and showed off their whitest whites against sun-kissed, perfectly toned skin.

They pulled up to a nightclub, and Billy handed his car over to the valet. Georgia looked at the long line snaking around the corner and seeing the crowd gave her a sudden flash of paranoia. What if she were to go in and they told her she'd been wrong? What if the poor, priceless pony had been ruined and it was all her fault?

Her stomach churned with fear on seeing Sebastian rushing up the street toward them. She held her breath, for a minute thinking he was coming at her in anger, but he was running toward her only to sweep her up into a bone-cracking hug. "*Señorita* Fellowes!" he said, smiling. "Our genius lady vet!"

He introduced Georgia to Hendy. "This is Lord Henderson, our *patrón*. He is also in your debt."

Georgia looked at him, not understanding the term "*patrón*," and Lord Henderson smiled under his salt-and-pepper mustache. "A *patrón* pays to play, my dear. I bankroll half the team's costs, and in return, they put up with me on the field. A bit like owning a basketball team, except that they actually let me onto the court."

"Nonsense," said Sebastian with a wink. "We would let him play even if he only paid for a quarter of our expenses. Hendy is a fine athlete."

Lord Henderson waved him off. "I was once perhaps, but now I am old and slow. But anyway," he said as he gave her a stiff-armed British kiss to the cheek, "well done, Dr. Fellowes! You saved our best horse yesterday, my dear."

"So MacKenzie's all right?" Georgia asked as the bouncer took one look at Sebastian and pulled aside the rope for them all.

"Absolutely," said Lord Henderson. "She won't play any more this season, of course, but she should be back in the barn by tomorrow and ready to go next year."

The club was loud and jam-packed with beautiful people looking all the more glamorous in the flattering ultraviolet light, but Georgia was too busy feeling relieved about the pony to remember to be intimidated. Beau dragged Billy onto the dance floor. Sebastian wandered off to secure a table, and Rory arrived and took her aside.

"Drinks are on me, Georgia. You saved my arse," he said. "Alejandro would have never forgiven me if that sweet filly hadn't recovered."

Georgia smiled at him over the glass he gave her. "Actually, I don't think he would have ever forgiven himself."

Sebastian waved them over to the table. Billy threw her a wink from the dance floor, his smile telling her it was time to shrug off all worry and have some fun.

And it was a fascinating spectacle, this horsey set. Sebastian sat at her side giving her the lowdown on everyone they saw and repeatedly filling her glass.

There were jockeys hitting on big-bottomed show jumpers, Arabs renting yachts for a quarter million dollars a week, blond German dressage queens seducing billionaire hunter jumpers. "With that lot, it's not one Rolls Royce, it's a dozen—"

"Show jumpers. Dressage. That's not real riding," Rory slurred. "The only real riding is polo. That's a man's game."

Georgia smiled and politely nodded, raising her eyebrows at Billy on the sly as he rejoined them.

The apparently endless ranks of Sebastian and Rory's friends and fans and groupies kept stopping by the table to say hi. Within minutes Georgia had met Argentines, Jordanians, Americans, Indians, Brits, French, Swedes, and Germans. There were owners and riders—and the socialites, semi-celebrities, jewelers, and groupies in orbit around them. Talk was of St. Moritz, Buenos Aries, Santa Barbara, Windsor Great Park, and Paris. Georgia was reminded of a maxim of her mother's, "Polo is a passport to the world." She hadn't been wrong.

The real riders sported tan lines from their riding gear— polo shirt bands of pale skin beneath spaghetti strap dresses, tan wrists, and white hands from their gloves. They looked like striped and spotted animals on the prowl. Everyone in the room was dressed to seduce and hell-bent on partying hard.

Finally, Sebastian got restless and declared it was time they all head back to the Del Campo *hacienda* for a quick drink. There was a Del Campo open house tonight, and they were all invited. Georgia started to protest, saying another drink was probably the last thing she needed, but Sebastian insisted, saying his mother would be so disappointed if she didn't come along.

Georgia took Billy aside and hissed in his ear, "I can't go there, B. What if I run into you-know-who?"

"Oh don't worry, Peaches. I'm sure he never even comes out of his room at these things. And the house is huge; there's no way you'll cross paths. Besides, this is the first time

Beau and I have been invited to the *hacienda*, and you, Miss Wonder Vet, are our ticket in. Please say you'll go. This is an amazing networking opportunity. Everyone who is anyone will be there."

Georgia sighed. "As long as you promise to offer a quick escape if I need it, okay?"

Billy shook his head at her. "It was just a couple of silly kisses, G. You'd think the man had ravished you, the way you're acting."

Georgia closed her eyes and thought of strong, callused fingers that trailed sparks so hot, they melted her insides.

"You have no idea," she said.

Chapter Eighteen

Driving back to the *hacienda*, Alejandro was dismayed to see a crowd of cars. Christ, between practice and an extended workout to shake off thoughts of Georgia, he'd forgotten about the party. He knew his mother would want him to make an appearance, but he was hardly suitable for company at the moment. He slipped in through the kitchen and took the back stairs to his bedroom, hoping to avoid running into anyone before he could clean himself up.

He stripped off his clothes on his way to the bathroom, savoring the prospect of a long, hot shower. He realized that he hadn't cleaned himself since the night before, since he'd had Georgia in his arms, and for a moment, he imagined the phantom scent of her on his skin. He was suddenly jolted with lust. Every fantasy that he had worked so hard to push away came slamming back into his head. There was no holding them back. He stepped into the shower and gripped himself under the hot jets of water, pulsing with desire, helplessly reliving the way her silky skin had felt under his hands, the sound of her gasps and moans, the way she had writhed against his chest, urgently pressing her firm, full breasts against him. Imagining all he would have done if she had not stopped him, how her naked body would have looked in the moonlight, how he would have explored her every curve and secret shadow . . . until at last he braced himself against the tile and found explosive release, letting the water run down over him and rinse him clean.

* * *

Sebastian led as they picked their way up a brick path toward the entrance, breathing in the heady, burnt-sugar scent of the jasmine and magnolias that bloomed all around them. Everywhere Georgia's eyes fell there was something lovely to see. The sprawling white adobe house glowed warm and welcoming through dozens of mullioned windows. Towering live oaks dripping with Spanish moss were underplanted with billowing hibiscus and floodlit from beneath. They entered through a stone arch into a private courtyard surrounded by a mossy brick wall. A tiny chapel stood across from the main entrance, and in front of the chapel was a small, shallow pool, bubbling with water that barely glazed the brightly colored, intricately painted tiles within. Nothing as splashy as a fountain, Georgia noted.

The party was met at the entrance by a slight, elegant, and rather forbidding older woman, her face framed by two snowy streaks in her otherwise jet-black hair. There was an emerald the size of a robin's egg resting at her throat. Sebastian introduced her as his mother, Pilar.

She smiled coolly as she took Georgia's hand in her own light grasp. "Ah, you are the *señorita* who saved our *yegua*— our little mare. *Bienvenida*. I am very happy to meet you."

She then turned her cheeks for Rory's kisses. She greeted Beau and Billy with the same easy welcome and then ushered everyone in before turning back to the door to meet more arriving guests.

Beau introduced Georgia to Cricket, a lush, platinum blond British girl who Georgia learned was an Olympic medalist in show jumping.

"Oh my God, I hate you!" was Cricket's opening remark. She paused long enough for Georgia to worry and then said deadpan, "You have the exact hair I've always wanted."

"Cricket, you're ridiculous," Rory said fondly.

Cricket took Georgia's arm and leaned in. Georgia thought she smelled like very expensive cotton candy. "I hear you're the hero of the day," she said, her voice dropping intimately. "Pilar told me all about it, of course, but I'd love to hear your version of events."

"Where were you anyway?" Sebastian asked. "Why weren't you at the game?"

"Being inducted into yet another Hall of Fame, darling," she drawled.

The group made their way through an impressive great room and out onto the back terrace, where low planter's chairs looked out over the lush landscape. Georgia was handed a glass of delicious ice-cold wine beaded with condensation. Billy begged to see the gardens, and he and Beau ran off together. Sebastian and Rory were busy talking to other players about horses and plays, conversations, Georgia could tell, that tended to go on and on...and Cricket followed Pilar back to the kitchen.

For a blissful minute, Georgia was on her own, stretching her legs and curling her toes, feeling the breeze drift through her hair, smelling the magnolia blossoms, and listening to the ebb and flow of conversation from inside the house. She realized she was a little woozy from the club cocktails and having had nothing to eat since lunch. She lay back in her chair and closed her eyes. This had to be one of the most beautiful places she'd ever been, and she wouldn't at all mind falling asleep here.

"Tired?" a low voice said. Georgia jolted upright and almost gave herself whiplash, turning to find Alejandro standing in the doorway, a silhouette like the statue of David backlit by the lights of the house.

Damn it, Billy. So much for the whole "he never comes out of his room" routine.

"Sorry. God. Talk about making myself at home." She got to her feet in what felt like a clumsy fluster.

He chuckled and stepped out of the shadows. "I'd say you've earned it."

Alejandro was casual and elegant in jeans and a thin red T-shirt, which clung to the rigid contours of his muscular chest. Georgia felt her face flush and quickly looked away. "How—how is MacKenzie?"

"She's doing well," he said. "Back in the barn by tomorrow, and the vet thinks back on the field by next season. Though, knowing that girl, she will be ready to ride by next month."

Georgia frowned. "Oh, but you really shouldn't push her."

He took a step closer to her, a smile playing at the corners of his mouth. "Don't worry, *Doctora*, I never push."

He reached out and swept a stray curl from her cheek.

Georgia froze. She knew she should step back, leave, go find Billy, but she found herself rooted to the ground, staring up into his pale blue eyes.

"*Doctora*," he murmured, "I've been thinking about you all day."

Georgia's heart fluttered. "Me, too," she admitted.

"Oh? What sort of thoughts?"

Georgia met his gaze. "Well, since you brought it up," she whispered, "I think maybe you should tell me first."

"I see." He moved even closer. Her breath caught in her throat. "I've been thinking about doing this," he said, and he placed his hands on her shoulders and kissed her.

She gasped, willing herself to resist, but he brought her closer to him still, searching her lips with his, moving with agonizing leisure over her mouth, his tongue delicately flicking, until she relaxed and involuntarily parted her lips for him. She moaned as he twined his fingers into her hair, positioning her head so that he could probe deeper, rhythmically moving his tongue in and out in a way that filled Georgia with almost unbearable heat, that made her want to press herself fully against him, to feel every part of his hard body against her own. He broke the kiss and looked into her eyes, searching. "And what about you? Is that what you've been thinking about?"

She nodded, barely able to speak. "Some—something like that."

"Show me," he said roughly.

Georgia smiled and took a hesitant step forward—but suddenly the back door slammed open, and the lovely young woman she had seen in the tent stood in the doorway.

"Ugh, this party is lame. I'm heading out," she said to Alejandro.

Georgia quickly stepped away from him, flooded with alarm at being caught.

Alejandro stood his ground and turned coolly toward the girl. He seemed more annoyed than anything. "You promised you'd stay at least a couple of hours."

She pouted. "I'm bored!"

Georgia looked at her, disbelieving. Up close, this girl looked even younger than she had thought earlier. She could hardly be legal.

"Valentina," said Alejandro, "now is not the time—"

"But Marcella wants to go clubbing and—"

"V—" He raked his hands through his hair and turned to Georgia. "I'm so sorry, Dr. Fellowes. This will only take a moment."

Georgia stared at him, completely confused. How could he act so cool? Didn't he care at all that his girlfriend had almost caught them kissing? What kind of unfeeling jerk was he?

Valentina curled her lip at Georgia. "Yes, please do excuse us, Dr. Fellowes," she said mockingly. "Apparently I need to be lectured."

Alejandro clenched his jaw, and the color heightened in his cheeks. "That is quite enough, Valentina," he bit out.

Georgia frowned. She didn't know what was going on between these two, but she knew she didn't want to be part of it. "You know what? I'm going to go. I never should have come. It was my mistake."

Alejandro blinked at her in surprise. "Georgia—"

"I'll see you around," and she left to find Billy.

Chapter Nineteen

Georgia pled sick and got Billy to drop her off at his house. He offered to stay, but she insisted that he go back to the party, and later on he texted her that he was going to spend the night at Beau's.

The next day, Georgia woke up early with a blinding headache so she swallowed some Advil, forced herself to eat a bagel, and then took a book and a giant pitcher of lemonade out to the pool and alternately read and swam and slept until her head stopped throbbing.

She was snoozing in the shade when she heard the toot of a horn to tell her Billy had returned. She opened the door to find him, freshly showered and skin happily flushed, holding a note he'd found beneath the door.

"For you. What's this? Georgia, have you been naughty? Ooh, which Del Campo brother did you mess with this time? Oh, no, wait, oh joy—was it both of them?"

"What is wrong with you?" she snapped, snatching the subtly expensive envelope out of his hand.

He seemed far too cheerful to be troubled by her cranky mood.

"What a night!" he said happily. "That party was off the

hook. The longer it went, the wilder it got. The champagne just kept getting poured, and people were getting rowdier and rowdier, and at one point, Rory was making out with two girls at once—but then Pilar walked in and put a stop to that with just one well-arched eyebrow. Man, that lady is super fierce, right?"

Georgia shrugged. "I guess."

"Oh, but she must have been in a terrible mood from the get-go, because right after you left, Alejandro and Valentina...Had. It. Out. Right there on the terrace. Yelling, screaming, exposing family secrets. It was crazy."

Georgia looked away, not wanting to admit that she had been the cause of that fight. "Don't you think there's something wrong with a guy who has a girlfriend that young? I mean, what's he trying to prove?"

Billy made a weird face. "What girlfriend? Oh, wait, you mean Valentina? Ew. That's his daughter, Georgia. She's sixteen! What is wrong with you?"

Georgia stared at him for a moment. And suddenly, the last of her irritable hangover dropped away, and she felt a ludicrous, completely inappropriate swelling of hope. Oh God, that made so much more sense. He wasn't some authoritarian asshole with a taste for young girls; he was just a protective father with a bitchy teenage daughter. She laughed with relief, aware she probably seemed a little unhinged.

"You're weird, Fellowes." Billy laughed. "But hey, who's the mystery note from anyway?

Georgia opened it and abruptly stopped laughing. She looked up at him, eyes wide, and said, "It's from Alejandro. He wants to meet for lunch at his club."

Chapter Twenty

The note was very formal. Alejandro requested a meeting at noon. By eleven, Beau was over, all oiled up, wearing barely anything, and stretched out alongside Billy on a sun bed by the pool. The pair had pushed the lounges close together so their hands could wander unhindered.

"I can't believe someone's finally taking Alejandro off the market," drawled Beau from behind his glasses. "The man's a proverbial island."

"No one's being taken off the market, Beau," said Georgia. "It's just lunch."

"It's not just lunch, it's a date," said Billy as he peered up at her, "and you look sexy as all hell, Peaches."

"I feel like I'm hanging out on both ends," said Georgia as she tugged down the hem of her dress and tugged up her neckline. She'd let Billy dress her again—and this time he'd presented her with a tank dress made of butter-soft, rose-colored jersey. It flowed over her curves and dipped precariously low in the front. He'd twisted her hair up, letting a few soft curls spring free at her neck and temples, and finished her off with thin gold hoops and matching flat gold sandals.

Billy grinned. "You kind of are. But in the best possible way. Trust. You're the hottest thing in town."

Beau trailed a lazy finger down Billy's chest. "Well, maybe not *the* hottest."

Billy smiled at him. "Smooth as Southern silk," he said, and then he was kissing Beau on the back of the neck and they seemed to forget all about Georgia and her lunch date.

"Oh God. Are you going to drop me off or what?" Georgia said, fighting her nerves by telling herself that it was no big deal.

Billy sighed and stretched languidly before rolling off his lounge and slipping a tee over his trunks. "Yes, yes. Let's go."

"I'll wait here," Beau said, slapping Billy's butt as he passed.

"I wish we weren't going to the club," she said to Billy as they buckled into his little convertible. "What if I use the wrong fork or something?"

"No one's going to be looking at your fork, Georgia."

She ignored him, tugging at her dress, "Are you sure this isn't too short?" She looked longingly back at the house. "I could still change into jeans."

"Not a chance," said Billy as he screeched out of the driveway. "You look great."

"I feel ridiculous. I don't even know if I like this guy. Why am I so nervous?"

"Well, you know that you like kissing him, what more do you need? You're leaving tomorrow, Peaches. There are zero stakes here. Just take advantage of the man, use him for your pleasure, and then you'll always have the memory of his gorgeous Argentine body to keep you warm on those cold, snowy nights."

Georgia couldn't help laughing. Billy was right. What

was she fussing over? She had only one more day of freedom before going back north, and she was not going to waste that day worrying about what fork to use or if her dress was too short. She was going to enjoy her date—and it was a *date*, she admitted—with the best-looking man she had ever seen. And then, remembering the rough timbre of his voice the night before when he had looked her in the eyes and said, "*Show me*," she felt a little shiver of anticipation. Maybe she would use him for her pleasure. Just a little bit anyway.

She leaned back in her seat, determined to have a good time.

Billy pulled up to the club. "Have fun, darling. And call me if you need a ride home." He arched a brow. "Though I cannot imagine why you would."

* * *

The interior of the club was cool and quiet. Distant sounds came from the kitchen. Everywhere she looked, there were thick white table linens and sparkling glass, an army of waiters tending to their well-heeled clientele. A friendly maître d' in white tie showed her to an upholstered mahogany booth where she was told Alejandro would meet her. Out on the deck, a couple of older women in wide-brimmed straw hats sat in wicker furniture sipping mimosas.

The waiter asked if she'd like a drink while she waited, and still resolute about having some fun, Georgia ordered a glass of expensive pinot gris, which was swiftly brought to her. She sipped the refreshing, slightly fruity wine, and had just started perusing the menu, widening her eyes at the astronomical prices, when Alejandro appeared beside her table.

"*Doctora*," he murmured as he slid into the booth across

from her. He smiled briefly, and Georgia felt a sharp sense of disappointment that he had not kissed her in greeting. It seemed he hadn't shaved that morning, and as Georgia eyed the dark shadow of stubble along his strong jaw, she longed to know exactly how it would feel against her skin.

He looked magnificent. He was wearing a perfectly cut charcoal suit with a crisp white shirt and a dark red tie. The top button of his shirt was undone, and the tie slightly loosened as the only nod to the tropical Florida weather. The suit acted like armor, only making his powerful, athletic strength seem even more impressive than usual. He was carrying an expensive-looking leather briefcase, which he carelessly placed on the seat next to him.

Perhaps he was coming from a meeting, thought Georgia to herself.

"A cranberry and soda, *por favor*," he said to the waiter.

"Oh," said Georgia, feeling bold, "have a glass of wine. It's not too early, is it?"

For a moment, she felt his eyes linger over her. His gaze was so intense that it was almost as if he had reached out and touched her. She could trace his path as he looked at her: starting at her eyes, drifting to her mouth, and then trailing down over her neck and shoulders, pausing with a sharp intake of breath at her décolletage. She suddenly remembered the feel of his hand on her breast, his thumb brushing so tantalizingly over her nipple, and it was all she could do not to suggest that he follow her to the bathroom and have his way with her right then and there at the club.

He broke his gaze, a look of regret on his face. "The wine looks very good, but it's not usually wise to mix business with pleasure, no?"

Business? Georgia blinked. "I'm sorry?"

Alejandro took a deep breath, seeming to steel himself a bit. "Dr. Fellowes—"

"Georgia."

"Okay, yes, Georgia. I'm afraid I owe you an apology."

"For last night? No, I think I owe you an apology—you see, I didn't realize that Valentina was your daughter and—"

He shook his head. "No, no. Please, you do not have to explain. You were quite right. Everything that had happened was, as you put it, a mistake."

The smile froze on Georgia's face.

He ran his hand through his hair, frowning. "You see, I have not been myself, exactly, these past few days. Normally, I never would have placed you in such a compromising position, but I was thrown off, I think, by MacKenzie's accident and…" He stopped for a moment, at a loss for words. "I don't imagine you have a daughter, do you?"

She shook her head. "No. No children."

Alejandro shrugged helplessly. "Since her mother died…the shock. It has flung us so far apart." His hands mimed a blast, and then he rested them on the table. She continued to look at his fingers as he said, "I can hardly reach her anymore."

He met her eyes with an appeal so direct she had to forcibly quell the urge to reach across the table and take his hand in hers to comfort him. Instead, she rapidly smoothed the thick, soft tablecloth under her palms.

"I understand," she said softly. "I lost my mother. I mean, she's alive. It's very different, but it's been a long time since I've seen her. She left when I was a teenager. So I think I might have some idea what…"

She faltered and nervously took a drink of water. This kind of conversation was new territory between them—and it somehow felt even more intimate than their kisses. She risked a glance up at him, and the look in his eyes encouraged her to go on.

"I was lost for a while," she said, "but I came back. And I bet Valentina will, too. You'll just have to be patient. With time and care, she'll start to trust again."

Alejandro cleared his throat. "Thank you. That means more to me than you can imagine." He took a sip of his drink, silent for a moment, and then clapped his hands together. "But I'm afraid that we have wandered a bit off track. So, what I was trying to say is that I have a business offer for you."

She nodded slowly, wondering where all this was leading.

"I do not know if you follow polo, but for our team . . . well, let's just say it has been a disappointing season so far. But I mean to turn this around. To make a new beginning. What you did for MacKenzie, you have proved yourself to be a remarkable veterinarian. I have a gut feeling about your judgment, your courage. And I think you might be able to help us. I am not a vengeful man, but our deputy vet's negligence was unforgivable. He won't be getting work for a while here in Wellington."

Georgia dropped her eyes tactfully.

"So, you see, we are in need of a new number two."

Alejandro paused for a moment, looking out over the water, running his hand through his thick hair. He was anxious, she realized, and it was endearing to see.

"Georgia, I think that hiring you to assist Gustavo, as our American vet—just for the remainder of the season, of course—six weeks—would be an excellent idea."

She stared, not sure she could have heard him right.

"I know you'll need to think about it. I understand that

you have responsibilities. Obligations. But I believe the job offers an interesting experience and a manageable challenge for a vet at your level."

Her mind ran rapidly, trying to accept the fact this was not, as it turned out, a date at all. This was a business meeting. That, actually, she had just been offered a job...and a rather dazzling job. But there was no way she could be apart from her father and the farm for over a month, was there? And what about her work at the clinic? But then she thought of that incredible fleet of ponies needing so much time and care, and the amazing, adrenaline-filled rush she had experienced watching the game in full swing...

And of course, there was Alejandro himself. She stole a look at him as he rummaged through his briefcase. His eyes were downcast, his long, spiky lashes feathering over the taut, tan skin of his high cheekbones. His wavy, coal black hair just barely touched the collar of his shirt. She didn't think she had ever met a man so infernally sexy, and just now, he'd shown her a vulnerable side of himself that made her ache. She wanted more. In every sense of the word.

He pulled a piece of paper out of his briefcase. "Sebastian has gathered from his friend Beau that you're very valuable to your practice in New York, so I know that you will have to be well compensated. Lord Henderson, our team *patrón*, was very impressed with you as well. We are prepared to be quite generous."

He slid the piece of paper across the table. Georgia unfolded it, and she almost laughed aloud. The sheer size of the number made it hard for her to keep a poker face. It was more than she'd make in a year at the vet practice back home. She thought of all the things she could fix around the farm with this money—how much it would mean to have a little cushion left each month for the first time. But she also thought of her father and what he'd think and say.

Alejandro leaned toward her across the table. She hoped for a moment that he might take her hand, but instead he ran his finger along the edge of his glass.

"Georgia," he said quietly, "I want to assure you that this would be a purely professional relationship. I do not want you to worry that what has already passed between us had anything at all to do with my offer. As I said, I have not been myself the last few days. Normally, I would have never . . . We have very strict policies about fraternization in our organization. You would be *la doctora*, and I would be your boss. Nothing more complicated than that."

Georgia swallowed her sudden disappointment. He was absolutely correct, she reminded herself. Obviously, she couldn't take a new job while being romantically involved with her future boss. She forced herself to smile. "Of course."

He smiled back. "So you accept?"

"Yes," she said, surprising herself as the word came out of her mouth. "I do."

He offered his hand to shake on the deal. She took it, and prayed he wouldn't notice the powerful rush of heat that surged through her entire body at the touch of his fingers.

For a moment, Alejandro's smile faded. He looked almost regretful, and his hand lingered on hers perhaps a shade too long. Then he broke contact and lifted his glass.

"*Salud*," he said softly. "I have a very good feeling about this."

Chapter Twenty-one

Leaving the club and putting his Tesla Roadster into gear, Alejandro was annoyed with himself. It was stupid, really. He'd gotten exactly what he wanted from Georgia Fellowes—the team needed a decent vet, and like magic, an incredible one had appeared. But when he told her that they would be strictly professional—and she had so readily agreed—he'd experienced a sharp pang of what could only be described as loss. It was as if, by giving him what he asked for, she had taken away something much more valuable.

He'd decided to offer Georgia the job last night, after his horrible fight with Valentina. It had been humiliating, all those people privy to his family's problems. His daughter hadn't held back—howling that he was a terrible father, that she hated Wellington, and that she hated him. He had finally sent her to her room, and she had slammed and stomped all the way upstairs, making sure that everyone knew exactly what an unfair beast she felt her father to be.

He knew, rationally, that she was just being a teenager—

a teenager who had lost her mother, no less—but her fierce
defiance had felt like just one more thing that proved how
out of control everything had become. First, all the lost
games, then missing MacKenzie's injury until it was almost
too late, and then his rash behavior with Dr. Fellowes...Je-
sus, where had that come from? When he'd found her out
there on the veranda, half-drunk in the twilight, wearing
that skimpy blue dress that looked as if it had been poured
over her, he'd instantly gone rock hard—no matter that a
mere fifteen minutes before he had exhausted himself in
the shower. She'd looked up at him with those changeable
eyes, and every reasonable thought had flown out of his
mind. He'd wanted nothing so much as he'd wanted to take
her right there; kiss her, lick her, bite her, strip her, and
have his way with every inch of her luscious body, party
be damned. And he would have done it, too, if Valentina
hadn't interrupted them.

Offering her the job was his way of proving that he could
control himself. He knew that it would have been easier had
he simply waited it out, let her go back to New York, probably never seeing her again. But the team needed a vet and
she was a damned good one. It would have been ridiculous
for him not to take advantage of such an opportunity. If he
had let her slip away, it would have been proof that he was
putting his needs ahead of the team.

And so he had deliberately placed her firmly out of reach.
She was an employee now, and there were iron-fast rules
about fraternization on his team. Alejandro had made those
rules himself, in fact. And the last thing he was going to do
was break them.

This was exactly the kind of thing he needed to get back
on track, he told himself. He had corrected one bad decision

and replaced it with a good one. He'd tackle each element of his home life and the team that needed fixing in turn. One task at a time until he restored order and championship form. Discipline. Self-control. A singular focus on winning. These things would fix it all. He was sure of it.

Chapter Twenty-two

Alejandro walked into the house as his mother and Corinne, the housekeeper, were putting the finishing touches on lunch. Pilar smiled at him and raised her cheek for a kiss.

His mother was amazing, Alejandro thought, throwing together feasts day after day so effortlessly. His father had always loved inviting friends—repeatedly springing dozens of people on her for dinner—and Sebastian was the same. With a little discreet help, she made sure the place was impeccable and everyone was comfortable, day after day.

"Anything I can do to help?" he asked.

"Call your brother and Valentina?"

"Isn't Sebastian on the field?"

"In the media room, I think," Pilar said, sprinkling basil over the salad.

Alejandro scowled. Sebastian should have been at practice.

Alejandro went down to retrieve his brother from the lavishly designed basement theater. Seeing him lounging on the giant leather couch, feet up, a drink in his hand, enjoying the closing moments of the latest Christopher Nolan movie, took a large bite out of Alejandro's mood.

"Hey," Sebastian said, not taking his eyes off the screen.

Alejandro fought back a wave of annoyance. "Hey. Get any riding in?"

"Not yet," Sebastian said. "Hoping we can head down together after lunch."

"I have to fly to Kentucky," Alejandro said. "See a pony to potentially replace MacKenzie in the string."

"Yeah? I might watch the sequel to this, then." Sebastian said, eyes still on the screen.

"Rory and Hendy are on the field. At least one of us should put in an appearance," Alejandro said.

"Enzo can handle it. That's what we pay him for."

"No, Seb, we pay him to be the *piloto*. He's in charge of the horses. He doesn't take your place on the field," Alejandro said.

"Enzo won't care," Sebastian said to his brother's retreating back. "Lighten up."

Alejandro stalked upstairs, where he found Valentina lying on her stomach watching makeup tutorials on YouTube.

"Valentina, lunch is ready."

She slid off the bed and slouched toward the door in her socks without looking his way.

"Shoes?" Alejandro suggested. "*Abuela*'s been to so much trouble."

Valentina rolled her eyes and pulled on a pair of Toms.

Pilar had laid out lunch on the terrace beneath a sailcloth shade, which snapped and billowed in the breeze. Thick-petaled peonies and bright floral print napkins decorated the table, along with tall flasks of chilled water and wine from the family's Argentine estate. Pilar made even a simple family lunch look ready for a *Bon Appetit* photo shoot.

"So, how'd it go at the club?" Sebastian asked as he helped himself to risotto.

"Dr. Fellowes accepted," Alejandro said. "Hendy will handle the contract, but we shook on it. Looks good."

"Doesn't she?" Sebastian drawled. "There's something intoxicating about that one, headstrong and sexy."

Alejandro felt a flare of annoyance. "She's a professional," he said grimly.

"She's also very pretty," Sebastian said. "Don't be so uptight, Jandro."

Pilar brought out another dish from the kitchen and sat down to join them. "Who is this we're talking about?"

"The lady vet," Sebastian said. "You met her at the party. Slinky blue dress. Curls."

"I remember," Pilar said. "*Que linda.*"

"See?" Sebastian threw up his hands in triumph. "I'm sorry, Jandro. I'm not suggesting Dr. Fellowes is not a good vet, or the fact she's pretty is the entire reason you hired her, but I don't see why I have to pretend to be blind just because you insist on it. The fact is, we're discussing a beautiful woman. Valentina? You with me?"

Valentina shrugged. "Yeah, she's all right. Whatev."

"Whatev," Sebastian mocked, and Valentina swiped him with her napkin.

Sometimes they acted more like siblings than uncle and niece, Alejandro thought. He threw a glance of apology at his mother and set his water glass down heavily. "Look, Sebastian, maybe you spend more time watching movies than you do on horseback, but that does not mean that you are not part of this team. You have to act accordingly. She works for us now, and you can't treat her that way."

Sebastian threw up his hands in frustration. "In what way have I treated her? I haven't done a thing to the woman. I'm just saying she's attractive."

"We have to focus. We can't be distracted. Do you know how close we are to being out of running for the cup?"

"So, we've had *un poco de mala suerte*," Sebastian said. "A little bad luck. Nothing terminal. Give it a break, Jandro."

"No, it's not bad luck. It's lack of discipline. It's disorder. Hiring Dr. Fellowes is going to help us get back on track."

"What about Gustavo?"

"What about him?"

"How is he going to feel about working with a woman?"

"I didn't ask him," Alejandro said. He felt himself flush in annoyance. "It's not his decision to make."

"Hmm." Sebastian raised his glass. "Well, *buena suerte* to Georgia. I hope the poor girl knows what she's getting into."

Chapter Twenty-three

Billy and Beau ignored all of Georgia's protests about everything she had to do and insisted on taking her out to celebrate. Between their own plans for collaboration and her new job, Billy assured her that it would be rude not to drink midday.

The three of them drank stone cold rosé at a little restaurant overlooking the water while the men told her everything they knew about working for the Del Campo family.

"It'll be a lot of work," said Beau. "You'll need to be strong to handle that responsibility. It's a thirty-horse barn, and a highly volatile environment even when the season's going their way. Horses are extremely vulnerable down here. Even a scratch can be a calamity in this heat. How much are they paying you?"

Georgia took a sip of wine. "They've been very generous. Plus they're giving me the cost of travel home at the end of the season, a car to use, and room and board."

"Well, just be sure you're getting what you're worth, Georgia. Think what it would cost them to get a good deputy vet on a day rate. The temps down here make a fortune. Injured horses are dangerous. Vets get hurt all the time."

"And remember, money's not an issue with these guys," Billy said. "The family's worth millions."

"Billions," Beau confirmed.

"Squillions," Billy trumped. "And G., there's other stuff to consider besides the actual work-work. They've got a small army of people working for them. Someone told me that they have a handler-to-pony ratio of something like five-to-one. And half of the grooms are young girls—they practically work for free in hopes of getting time on the horses or a lesson from one of the players. So you know that kind of crowd is going to be a bitch to handle. The politics in those barns are pure poison. The whole La Victoria team is a mess of scandal and intrigue."

"Well, at least it will be more interesting than worming terriers." Georgia smiled.

"Now that's a whole other point. What about your boss upstate?" Beau said, waving a forkful of asparagus. "Will you even have a job to come back to?"

"I think so. I mean, I haven't talked to him yet, but winter isn't a very busy season and . . . Oh God, maybe I accepted too soon." Georgia threw down her spoon. "You guys are making me too nervous to eat."

"Well, you haven't signed anything yet, darling. You don't have to do it," said Billy.

"Yes, it would be simple enough to back out," said Beau.

"But I want to do it!" blurted Georgia. "I don't care if it's hard work and that everyone behaves badly. I want to work with those ponies and I want to work with—"

She caught herself and quickly shut her mouth.

"Now who is it that you want to work with so bad, Peaches?" teased Billy.

Georgia glared at him. "The team," she said. "I want to work with the team."

"Uh-huh," said Deau.

"Okay then. If you're hell-bent on doing it. Call your boss in New York now," advised Billy. "Get it over with. Make it official, G."

Georgia took one last gulp of wine and then walked out to the deck to call her boss at the clinic.

Dr. Jackson was genuinely delighted for her. Georgia had been right. Given that the town emptied so dramatically over the winter, he was more than happy to reduce his over-head until the spring. He promised to give her a dream reference if anyone called, and he assured her that the job would be waiting when she was ready.

Georgia stepped back in from the terrace relieved and beaming, which Billy decided warranted a second bottle. She sat down and sipped her wine, feeling each anxious knot in her back slip loose as the moments ticked by. She was happy to relax and let her friends dish gossip and intrigue while she basked in the rays of the warm Florida sun pouring through the window and the odd and delicious feeling that, for once, she was exactly where she wanted to be.

* * *

Alejandro was wondering how it was that family had the ability to kill a good mood so quickly. It nearly winded him watching his daughter finishing her meal with that shuttered expression. They had been coming to Wellington for years, and it seemed only yesterday she'd been eleven, and seven, and five, and her happy chatter and easy peals of laughter had been the warmth which bound them as a family. Now he could barely remember the last time he'd even seen her smile.

After picking at her food, Valentina asked if she could be excused.

"Say thank you to your *abuela*," Alejandro said automatically.

"Thank you, *Abuela*," Valentina parroted as she slid from her chair.

It had been so much easier when Olivia was alive. They'd had a traditional marriage. Olivia managed the home. Alejandro the barn. And Olivia's constant vigilance over their daughter had left him free to be the fun *papá* when it came to weekends and bedtime. It was only now he found himself having to nag Valentina about manners that he realized just how much work Olivia had actually done. His throat felt constricted with guilt.

"Valentina?" he called after her on impulse.

She turned back.

"Come with me, to Lexington? We'll see a couple of ponies, maybe bring one home. It's a short flight. Should be fun."

She looked interested for a moment. "Can I try them out?"

Damn. He should have seen that coming. "Well...no, I think it's better if I ride."

She rolled her eyes. "Nah, then," she said. "What's the point?"

Snubbed and trying not to mind, he helped his mother clear the plates.

As he stacked the plates in the sink, a deep urge for privacy triggered a pang of homesickness. It wouldn't be like this if he and Valentina were at home. He missed his own *campo*, the glorious rambling kitchen and flagstone floors, the worn wooden surface of his enormous kitchen table. This Florida house still felt more like his father's home than his own. There was something about the gleaming and impeccable look of the kitchen—the wraparound granite and stainless steel—that left him ill at ease. He missed the warmth of Argentina. It was a relief at home to be able to leave things where they fell, among the dogs and a comfortable amount of dust. This place was just too antiseptic for his taste. Still, he knew that the interior decorating was less of an issue for him than the fact that, here, he and his daughter were never alone.

He loved his mother and was glad to have her fixed presence in their lives, for Valentina's sake as much as his, but he couldn't help feeling that his daughter's transgressions were somehow magnified under her gaze.

As his mother and the housekeeper restored the vast kitchen to order, Hendy called to ask Alejandro about the deal he'd struck with Georgia.

"You offered her room and board?"

"Of course," Alejandro said.

"Where do you propose we put her?"

"I'm not sure yet. I'll need to figure it out."

"Good. Oh, and I had a thought. Why don't you take her with you to Kentucky, eh? It's always better to use our own vet when we're buying."

Alejandro was silent for a moment—imagining himself traveling alone with Georgia. His heart hammered in his chest.

"Alejandro? Did you hear me about the trip?"

He shook his head. "Yes. Sure. That's a good idea. I'll call her."

"Excellent. All right then, my boy. Have a good time."

Alejandro hung up and filled his mother in on their need to find someplace for Georgia to stay. He wanted the vet to be a fully integrated member of the team, close to the barn and on call for Gustavo at all hours, but of course, finding a rental now that the season was under way would be a hopeless task.

"The motel?" Pilar suggested, but he knew the place would be booked solid since this time last year, often with three or four girls to a room. There were plenty of young people in Florida sleeping out in trailers, happy to have the experience of working with world-class trainers and horses, but that was hardly a setup he could propose to Georgia.

It occurred to him to enlist his brother's help, but after the exchange they'd had at lunch, Alejandro thought that Sebastian would probably think it totally reasonable to offer Georgia to share his own bed for the season.

Help from Gustavo was out of the question until news of Georgia's hiring had been properly finessed, and Rory was off wining and dining with possible sponsors, fishing missions at which he had had limited success but fun trying.

Alejandro rubbed his hands through his hair in frustration. Seeing this, Pilar came over and smoothed it back down again. "You need to get ready to go, *hijo*. Let me figure this out for you."

"You don't mind? It's a lot."

"*Querido*, it's the least I can do. I may be decorative, but I'm not completely ineffective. In forty years with your father, I learned a thing or two. You should use me. There's so much more I could do to lighten the load if you'd let me."

"Just this one thing would be amazing, *Mamá*," Alejandro said, already on his way out to the barn. "Thank you."

* * *

Back at Billy's place, the boys took a nap, leaving Georgia no further excuse not to call her father. She dialed his number with a rising feeling of dread. She was doing exactly what she had said she would never do, leave him in the lurch in order to run off with the equestrian jet set.

The conversation went even worse than she'd expected. As she described the offer, Georgia could feel her dad's hurt and disapproval all the way down in Florida.

"You have commitments here, Georgia," he said.

"I know, Dad. That's why I'm taking the job. Think how much we'll be able to do with what I make down here. It includes room and board, so I can save everything I make. We can fix the rotten siding, get going with the new roof, maybe even get a second car so that I won't have to bum all those rides from you."

He was silent for a moment and then said, "Who's going to look after the animals while you're gone?"

"Dad, I'm sorry, but you did fine looking after everything when I was at college. And we can get some help. I can arrange that from down here. Plenty of locals I know from the practice are good with animals and would be happy for some extra work in winter. I know it's a pain in the neck for you now, but the payoff could really make life simpler."

"What about your job at the clinic?"

"I've spoken to Dr. Jackson, and he was super supportive."

Too late Georgia realized that was a mistake. She could hear her dad's anger like white noise around her words.

"You've already gone ahead without talking to me? Why are we even having this conversation, then? I thought you were calling to ask my permission. Why bother even asking me when your mind's made up?"

"Dad," Georgia said slowly, trying to keep her voice calm, "I wasn't asking, so much as explaining. I mean, I have made my mind up, but I would love your understanding. Your blessing—"

"Well, I'm sorry to rain on your parade but the whole idea seems flaky to me. Giving up a good thing at the first hint of glamour—"

"Dad, it's not like that. And it's temporary. Six weeks max and I'll be back on the farm. Back at work in the clinic with that extra savings in the bank."

"What about Sam? Have you told him? What about the rental?"

Georgia felt a flash of annoyance that her father thought Sam should have any say in the matter. "I'll send him an e-mail. And if I decide later that I want the place—who knows? Sam didn't seem in a hurry to rent it to anyone else."

"Who do you think you are, expecting the world to wait around for you? Do you think a man like Sam doesn't have options?"

Georgia felt her anger rising. They were clearly talking about more than a lease.

"I've said yes to the Del Campos, and that's that. I can't go back on it now."

"Well, what can I say, Georgia? You are your mother's daughter," he said wearily and hung up on her.

She felt the tears smart in her eyes. His weariness was worse than anger.

Her phone rang again, and she snatched it up.

"Dad, please," she cried. "That was completely unfair! Just

because you don't want me down here doesn't mean you can compare me to Mom!"

There was a silence and then, "*Doctora?*" a deep, accented voice asked.

Damn.

Georgia flipped the phone in her hand to see the caller ID. Private Number. She cringed as she put the phone back to her ear. "Um, Alejandro?"

"Yes? Georgia? Is everything all right?"

"Yes, yes. I'm fine," Georgia said.

"You sound upset."

The obvious concern in his voice created a little warm spot in her chest. She couldn't help smiling. Suddenly what had just happened with her father didn't seem like the end of the world.

"No, I'm fine, thank you. I just thought you were . . . someone else."

"*Bueno*, I am calling to ask if you could start work a bit earlier than we discussed."

"Of course. How much earlier?"

"Would an hour from now be a possibility?"

Chapter Twenty-four

"Wheels up in five minutes," the flight assistant announced as she passed Alejandro a drink. He settled contentedly back in his seat. The family Cessna was a luxury that never got old.

"When you said work, I expected it to be in your barn, not your jet," said Georgia.

He smiled at her across the aisle. She looked charming and casual in jeans and a yellow T-shirt. Her cheeks were pink with excitement, her curls in slight disarray. "You like to fly?" he said.

"Well, sure, but usually I'm stuck between two talkative old ladies who smell like cats. I mean, I've never even flown first class, never mind a private jet." She turned around and peered at the back of the cabin. "Is that a bedroom back there?"

"*Sí*, but it's a short flight. I don't imagine we'll be using it."

The dimples in her cheeks flashed as she tried to suppress a mischievous smile. He cleared his throat. "I just meant, we won't want to sleep."

The dimples deepened. "Oh?"

"So," said Alejandro, suddenly desperate to change the

subject, "I have the specifications on the stallion we'll be looking at today, if you'd like to see."

She nodded, and he passed over the printout. She scanned the pages, her nose wrinkling.

"It's unusual for polo, that he's a stallion. Typically the game's played with mares but this horse—Temper—looks an unusually good prospect, and he might be good for breeding as well. We'll see what you think."

"Whoa," Georgia exclaimed. "Is this really the asking price? One hundred thousand dollars?"

"Well, I think we have some room to negotiate."

She blinked. "I'm sorry. I'm trying to act cool about this but kind of failing miserably. That seems like an awful lot of money for just one horse."

He looked at her sharply. "In polo, the horse is everything. Without world-class mounts, we cannot win, and I play to win."

She nodded. "Of course. I just didn't realize that a world-class mount cost quite this much."

He relented a little. "Not all do. And of course, you're right, it is a lot of money. But you must understand, the game begins and ends with the pony you ride. The horse is as much of an athlete as the rider. I am only as good as my mount, and at the level I play, I have to be sure that I am riding the very best."

"Because—because it's so dangerous?"

He shook his head. "No. I mean yes, polo is dangerous, and the better the horse, the safer the player, but even the best horse can stumble. I am talking about winning."

She nodded again, thinking. "Alejandro, I know this isn't going to exactly reward your confidence in me, but I have to tell you something."

His chest tightened. "Yes?"

"Your game the other night? That was the first time I'd ever seen polo."

He let out a bark of surprised laughter. "You're kidding me."

"I'm sorry, but I'm not. And since, thanks to me, it all kind of ended before it began, I wonder if you could tell me the basic rules? I mean, if I'm going to be taking care of priceless horses, I should probably have at least some idea of what we're doing with them."

"Yes, I imagine that might be useful." He unbuckled his seatbelt. "Do you mind if I come sit by you? It will be easier if I can put some of this on paper."

She nodded and scooted over to make room.

He sat down next to her, exquisitely aware of how close she was. He dug a pen out of his jacket pocket. "May I?" he said and took the papers she had been looking at and flipped them over, quickly sketching out a polo field.

"This is the field of play," he said. He touched his pen to the paper. "This is the halfway line. These are the score lines. Do you know *fútbal*?"

She leaned closer to look. He could smell her hair—like sweet almonds. "You mean soccer? A little."

He shifted away a bit. "Okay, imagine *fútbal*—soccer— played with only four players on each side and no goalie. Plus, every time a goal is made, the players change field direction."

"Like halftime at basketball?"

"*Sí*, but for us, this happens every time we score a point. So you know the basics—we ride the ponies, we hit a small plastic ball with a wooden mallet. The ball goes very fast— up to one hundred miles an hour—and we try to get the ball through the goal. Whoever has the most goals at the end wins."

"Right. But it seemed like you were stopping and starting every five minutes or so, switching ponies."

"*Sí*, each period is called a chukker, and it's every seven and a half minutes, actually. We need to switch out the ponies because we ride them so hard. Sometimes a pony can do two chukkers, but that's not so common. Usually only in the semifinals and finals."

"But MacKenzie did two."

He smiled, pleased that she had noticed. "Yes. MacKenzie has a rare heart. She lives to play so we gave her two even though it was not a final. Now, in Florida, we play only six chukkers, but in Argentina, we play eight."

She laughed. "So, they're tougher in Argentina."

"Oh, yes. Definitely." He leaned over the paper again and drew four X's on each side of the paper. "There are four positions, each very important. Number four—on our team this is Hendy—is the closest thing we might have to a goalie. He is all defense, blocking shots. Number two—that is Sebastian—plays both offense and defense. He runs the ball back and forth and sets up shots. Very hard worker usually. Which is ironic considering my brother."

Georgia smiled.

"Number one—this is Rory—is all offense. He is just waiting for the ball to be sent his way, and he usually scores the most goals. And then, Number three—that is me—*el capitán*—the captain. Three hits the ball the hardest, decides all the strategy, also gets a goal or two through when I am lucky."

"And do you ever switch positions?"

"No. We know what we are best at. There are different

types of players, you know? Guys who are amazing with the ball, who have real finesse, and then there are guys who are just *guerreros*—warriors—if that makes sense? They play as hard as they can. Nothing stops them."

She looked up at him. Her eyes sparked. "Let me guess. You're a warrior."

He gazed back at her. "I like to play hard."

"And the ponies, they like to play hard, too?"

"The ponies, they are all heart. A good polo pony is a perfect athlete. A good pony will instinctually know what you want before you even tell them. You cannot love polo if you do not love the horses."

"But it looks so dangerous, though. For the players and the horses."

"It is. Every time you go out on the field, you know there is a chance you could get seriously hurt, or die even. But it's an ancient game, Georgia. Thousands of years old. And there is a reason people have played it for so long, even if it is risky. When you are out on that field, if everything goes correctly, it's like you and the pony are one being. You cannot tell where you end and the horse begins. And when you are chasing that ball, and everything is happening so quickly— it's like you are flying together. And when you win..." He sighed and closed his eyes for a moment. "There is no feeling like that anywhere else in the world."

"You really love it," she said huskily.

"I do," he answered. "Maybe more than anything."

Chapter Twenty-five

The Lexington horse farm was a glorious piece of property. Georgia took a deep breath of the crisp air as she looked out over the endless, rolling fields of bluegrass.

"It's nice, no?" said Alejandro as they stood waiting for the pony to be brought out. "Not so hot as Florida."

"And not as cold as New York."

The farm owner, Mr. Yates, was a gruff sort with the facial capillaries of a drinker but a keen and beady eye. He shook Alejandro's hand, nodded politely at Georgia, and then stood in silence, not bothering to make small talk.

A young groom led out the bay stallion, Temper. He was a beauty, nickering and stamping to live up to his name, his muscles veined and gleaming.

"Hey, good looking," said Georgia and scratched him under his chin. The horse threw his head back and snorted, rolling his eyes. "Whoa there, a little touchy," she said, taking a step back.

Yates frowned at her. "He's not touchy. He's sensitive. A good polo horse is always sensitive."

Georgia shot a questioning look at Alejandro, who shrugged. "High spirited is not necessarily a bad thing," he conceded as he ran his hand along the pony's neck. He looked at Yates. "May I?"

Mr. Yates nodded, and Alejandro swung up into the saddle. He rode a small circle, and Georgia saw his eyes light up and a tiny smile play at the corners of his mouth, but when he looked back at the owner, his face slid into a composed and neutral mask. "Nice horse," he said carelessly.

Mr. Yates raised an eyebrow. "A damned nice horse," he returned. "Go ahead. Take him out."

Georgia watched as Yates swung open the gate and Alejandro headed out into the open field. The pony was a bit wayward at first, but Alejandro quickly seemed to find a rhythm with him, and soon they were moving together with sweet ease and precision as they went through their paces.

Georgia leaned against the fence, her heart in her throat, as they opened up into a full gallop, streaking across the grass. *God*, she thought, *what a horse. And what a rider.* She couldn't say who was more beautiful—the man or the stallion.

After about twenty minutes, Alejandro cantered back up, swung down, and handed the reins to the waiting groom.

"You want to give him a try?" he asked Georgia.

Georgia blinked. It had been a long time since they'd had a ridable horse at the farm. She hadn't been in the saddle for years. "Oh, no, that's probably not a good idea. I'll just check him out from the ground," she said, embarrassed.

She asked Yates questions as she did an inventory of the pony. What was his history? How much feed did he consume, and how often? How about water? Any previous health issues? She took the stallion's temperature and checked his pulse and respiration. She peered inside his ears, looking at his teeth and hooves, running her hands up and down his legs and then the rest of his body, checking for any lumps or sores or scars she might have missed.

She couldn't find a thing wrong. He was immaculate. She'd never seen a more exquisite horse. "He seems to be in decent shape," she said carefully, not wanting to tip Alejandro's hand.

Yates snorted. "He's in perfect health," he said, "and you know it."

"Yes, well," said Alejandro, "he's a nice type, but maybe not at this price."

The owner sighed and looked greatly put upon. "Well, I suppose I could drop a thousand off. But you'd have to pay for shipping."

Georgia inwardly rolled her eyes—even she knew that the cost of shipping would easily come to a thousand.

"How about ten thousand off, and I pay for shipping?" countered Alejandro.

Yates bit his lip. Considered. "Five thousand."

"Seven-five. You ship. And I'll take him. Can you have him delivered this week?"

"You pay for the shipping and I'll have him loaded up before you leave the farm."

Alejandro laughed and shook the older man's hand. "Done."

Georgia watched him as he turned back to the horse, finally letting his real feelings show as he ran his fingers down the stallion's long neck, and graced the animal with a heart-stopping smile.

Georgia stepped up closer. "So, I guess you like him," she said teasingly.

He turned his head, the same magnificent smile now focused on her. "Maybe just a little bit," he murmured.

Chapter Twenty-six

Temper didn't want to go into the trailer. He balked as soon as he saw it, let out a high whinny, and refused to move forward, leaving the groom futilely tugging at his lead.

Alejandro watched, a bit amused, as the farm owner tried to cajole him on from behind.

"C'mon, boy!" Yates said, and slapped the horse's rump. The horse just flicked his tail in response and whinnied again.

From inside the stables came an answering whinny, higher and more desperate than Temper's.

"Aw," said the groom, "it's like she knows."

Mr. Yates snorted. "That damned nag. I'll sell her as soon as she foals."

"Wait, what nag? What are you talking about?" said Georgia.

Temper neighed again—a trumpet-like noise. The horse in the barn answered. Alejandro raised his eyebrows questioningly at Mr. Yates.

"They're in love," said the groom.

"In love?" repeated Georgia. She looked stricken.

Mr. Yates grimaced. "Don't be ridiculous. They're horses.

They're not in love. They're just...attached." He shoved at Temper. "Walk on!"

The stallion didn't budge. The sounds from the stable grew ever more hysterical.

Georgia looked at Alejandro. "Maybe we can just take a look?" she said hopefully.

Temper pawed the ground and snorted. Alejandro sighed. "Show us the horse in the barn."

* * *

"No," said Alejandro as soon as he saw the mare. "Absolutely not."

The horse was bewilderingly average. A weathered palomino, with short bandy legs, a scrubby little mane, and a huge, distended belly. Standing alongside Temper, she looked like a warthog next to a gazelle.

Temper nickered softly and gently nibbled along the little mare's neck. The palomino closed her eyes in bliss.

"Aw," said Georgia. "Look at how sweet they are together."

Alejandro shook his head, amused. "Why do you even have a horse like this?" he asked Yates.

"A groom left her behind when he went back to Mexico. She was his own personal pony. I was gonna sell her for dog meat, but then Temper got loose and knocked her up. Just waiting to see what the foal looks like before we ship her off."

Georgia glared at him. "That's terrible!"

Mr. Yates smirked at her. "Lady, we breed and train Thoroughbreds here. The best horses in the country. This old nag is just taking up resources."

"She's not an old nag." Georgia reached over and patted

the palomino's nose. "Don't you listen to him, you're not an old nag."

Alejandro snorted. "No, he's right. She's pretty much an old nag."

"I think she's lovely," said Georgia. "Look at those gorgeous brown eyes."

"I think she might have worms," answered Alejandro.

Georgia ignored him. "What's her name?"

"Manuel called her *Azucar*," the groom piped in.

Alejandro laughed. "Sugar," he translated for Georgia.

"Oh," breathed Georgia, "that's perfect." She looked at Mr. Yates. "How much do you want for her?"

He smiled wolfishly. "Since she's carrying Temper's foal, I'd say ten."

"Wait—" interjected Alejandro.

"Ten thousand?" said Georgia.

"Hey," said Alejandro, "we are not buying this mare."

Georgia got a stubborn look on her face. "How about two?"

"I might do seven. That foal could be just like Temper."

"That foal could be just like her," protested Alejandro.

"Five," said Georgia.

Yates looked like he was considering it, but before he could answer, Alejandro yanked Georgia's arm. "Excuse me," he gritted. "May I speak to you privately for a moment?"

Georgia followed him out of the barn.

"What do you think you're doing?" said Alejandro.

She rapidly blinked her hazel eyes, all innocence. "What do you mean?"

"I mean, why in hell are you bargaining for a horse that I do not want?"

"Because you need her."

"No, I definitely do not need her."

She put her hand on his arm and looked up at him, beseeching. "Temper needs her."

He rolled his eyes. "Temper will get over her. Have you seen my horses? They are beautiful. He will fall in love with another mare."

She glowered at him. "But then Sugar will end up as dog food!"

He sighed, exasperated. "That is very sad, indeed. But I am still not buying that mare."

She got a dogged look on her face. "Fine. Then I will buy that mare. And I will give her to you as a gift."

He laughed. "Are you crazy? Do you even have five thousand dollars?"

She jutted out her chin. "Well, no, actually. But I will. Because you are paying me a lot of money, remember?"

"Yes, but I haven't paid you yet."

"You can dock me."

"You are actually serious? You want to buy me that horse?"

"Dead serious. I will absolutely buy you that horse...if you will loan me the money to do so."

He looked at her. Her pretty face was flushed, her curls were even more askew than usual, her little nose crinkled...

He threw up his hands and laughed. "Fine. Fine! I will buy that ugly pony! I will buy the nag for Temper. And for you, *Doctora*. But you have to let me negotiate the price. She is definitely not worth five thousand dollars."

Georgia squealed and threw her arms around him. "Yes! I knew you wouldn't let her be dog food! Thank you!" She reached up and quickly kissed his mouth in innocent joy.

The moment he tasted her lips on his, he stopped thinking. Pure instinct took over. His arms reflexively locked around her waist, he crushed his body to hers, and pinned her up against the barn, intent on finishing what she had started. Breathing heavily, he trailed his hand over her cheek and bent toward her mouth. He could feel the warmth of her breath tremble against his lips, her eyes locked onto his.

"Alejandro, I..." She trailed off, not able to finish her thought.

He knew that he could still do it. That she wasn't saying no. That she wanted him as much as he wanted her. He could feel her heart hammer against his chest. He could feel her trembling in his arms. But he also knew that if he kissed her, he'd be crossing the line. The line that he himself had created. He closed his eyes. A long shudder tore through him.

"Ahem," said the groom, who had poked his head out of the barn.

They leapt apart. Alejandro cursed. "What?" He snarled as he turned on the groom.

The groom stepped back nervously. "Uh, Mr. Yates just wondered where you got to. But I can—I can tell him y'all are busy."

Alejandro took a ragged breath. "No, tell him we'll be right back in. Just give us a second."

The groom nodded and hustled back inside. Alejandro looked at Georgia, who stood where he had left her, propped up against the barn, her eyes glazed over, her chest heaving.

Their eyes met.

"Do you still want the horse?" he said to her.

She blinked. "Ye-yes," she stammered.

"Then we need to go back in." He yanked open the door, striding into the barn, and offered the full five thousand, not bothering to negotiate at all.

Chapter Twenty-seven

Alejandro decided to rent a trailer and drive the horses down to Florida himself. He needed time to think and cool down. A solid day behind the wheel would be a good way to get himself under control, remind himself of his priorities. Plus, he didn't trust himself to be alone on the plane with Georgia again. When it came to this woman, he had realized it was better to avoid private, confined spaces.

As they watched the horses get loaded into the trailer, he told Georgia she'd be flying back alone. She didn't show any surprise, just nodded and dug her foot into the gravel.

"Alejandro. Can I ask you a question?"

"Of course."

"Did you hire me because you think I'm a good vet or did you hire me for other reasons?"

He looked at her. "I meant what I said when I offered you the job."

"That this is purely professional?"

"*Sí.*"

She was quiet for a moment, thinking. "You know," she said at last, "though I am fully aware of the fact that I have shown you almost nothing in the last few days to prove this—I *am* a professional. And I am excited to work for you. I actually think I'm pretty good at my job."

"I agree," he said.

"But the thing is, there is pretty much nothing professional about how we've been behaving. I mean, I can't even really explain what has been happening, how we keep ending up in the same situation—but I have never worked anywhere where almost making out up against a barn was part of the job description."

"Nor have I."

"In two days, I start work at your barn, and you are officially my boss, and I want to be able to do my job and take care of your ponies, and I imagine you would probably like to get back to polo and doing whatever it is you need to do. So, it would probably be good if we could both just act like the professionals that we claim to be."

"Of course."

She bit her lip and nodded. "Okay, then. We do not have to talk about this anymore. I will take care of your ponies. And you will be my boss. And we will be professionals, and"—she looked up and met his eyes, a small smile playing around her mouth—"we will definitely not almost make out against any more barns, okay?"

He tried not to smile in return. "Okay."

She kept looking at him. "Alejandro?"

"Yes?"

"I think it would be much easier for me to be a professional if you would stand a little bit farther away from me."

He blinked. There was a pause, and then he took an enormous step back.

She grinned. "Thanks, boss."

Chapter Twenty-eight

Billy crammed the last bag into the trunk of his tiny car and slammed it shut.

"You sure you don't want a ride, Peaches?" he said. "It's on the way."

Georgia shook her head. "No, they're sending over a car. Pilar Del Campo called this morning."

"Well, of course they are," said Beau, who came out of the house carrying two large and exquisitely wrapped packages. "The Del Campos don't do anything half-assed."

"You can say that again," snorted Billy. He looked at Beau. "Better give her the presents. She'll need something to wear to suitably impress *La Familia*."

Beau passed over the boxes to Georgia. "Just a little going-away gift from us boys," he said.

Billy was traveling back to New York City that night, and Beau was going with him—a pit stop on his way to Italy, where he had to source a new tannery.

Georgia opened the first box—in it was nestled one of Billy's perfect bags, glossy chestnut brown, with a subtle reddish trim and silvery burnished hardware. The leather was so soft that it felt like it was melting in her hands. She buried her face in it. "Oh, Billy, it's gorgeous!"

Billy shrugged, obviously pleased by her reaction. "I just couldn't stand another moment watching you carry around that green pleather thing you call a purse."

Georgia laughed. "I love it!"

"Now mine," said Beau.

She opened the other box and gasped—a pair of tall, cocoa-colored polo boots.

"Beau, these are too much!"

"Nonsense," said Beau. "It's not like I gave you a saddle."

"But—" said Georgia.

"Just try them on, G," said Billy. "You'll look amazing in them."

She pulled the boots out of the box, admiring their luster, running her fingers over the intricate toolwork. They had to be handmade. She kicked off her flip-flops and slipped her feet in; even without socks, they felt like they had been made to fit her feet exactly.

She sighed happily. "They're absolute bliss. I don't think I've ever owned anything as nice."

"It's purely self-serving on our part," Billy said. "We're branching out from just saddles, trying to compete with Fagliano boots. You'll be our very own product placement, embedded among the equestrians."

"I'm going to miss you guys so much."

Billy grinned wickedly. "I want you to remember this next time I ask you to drop everything and come visit me, Peaches."

Georgia smiled and got a little teary. She hugged Beau and then Billy.

"Okay, Peaches, we gotta roll," Billy said. "You all good?

Just close the door behind you and key in the code when you leave."

"And then remember that code," Beau quipped, "in case you need a place to hide from the Del Campos."

Georgia smiled and shook her head. "I'm sure I'll be fine."

They drove off with a last flurry of advice.

"Don't sleep with anyone!" said Beau. "Unless you want to, of course!"

"And don't forget, just because everyone here has money doesn't make them better than you," Billy said. "Oh, but get some new jeans."

Georgia blinked. "Wait, what's wrong with my jeans?"

Billy laughed as he stuck his head out the window and yelled back at her. "You can do this! You're going to be amazing! Love you!"

Georgia sighed as she watched them drive off. A silver Bentley passed them going the opposite direction. Georgia laughed softly to herself as it pulled up in front of her, its engine purring.

"Dr. Fellowes?" the driver said, "*La Señora* Del Campo sent me for you."

No, she thought, the Del Campo family did nothing halfway at all.

Chapter Twenty-nine

The driver watched her in the rearview mirror as she tugged nervously at her sleeves. He pulled the car to a stop in the villa's circular driveway and took her small carry-on from the trunk. Georgia had no idea about the etiquette of tipping in this situation, but pulled a crumpled bill from her pocket and slipped it to the driver with what she hoped might pass for casual aplomb.

The place was even more beautiful in the daylight. The white adobe gleamed against the red terracotta tile roof, and the huge, stone framed glass windows reflected the acres of gardens surrounding the house.

Georgia was nervous as she wheeled her bag to the door, wondering just how close Alejandro and his mother really were, and what Pilar Del Campo might know about all that had happened between Georgia and her son.

Before she could ring the bell, the door swung open, and Valentina, wearing tiny shorts, a skintight tank top, and enormous sunglasses, appeared. She looked blankly from Georgia to the car.

"Uh, hello. Valentina, right? We met—well, sort of met

anyway—at the party the other night? I'm Dr. Fellowes—
Georgia."

"Okay?" said Valentina.

"Uh, your grandmother is expecting me, I think."

Valentina shrugged and stepped aside. Georgia, deciding
this was as much of an invitation as she was going to get,
walked in.

"You can wait in the library, I guess," said Valentina—
waving vaguely behind her while heading out the front door.
"I'll tell her you're here...if I see her."

That didn't inspire much confidence but since Valentina
had already disappeared down the steps, Georgia did as she
was told.

The central hallway was incredible, with vaulted ceilings
and dark parquet floors. Georgia felt a little dizzy, staring up
the enormous, sweeping staircase, from where she could hear
the distant sounds of cleaning.

She glanced into a dining room with a table that could
comfortably seat twenty and, beyond that, tall glass doors,
which led onto beautifully planted sunken gardens.

She should find the library, she thought, not wanting Pilar
to walk in and think she was snooping. She looked for a room
with books.

She found it off the main hallway. Unlike the rest of the
house, the room was small and almost cozy. Dark blue linen
curtains piped with gold and rich, thick silk tassels framed
the windows. Floor-to-ceiling white oak shelves were filled
with books on photography and interiors, arranged by color
and size. Another wall of biographies, another of history, and
an alcove of novels, classics to *Gone Girl*, a proper cornucopia
of titles. Georgia imagined herself curling up in here and not
coming out until she had read everything wall to wall.

Resisting the urge to kick off her shoes and climb onto the window seat to get started on the latest best-seller, Georgia turned to a vast rosewood desk, where, practically jumping up and down for her attention, were a cluster of silver-framed pictures of the Del Campo family.

She squinted, surprised, at one of a young Pilar. She looked like a cross between Bianca Jagger and Angelica Huston in their Studio 54 years—wearing a slinky black jumpsuit, with hair frizzed out to the max and a huge smile on her face as she hung on the arm of a man Georgia had to guess was the Del Campo patriarch himself, Carlos, Billy had told her his name was. Aside from his extravagant 1970s facial hair, he was every bit as good looking as his sons, but unlike his sons, he wore the look of a man who was deeply satisfied with his lot in life.

Georgia picked up another picture and felt her hands turn clammy. Alejandro's wedding portrait. God, they were young. He couldn't be more than early twenties and his bride looked even younger, no more than nineteen. She was very pretty and, in a heartrending way, looked like a less-jaded Valentina, with wide, kind eyes, a small rosebud of a mouth, and rather severe dark hair softened with a crown of gardenias. Her smile seemed a bit hesitant, but her eyes were hopeful.

Alejandro was every bit as good looking as now, but there was an openness and optimism about his face that Georgia hadn't seen yet. His hair was longer, the curls more pronounced. He was turned away from his wife and caught mid-laugh.

Georgia brought the picture closer and then jumped as she heard the click of a heel outside in the hall. She set it down quickly as Pilar entered the room.

"Oh!" said Pilar, clearly startled. "Dr. Fellowes. But what are you—"

"I'm so sorry, I didn't mean to surprise you. Valentina let me in. She didn't tell you?"

Pilar's mouth thinned. "*Mi nieta*, Valentina, she thinks that the only time that might be valuable belongs *solamente* to herself. I will speak to her."

"No, no, please, it's fine. I wasn't waiting long."

Pilar raised one eyebrow, which made Georgia feel sure the older woman thought she was more weak than polite.

"She has been given a certain...latitude since her mother died. We are soft on her. Maybe too soft, but, eh, what can you do?" She crossed over to Georgia and took her hand between her own. "But *bienvenida*, welcome, Dr. Fellowes. My son has high hopes."

* * *

The pool house was breathtaking. Modern and sleek, with a whole wall of windows overlooking the infinity pool and a tennis court beyond.

"It is maybe not the most private of places," apologized Pilar. "The family will need use of the pool, but at this time in the year, finding a rental would have been *muy difícil*."

"It's lovely," said Georgia as they moved through the light-flooded space. "I hope I won't be putting anyone out by being here."

There was the large, open-plan living room that overlooked the pool. A luxuriously deep couch, upholstered in grass green linen, sat in front of a delft blue tiled fireplace and a low coffee table piled high with photographic books on polo. The walls were lined with white bookshelves stocked with a complete set of modern classics.

Through French doors was a sweet little kitchen with a shiny red refrigerator and stove. Pilar opened a door to show a fully stocked pantry and then opened another cupboard that worked as a well-provisioned bar. Next, they looked at an airy bedroom with a bed so big that Georgia was pretty sure it could fit her and a horse if need be, and a second, smaller room, which Georgia thought would be a perfect little office.

Pilar opened the door to the bathroom—tiled and filled with light, with a deep Japanese soaking tub that Georgia was already dying to try. Two vast baskets of soft, rolled towels sat by the glassed-in shower.

"*Bueno.* I will just leave you to settle in, then," said Pilar. "I'd suggest you check with Enzo at the barn in the morning. He's the *piloto* and knows as much as anyone here. Consuelo will be in to clean every day while you're gone and just leave a note on the counter with any supplies and food you need."

Georgia looked around the thoughtfully stocked little home and she couldn't imagine needing anything that wasn't already here even if she stayed the whole year.

Chapter Thirty

Keen to make a good start at work the next morning, Georgia snuggled up on the soft couch, pulled a cashmere throw over her lap, and opened the book she had found. *Polo: A Primer.*

She flipped through the pages, looking at the brightly colored photographs of finely muscled men and women, and all their gorgeous ponies in action. The photos were beautiful, she thought, but they didn't really catch the crackling thrill of seeing the game live. She started to read, but found that the words paled in comparison to the lively explanation that Alejandro had already given her on the Cessna.

Alejandro...

She wondered if he had made it back from Kentucky yet. Perhaps he was already at home. Maybe he'd even been in the house while she was there...

She exhaled, determined to push him out of her head. *Boss. He is your boss. That is all. Now think of something else.*

A little hummingbird hovering outside the window caught her eye. The bird darted from flower to flower in the garden around the pool, its wings a whir of miraculous motion. Georgia put the book down and sighed. She could feel the warmth of the late afternoon sun through the windows, hear the whip of the sprinklers, smell the winter roses and gardenias, sense the breeze coming in through the open glass doors.

Suddenly she thought of her missing mother.

This must be the world that had won her over. This amazing place where the best trainers and horses and facilities were all available, where everything was beautiful and luxurious and exciting. If this was the seductive setup where she spent each winter, it was no wonder she was always in a hurry to leave her husband and daughter.

This would have been her element, thought Georgia, the place she made sense. Really, it was ridiculous that someone like her mother had ever ended up stuck on a teeny little farm outside a teeny little town in upstate New York.

Georgia had asked her father once, while her mother was away—before she left for good—how did they meet?

Her father had smiled almost dreamily. "Oh, she was just passing through," he said. "On her way to a horse show in Millbrook. Her trailer got a flat tire at the end of our road, and your mother—well, you know she's a looker—came walking up to where I was working and was just about the prettiest thing I'd ever seen. And not to brag, but I've been told that I was a bit easy on the eyes back then as well. Or at least your mom must have thought so. For a few minutes anyway. I always say that I changed her tire but she—she changed my life."

Not wanting to think any more about her mother and refusing to think about Alejandro, Georgia picked the book back up and stretched out on the couch, resolving to do her homework. But as she read, the words started to swim before her eyes, and she yawned. She'd just rest for a moment, she thought as she lay the book down on the floor and closed her eyes.

Chapter Thirty-one

Alejandro pulled into the gas station in Tallahassee, and got out to check on the horses. He'd driven straight through, only stopping for coffee and to give the horses parking breaks. It was hard for the animals to balance when the truck was in motion, and they needed frequent stops to rest their legs.

Alejandro knew that he should be weary, but he felt wired, and was certain that this restlessness wasn't just from the amount of caffeine he'd been consuming. He stretched next to the truck for a moment, relishing the feeling of being on his feet after sitting for so long.

He entered the trailer to give the horses some water and check their hay. Temper nickered nervously and snorted and Alejandro scratched the high-strung stallion's neck, speaking soothingly to him. The little palomino, Sugar, huffed at him and bumped his shoulder with her nose, wanting her share of the attention.

He turned to the mare, amused. She might not be much to look at, but unlike her mate, she had a sweet and playful nature, and definitely had a calming effect on Temper. Alejandro wouldn't ever admit it to Georgia, but she had been right to insist they buy Sugar, too. He had seen horses suffer and pine when separated from their mates, and these two were definitely bonded. It would have been stupid to risk harming a pony as valuable as Temper just because Sugar wasn't pedigreed.

He patted the little horse, enjoying the feel of her rough coat beneath his hands. She turned her gaze upon him, and he smiled ruefully. Georgia had also been right about the fact that the pony's big brown eyes were rather nice.

Satisfied that the horses were comfortable, Alejandro bought himself a sandwich and got back on the road.

When he first left Lexington, he had tried hard not to think about Georgia, doing his best to shove any thoughts of her out of his head as soon as they entered. What she had said on the farm was absolutely true. He was her boss. They were working together, and they needed to be professional about things from here on out. Setting up these rules about workplace fraternization was one of the first things Alejandro had done after his father died. He had spent far too many years watching his father and his father's cronies cut a swath among the young female students and grooms, bedding whomever they wanted with no thought about the consequences—not only to the team and the barn—but to Alejandro's mother, as well.

Pilar had fought for Carlos at first. When Alejandro was a boy he remembered horrible, screaming fights between the two of them. He and Sebastian huddled together upstairs while Pilar pleaded desperately with Carlos to be faithful to her, and Carlos had denied everything, swearing that she was paranoid and crazy. But it had been almost worse when Pilar had finally lost heart and surrendered. A cold and angry silence took the place of the fights. That silence had lasted between his parents for years.

After Carlos had died, Alejandro had found that his father's *peccadillos* had not been limited to the barn. Carlos had left a large bequest in his will to a stranger—a young woman in Germany—who turned out to be Alejandro and Sebastian's half sister, Antonia. Someone they had known nothing about until the lawyers had informed them of her existence.

Fueled by the pain of this discovery, Alejandro laid out the new rules in the barn as soon as he decently could, calling together the team and telling them that things would be different now that he was in charge, that he expected no less than absolute professionalism from the people who worked for him, and that they could receive the same thing from him in return. Sebastian and Rory hadn't cared—they didn't need the barn to meet women, and they were content to do their partying on their own time—and Hendy, of course, had never been anything but absolutely upright. But a lot of the old guard had grumbled—they'd done things a certain way when Carlos was alive and didn't see why they should have to change anything now. Alejandro had swiftly given them their walking papers, firing them one by one as soon as he caught wind of any wrongdoings, secretly pleased to rid the team of these men who did nothing so much as remind him of the things he couldn't stand about his dead father.

Soon, the only man left from Carlos's original staff was Dr. Gustavo. Alejandro didn't kid himself that the old vet had any particular respect for him, or that he cared about anything other than keeping his well-paid job. Gustavo reliably showed up for what was a long day—5 a.m. to 9 p.m.—and had always kept his drinking misadventures limited to his private life.

Until recently, that is, thought Alejandro as he turned off the highway to search for another place to let the horses rest. He hoped that bringing Georgia onto the team instead of letting Dr. Gus surround himself with sycophants would help correct the course. But he'd also hoped that making her an employee would shake her from his thoughts, and then he'd been sure that this drive down from Kentucky would give him enough time to end the aching temptation she had become to him...

That was the idea, so why did his heart beat faster with every mile he got closer to home?

Chapter Thirty-two

Georgia awoke to the scent of roses carried on the breeze through her open window. The sun was just beginning to set, and the room was filled with a soft, pink-gold glow. For a moment, she lay on the comfortable couch, content to watch the play of light and shadow dance across the ceiling.

Finally hunger propelled her up, and she wandered into the kitchen. She opened the refrigerator. How perfect, she thought as she gazed at the bottle of milk, the small buttons of goat cheese, a bowl of eggs (Do these people have some aesthetic objection to egg cartons? she asked herself), a container of washed salad greens, a cluster of frosty red grapes, a crisper full of brightly colored lemons and limes, and a magnum of Dom Perignon Limited Edition Rosé.

She pulled out the heavy bottle and examined it. For a moment, she was tempted. The whole situation seemed celebratory, after all, and she did love champagne. This outsized bottle looked dangerously expensive, though, and once begun, it would be wrong not to finish. She imagined herself passed out on the couch, the empty bottle lying next to her...and Pilar and Alejandro discovering her the next morning.

She put the bottle back.

She thought about going out on the town—finding some dinner and looking around—but she felt shy about asking for the car and driver, even though Pilar had assured her that they were to be hers whenever she needed them. Georgia reminded herself that she needed to save her money anyway. It was better just to make herself dinner instead. She found a good loaf of bread in the pantry, smeared a slice with the goat cheese, broke off a bunch of grapes, made a little salad—and decided to leave the champagne, but help herself to some Malbec. Not bad at all, she thought as she popped a grape into her mouth and leaned against the kitchen counter.

After dinner, she poured herself a second glass of wine and took it into the bathroom, dying to try out the soaking tub. She turned on the taps, sighing happily at the extravagant gush of hot water. Back home, there was something wrong with their water pressure. She was usually lucky to get even a tepid sprinkle when she showered.

She found a jar of lavender bath salts and sprinkled them in, enjoying the sweetly floral burst of scent that arose in the steam. While she waited for the tub to fill, she turned down the lights and lit some candles, and then she slowly undressed, peeling off her shirt and bra, followed by her jeans and panties. She neatly folded her clothes, took another sip of wine, and stepped into the tub, sinking beneath the steaming water, holding her glass above the surface, giving in to the absolute glory of a hot bath and the intense red wine.

A mirror on the wall had been hung at just the right angle to reflect everything that was happening in the bath. Georgia looked away at first. She'd suffered from spending a lifetime of comparing herself to her mother, who had been a world-class beauty. Georgia always thought of herself as too short, too pale, too curvy, too soft, in comparison. But tonight, bathed in the forgiving glow of the candlelight and immersed in the sudsy water, she saw herself differently. Her skin was rosy and glowing from the steamy heat of the bath. Her hair was in tight little ringlets, springing out all over her head in a sort of halo effect. Her eyes were still dreamy from her nap, and her cheeks were flushed. Her curves, which she had always thought of as simply *too much*, now looked inviting and lush.

Pleased, she ran one damp hand along the flare of her hip, slipping her fingers down her leg and over the soft skin of her inner thigh. With the other hand, she cupped one of her breasts, slowly rolling the nipple between her fingers . . .

Alejandro.

Damn it.

She sat up so abruptly that the water sloshed over the edges of the tub and down onto the floor below. Of course he had popped into her head just as she was about to give herself a good time. Why wouldn't he, this man who, with just a few kisses, had made her feel things that she hadn't felt in her entire sexual life? For God's sake, he hadn't even kissed her at the barn—just pressed up against her and held her gaze, and she'd felt a rush of desire so intense that her bones turned to liquid and she thought she might climax simply from the way he was looking at her.

No, she thought, forcing herself out of the tub, she could not indulge in these dangerous fantasies. She was going to be standing right in front of the man again tomorrow morning, surrounded by grooms and horses and the other players. The last thing she needed to take to her first day of work was the memory of pleasuring herself in the bath while fantasizing about her boss.

She vigorously dried herself off and tipped the rest of her wine down the sink. Enough was enough. Time to read that damned polo book and go to sleep.

Chapter Thirty-three

The house was dark and quiet when Alejandro arrived home. He had dropped off the ponies at the barn, settled them in, and then headed back to the house.

His mother had left a bowl of *carbonada* for him in the fridge, but he wasn't hungry.

Alejandro hesitated and then poured himself a glass of brandy to take back to his room. Turning out the kitchen lights, he walked through the silent house and padded softly up the stairs. He looked in on Valentina, asleep on top of the covers with her headphones on and the music still playing. Alejandro gingerly removed the headphones and pulled the covers up and over her. She groaned in her sleep, flailing one arm out at him, but then snuggled down in her bed, oblivious, as he gave her a soft kiss on the top of her head.

In his bedroom, he changed into shorts, sipped the cognac, and opened the French doors to his balcony, enjoying the night air. He liked these hot, humid nights—they reminded him of summer at home.

He stood on his balcony and watched the way the moon hung over the sky and reflected in the pool down below. He looked back at his bed and the uninviting prospect of another sleepless night—and then back at the pool.

* * *

Georgia couldn't sleep. But the bed was not to blame. In fact, it was quite possibly the most comfortable bed she had ever not slept in. The mattress was just the right shade of firm, the sheets were silky and cool, the duvet was whisper light but just warm enough, and there were more pillows than she knew what to do with. No, the bed was fine. It was just the whole place—so foreign and warm and bright. The buzz of the insects in the garden, the scant breeze rustling through the trees. Even after dark, the wavering blue light from the pool reflected on her walls, and the moonlight streamed in through all the windows, brighter than a streetlamp. It was beautiful, but it was a sensory overload and definitely not home.

She turned over and kicked her legs in frustration, and then gave up, rolling out of bed, closing the windows and turning on the AC—not bothering to turn on the lights. Wanting a glass of water, she stood at the counter in her briefs and a tank top, sipping her drink, looking at the moonlight sparkling on the pool.

She was just about to go back to bed when she saw the back gate of the pool house open and a shadowy figure emerge and walk toward the cottage.

For a moment she was terrified, imagining an intruder—but then she recognized the tall and broad-shouldered figure of Alejandro. Fear subsided to butterflies.

As he approached the window, she slunk back, her hands flying instinctively to cross her chest, but then she realized that her place was dark, and with the window closed and the light on outside, there was no way he could see her. The right thing to do, of course, was retreat from the window, to give the man his privacy. The right thing was definitely not to stay riveted to the spot.

She watched as he approached the pool, illuminated by the lights in the water and the bright moonlight pouring down. He stood at the edge of the water, sipping a glass of some amber spirit. He kicked off his shoes and touched the pool with his bare foot, sending ripples through the glowing blue liquid.

When he set his drink on the edge of the fence, Georgia's breath quickened. She knew she should stop watching—knew that something was about to happen that was out of bounds—but the voice of reason and decorum whispering in her head was very feeble indeed.

He slowly unbuttoned his shirt, and Georgia unthinkingly slid an answering hand beneath the strap of her camisole. He dropped the shirt behind him, exposing his smooth, sculpted chest and shoulders.

Georgia's breath caught as he lazily stretched, the muscles in his arms and shoulders rippling in arcs and planes. And then he unzipped his shorts and stepped out, completely naked.

Georgia's cheeks flamed. Her breath came in a gasp. Her hand, still lingering at her breast, felt her heart beat an urgent tattoo. He was incredibly sexy...beautiful really, she thought. And a man to the max. The intense eyes, the full mouth, the cords of muscle, the breadth of his shoulders, the way his skin glowed, with just the perfect amount of chest hair that tapered down to his belly and below.

With quick grace, he dove into the pool, hardly making

a splash. Georgia found herself holding her breath as she waited for him to resurface. He emerged—his hair sleek and iridescent against his skull. He cut through the water with long, sure strokes, moving almost silently, his body a bronze blur under the ice blue water, turning a backward circle to change direction and power on.

He swims like he rides, thought Georgia, *almost as if he's being pursued.* Beneath the power and precision, there was a distinct feeling of escape.

He touched one end of the pool and then turned and circled back—over and over, never breaking his stroke. And as she watched him, Georgia unthinkingly drifted closer to the windows, reaching out and touching the cool glass with her fingertips. Her body burned, every nerve ending alert.

Finally, he slowed and drifted, allowing himself a few lazy backstrokes before gripping the edge of the pool and pulling himself out. Water streamed down his body, flickering in the light, catching in glimmering drops on his skin. He shook his head like a great dog—flinging droplets of moisture from his hair—and then pulled on his shorts. He reached down to grasp his shirt and, as he straightened, looked directly into Georgia's eyes.

There was no mistaking the fact that he saw her this time. He could see all of her, standing in the floor-to-ceiling window, wearing next to nothing—but she felt petrified, unable to break his gaze.

Their eyes locked, but except for the faintest flicker of surprise, his face remained impassive, almost as if he'd been expecting this, as if he caught women in their underwear watching him skinny-dip every day. Without looking away, he dropped his shirt back to the ground and started walking toward her.

Georgia gasped and hurled herself backward—away from the window, back into the darkness of the house. But that didn't stop him. In three quick steps, he had opened her door, and then he was over the threshold, and he had her in his arms.

Chapter Thirty four

He would not be stopped this time. The sight of her watching him—the sexy flush that lit up her face when she realized she was caught, the shock in her eyes, which had almost instantly turned into an urgent invitation, the way he could see each luscious curve of her figure in her panties and translucent tank top—had caused his body to roar into life. Every well-trained reflex, every fierce and brutal instinct to take what he wanted, to win at all costs, had thrown him into action. He did not stop. He just closed the distance between the two of them and took her in his arms.

She smelled like lavender and honey, sweet almonds, and under all that, a faint musk that he immediately recognized as sexual excitement. Without even kissing her first, he ran his hand down her body and cupped her crotch, feeling the warm, soaking wetness that he had instinctively known would be there.

She gasped and quivered under him, pushing her hips against his hand. He reached up with his other hand and tore off her tank top, letting her glorious breasts come unbound with a gentle bounce, feeling the full extent of her hot, silky skin smack against his own damp chest as he pressed his body to hers, and claimed her lips with his.

He roughly pushed his tongue past her lips, plunging and exploring, tasting the sweetness of her, taking her lower lip between his teeth and biting down until she groaned and twisted against him.

"Oh God," she breathed, and one hand rose to twine itself in his hair, while the other grasped his rear, pushing him even farther against her until he felt he might burst, he was so hard.

With a growl, he tore his mouth from hers and brought his lips to her throat, finding the sensitive spot just above her collarbone, pausing a moment to nibble and tease her there as she sighed and writhed. He moved to her breasts, urgently kissing, licking, and biting first one and then the other, and then sucking her nipple into his mouth, feeling it tighten under his tongue as she threw back her head and cried out in pleasure.

She grabbed at the button on his shorts and pulled them open, grasping the length of him in her hand. He shuddered, her hand felt so good. She sank to her knees, dragging his shorts off him, and her mouth closed around him, swirling and sucking, and for a moment he shut his eyes and lost himself in the warm wet of her tongue and lips and mouth, felt himself getting harder and harder, until he pulled away with a hoarse, "No! *Todavia no.* Not yet."

"Alejandro," she whispered as he pulled her back up and against him, "I want—"

He interrupted her with another kiss, deep and searching, as one hand cupped her breast, finding the hard, pink tip and pinching it softly between his fingers, rubbing and teasing, while his other hand hooked her panties and pulled them

down and off her. He ran his fingers through her soft, tight
curls until he found the molten wetness within.

She moaned as he parted her, searching out her rigid little
clit, and caressing it gently as she bucked against his hand.

"Please," she groaned, and he turned her away from him
and braced her against the wall, enclosing her body within
his and pushing the length of himself against her luscious
curves. He reached around and continued to circle the sensitive little bud with one hand, and with the other, he found
her entrance. He slowly pushed a finger inside her, feeling
the plush slickness, and then another, finding the spot that
made her suddenly cry out, jerking her hips over and over,
contracting against his hand as she rode the waves of her
climax. Her pleasure made him ravenous. He could hardly
contain his need to be inside her, to feel her around him, but
he forced himself to wait. He wanted to savor every moment
of this night.

She collapsed against the wall for a moment, her shoulders
heaving, and then turned around and pressed herself against
him. He groaned, feeling her slickness, and then he reached
down and swept her up into his arms and carried her into the
bedroom.

He laid her on the bed, and she gazed up at him, so
gorgeous in the moonlight, her long, honeyed curls spread
out behind her, her hazel eyes half-closed, her lips red and
swollen. He kissed and licked his way down her pearly skin,
lingering at the soft curve of her hip, the little dip of her
belly button, and then placing his mouth over the mound of
her curls, breathing softly, kissing gently, tasting the salty
sweetness of her, until he could feel the nib get hard again,
until her breath came in little gasps. She wriggled under his
tongue, greedily pushing herself against his mouth.

"*Shh, shh, quedate quieta*, let me take my time. You taste so good."

"Oh God," she moaned, "I don't think I can wait."

He kissed her again, softly, and then harder, teasing her with little flicks of his tongue, driving her to greater and greater heights of desire as she writhed and pulsed under his mouth. He slid his hands under her, grasping her behind, pulling her closer, bringing her silky thighs against his face, and then immersed himself into the soft wetness of her, losing himself in her sweetness and the sound of her pleasure.

She cried out, her hands gripping his hair, her hips pulsating against him. She shuddered uncontrollably under his touch.

"I need to feel you inside me. Please, please—do you have a condom?"

He rested against her a moment, thinking, and then laughed and sat up. He opened a small silver box on the bedside table and showed her the contents. Her eyes widened. "This place really does have everything," she murmured.

"I never thought I'd say this, but thank God for Sebastian's bad habits," said Alejandro as he ripped open the little packet and rolled the condom onto himself.

He lowered himself over her, searching out the silky wetness between her legs. She shuddered under his touch. "Please," she whispered.

He paused to look at her face; her hazel eyes glossy with need, the pretty constellation of freckles against the cream of her skin, her delicious, irresistible lips. He wanted her so badly. He was nearly wild with it. He parted her legs with his thigh.

Suddenly, her eyes went wide. She pushed him away, scrambling back in the bed. "The light! Alejandro!"

He turned around, confused.

Through the window he saw the back porch light had come on at the main house. Someone in the household had come outside, most likely his mother, or Valentina, looking for him.

"*Mierda*," he swore as he leapt out of bed. She followed. He went into the living room and retrieved his shorts, pulling them on. He looked at her and ran his hands through his hair, an apology on his lips.

"Go. Go, quick!"

He slipped out the door, quickly snagging his shirt from the ground as he strode toward the porch.

Chapter Thirty-five

Georgia watched Alejandro duck through the back door and then the porch light went out again.

She stood naked in her living room, trying to catch her breath, her entire body trembling with adrenaline. She could barely stand, she felt completely wrung out, but at the same time—as if something had been ripped from her—empty and unfulfilled.

What had she done?

After all her big words about professionalism. After practically lecturing him on the need for them to be nothing more than employer and employee. She'd acted like a cat in heat. She hadn't even tried to stop him.

But God, how could she have stopped him? The way he looked, the way he smelled, the way he held her, everything he did, every single touch, felt like absolute bliss. She must have come half a dozen times—and she was still standing here, aching for more.

She took a deep breath and shivered. Well, mistake or not, it was her first day of work tomorrow. It might begin with her being fired, but she supposed she would have to show up to find out.

Chapter Thirty-six

For the first time in a long time, Alejandro overslept.

Normally, he never even bothered to set an alarm, he was so predictable in his habits. As soon as the sun was up, so was he. Usually long before anyone else in the household. But this morning, when he opened his eyes, the light was much too bright, and he heard the distinct sounds of breakfast being consumed in the kitchen.

He groaned in frustration. He thought of the confused look on his mother's face when he had opened the back door the night before and found her standing in the hall. "*Hijo*, I thought I heard—what in the world?"

He'd marched past her, barely making eye contact, "Swimming," he muttered as he sent himself straight to bed.

He checked the clock and cursed. A full two hours later than he'd meant to get up. He had planned on slipping out this morning and finding a private moment to talk with Georgia before they started work. He was determined to apologize, to take complete responsibility, to let her know that it would never happen again...

Never? Really?

He squeezed his eyes shut for a moment, feeling the insane

amount of longing from last night. Leaving her there like that, naked, and trembling, with his desire unslaked, had been one of the hardest things he'd ever done. It was only the thought of his mother, or worse yet, his daughter, finding them there that had forced him out of her arms.

Now he would have to face her at work like the hypocrite he was.

His family was sitting around the kitchen table, finishing up *café con leche*, fruit, and croissants. They all stared at him as he entered the room and casually poured himself some coffee.

"*Papá*," said Valentina. "You're back."

He helped himself to an orange. "I am."

"But—"

"It was a late night."

Sebastian smiled knowingly. "Oh?"

"He was swimming," said Pilar. "At two in the morning."

Sebastian shot him a puzzled look. "Swimming?"

"Couldn't sleep," said Alejandro.

"Well, I hope you didn't disturb *la doctora*," said Pilar. "I didn't get a chance to tell you that I ended up putting her in the pool house."

"Yes, I don't know if that was the best idea, *Mamá*. Awfully close quarters. She may as well be living under our roof."

Pilar's eyebrows shot up.

"So you did disturb her, then?" said Sebastian silkily.

"No, I mean, yes, I may have seen her."

They all looked at him, waiting.

He threw his napkin down. "I need to get to the barn." He stood up and headed for the door.

Pilar called after him. "*Hijo*, just so you know, I was

thinking I would invite her to dinner this week. Make her feel welcome."

He briefly squeezed his eyes shut in frustration, but tried to keep his voice as normal as possible. "*Sí*, whatever you think is best, *Mamá*."

He waited until he was well clear of the house and then stopped, trying to gather his wits. He swore softly to himself. What was wrong with him? He hadn't even been able to face his own family without acting the fool. How did he expect to deal with a barn full of employees and Georgia herself?

He took a deep breath. He would just find her. Find her right away and take her somewhere private and . . .

Her breasts. Her thighs. The way she tasted. The look on her face when he caught her watching him in the pool . . .

Take her somewhere private and finish what we started last night . . .

He violently shook his head. "No," he said aloud. He would talk to her and apologize and be done with it, and then get back on a goddamned horse and get ready for the next game.

Chapter Thirty-seven

Approaching the barn, Georgia couldn't help being intimidated by the facilities. Though obviously built much more recently, the building's design echoed the Del Campo *hacienda*, with the same gleaming white adobe walls, and red terra-cotta roof. But it was, if anything, even more impressive than the mansion, with enormous arched windows and Corinthian pillars running the length of the building.

Georgia thought of her own little dilapidated four-stall barn at home and sighed. She was definitely in over her head.

Once inside the barn, though, she immediately felt at home. It smelled wonderful in there, of linseed oil and saddle soap, deep beds of fresh hay and clean horses, and every stall was alive with Mexican grooms and working students, many of them teenage girls, their ponytails swinging, as they raked hay and picked hooves and carried heavy buckets of feed through the corridors.

There were neat checklists for turnout and grooming and feed on every stall; clearly the place was run with military precision. Most of the staff paused in what they were doing to give Georgia a sweeping look that finished with the thousand-dollar boots Beau had given her, and then quickly dismissed her. She was starting to get a bad feeling that fitting in might be harder than she'd hoped.

"Where's Enzo, please?" Georgia asked one of the students, a young African-American kid busy changing feed.

"With the blacksmith," he said. "Last stall."

"Thanks," she said and offered a hand to shake, which he took very uncertainly. Obviously, that was not usually done.

She walked down the long central corridor, dust motes in the air, trophies lined up along the wall, framed black-and-white photographs of the team's triumphs displayed as if in a museum.

There were beautiful trunks outside every stall, topped with small colorful bins filled with curry brushes and combs and hoof picks, each one carefully labeled with the horse's names.

The horses all looked in such top health she wondered if there could possibly be enough for her to do. Every horse in the barn was better looked after than a Hollywood child star, groomed within an inch of their lives and tended to by a fleet of eagerly competing staff.

Before she reached the end of the barn, she noticed a group of grooms, students, and the veterinarian, Dr. Gustavo, all crowding around a stall and laughing.

Gustavo craned his neck to look into the stall, and his theatrical expression of astonishment triggered snickers from the grooms. "Is the *señor* out of his mind?"

Georgia saw a little spotted nose emerge from the stall, apparently hoping for a pat. It was Sugar.

"An interesting judgment call," one of the students drawled in a loud aside to Dr. Gus.

Georgia smarted, thinking that the judgment call had actually been hers.

"Apparently, this is what happens when I'm not in the decision-making mix," Gustavo said, stepping up to take a closer look at Sugar. The little horse gazed at him placidly, switching her tail and blinking her eyes. Gustavo shook his head and sneered at the palomino. "You think Alejandro plans to ride her or eat her?" he asked, and he poked the mare's ample belly.

"Hey," said Georgia, "she's not fat, she's pregnant."

They all turned as one to stare at her. Georgia bit her lip, embarrassed to be the center of attention.

Dr. Gustavo stared at her with frank dislike. "What are you doing here?" he said softly.

"I—well, it's my first day and—"

Gustavo blinked. "First day at what?"

Georgia was speechless. Apparently he didn't know that she'd been hired.

"I—"

"Gustavo," interrupted a calm, deep voice from behind her, "I'm sure you remember Dr. Fellowes?"

Georgia turned. There was Alejandro, wearing his riding gear, standing so close she could feel the heat coming off his body. His eyes met hers and flickered in acknowledgment, but then he looked past her back at Gustavo.

Dr. Gustavo's face was claret. "Indeed."

"I'm happy to confirm she'll be joining us for the season. I know you'll make her welcome, and she'll do everything in her power to supplement all you do."

Gustavo's face got even redder. Georgia extended her hand, but he ignored it, looking at Alejandro. "Perhaps I could have a moment of your time in your office?" he asked haltingly. He turned back to Georgia. "If you'll excuse us for one moment, *señorita*?"

"Oh," Georgia said, coolly taking note of the way he called her *señorita* instead of doctor. "Yes, of course."

The men went into Alejandro's office and closed the door, and the crowd of grooms dispersed, getting back to their work. Georgia hesitated for a moment, not sure what to do, until she heard the soft nicker of Sugar, calling her over.

"Hey, little girl," she said as she pressed her forehead to the mare's and scratched behind her ear, "at least someone's glad to see me."

Sugar huffed and nibbled at Georgia's neck. Georgia laughed, but then froze when Alejandro's irritated voice echoed out of his office and resounded into the corridors.

"Gustavo, you knew very well we needed a replacement and that Hendy and I were stepping in."

"Yes, but I did not expect you to hire some girl without even consulting me first."

Alejandro snorted impatiently. "First off, she's not a girl. She's a highly skilled and conscientious veterinarian. Which is much more than I can say about your choice."

The fight could clearly be heard by half the barn. Georgia stood frozen as all the grooms seemed to turn in unison to listen. She was mortified and then furious. What chance did she have of commanding any workplace authority with a beginning like this?

A slim young woman with silky, white-blond hair and eyes so dark they were almost black materialized next to her. "Hello," she said. "I'm Antonia, known to most as Noni. That or the blacksmith. You must be our new vet."

"Er, yes," said Georgia, her eyes darting between the woman and the office. The men's voices were getting even louder. "I guess you were told about me, then, even if no one else was?"

Noni smiled. "I suspect that most of us knew you were coming, but no one wanted to tell Gustavo."

Georgia shook her head and sighed. "Great."

"So, any questions so far?"

"A million," Georgia said, trying to ignore the rising voices from Alejandro's office.

"Let's start with one," Noni said, striding away from Georgia so that she was forced to follow her out of the barn and out of hearing.

"Okay." Georgia took a deep breath and tried to shake off her humiliation. Her gaze scanned the nearest corral. "Who's that guy?"

She pointed to the far field, where a handsome older horse chewed thoughtfully on his daily allotment of grass, and a tall, striking man with dark hair stood nearby filling a trough with water.

Noni smiled. "The horse is Tango. Elder statesman. He's the first pony on whom Alejandro won MVP. Most Valuable Player. He keeps him with him. Lucky talisman. The man is Enzo. He's the *piloto*."

Georgia nodded, her mind scanning rapidly. "Sorry, but what exactly does the *piloto* do?"

"He's like part trainer, part barn manager. He also gets to play polo in the practice games. And he exercises the horses. He's usually first here and last to leave—quite likely he'll be the one to call you if you're needed in the night."

There was another exclamation from the office. Georgia cringed.

"I think you should start by talking to Enzo," Noni said, walking rapidly out into the field, Georgia trailing behind.

"Hey, Enzo. Georgia has some questions for you about what you do as *piloto*."

Georgia turned to Noni to thank her but the woman had already moved on.

* * *

Gustavo jabbed a finger at Alejandro. "You're deliberately undermining me. I should have some say in who's assisting me. The girl made one lucky guess about an injured horse and has a pair of nice *tetas*—"

Alejandro slammed his hand against the desk. "Enough! We have done our due diligence, and I resent the suggestion we'd do anything less. Lord Henderson is satisfied and so am I. And if you're not capable of treating her as the professional she is, then you need to seriously consider your position."

Dr. Gustavo sputtered. "Your father would never have—"

Alejandro's voice dropped dangerously low. "As you have pointed out to me countless times, Gustavo, I am not my father. Now please get out there, take ten minutes, then come back and begin to teach her what she needs to know."

Gustavo eyed him belligerently, breathing heavily, clearly weighing his options while refusing to give way.

There was a soft cough behind them. They turned to see Noni, standing with her head cocked, unsmiling, but with a gleam in her dark eyes.

"Gentlemen," she said, "Everything okay?"

Alejandro took a step back. "Fine, Antonia. Did you need something?"

Noni nodded. "Yes, I just wanted to double-check about shoeing Rosa. I wasn't sure if it was time or not."

Gustavo nodded stiffly and turned to go. "If you will excuse me..."

Noni stepped back and let him pass. Alejandro made to

have the last word, but she gently laid her hand on his arm. "Let it lie for now, Jandro. You can talk to him when you are calmer."

Alejandro hesitated for a moment and then kissed his sister's cheek. "All right, Antonia. Thank you for your timely interference."

Noni shrugged it off.

"You met her?" Alejandro asked. "Georgia?"

"Yes. Very nice," Noni said. "She's not particularly happy with you, though."

Alejandro felt himself flush. What had she told his sister?

"She wasn't exactly pleased to be sprung on Gustavo like that. And I can't say I would be either. You just made her job that much harder."

He nodded, relieved. "Oh, *sí,* but that was a mistake. I thought Hendy had informed Gustavo already, and obviously, Hendy thought I had done the honors."

"Well, in any case, I believe you have some damage control to do."

Alejandro smiled ruefully. *More than you know.*

Chapter Thirty-eight

Georgia stood at the back of the barn, watching Noni shoe a pony. Noni's arms were flexed—sinewy and muscular—as she leaned into a gray mare, fitting on the new shoe with unusual economy of movement. Enzo stood by, comforting the horse, slowly scratching at the base of his mane.

Georgia felt, rather than heard, Alejandro's presence as he stepped up behind her

"So," he said softly into her ear, "I see you've met my sister the blacksmith. She's very good, isn't she?"

Georgia turned to him and felt her body burn with memories of the night before. "Noni is your sister? I hadn't realized."

"It's a complicated story. I'll tell you some other time. But for now, will you join me for a walk around the yard? We should talk."

She nodded and followed him out the back way. She felt compromised and confused. She didn't know if she wanted to kiss him or yell at him.

They stood at a corral and watched a small colt frolic with his dam. Alejandro kept his eyes on the horses. "This was not how I planned for your first day to go," he said stiffly.

Georgia frowned. "Yes, well, it might have been nice if the man I am working under had been informed of my existence."

"Yes. A team miscommunication. I'm sorry you had to go through that. I assure you that Dr. Gustavo has fallen into line."

Privately, Georgia very much doubted that, but she bit her tongue.

"As for what happened between us last night..." He paused, his face flushed. "I take full responsibility. I would feel very unhappy if my thoughtless behavior in any way made you uncomfortable or compromised your working here."

She looked up at him. "You were hardly alone in what happened, Alejandro. I was obviously a more than willing partner."

"Yes, well, thank you for saying so. But it is my responsibility, as your employer, not to put you into the kind of position—"

She let out a little huff of frustration. "Honestly, I am more worried about your behavior this morning compromising my position than I am about anything that happened last night."

His jaw clenched. "I said it was a mistake, and I have corrected—"

"How can you expect me to recover from the scene you made? The whole barn thinks I'm a laughingstock."

He looked at her. "The scene I made? I don't understand how—"

"You dressing Gustavo down in front of the entire barn, shouting like that, do you think that somehow helped me?"

Spots of red appeared on his cheekbones. "I was defending you."

"I don't need to be defended. I simply needed you to remember to tell people that I actually work here."

They were silent for a moment, glaring at each other.

He let out a long breath. "Yes, well, they all know that now. And as for last night—"

For an excruciating moment, their eyes met, and a longing that was almost tangible flashed between them before Georgia forced herself to look away. "It was a mistake," she said. "It won't happen again."

His lips thinned, and he nodded. "Indeed."

Chapter Thirty-nine

Alejandro fed the bit into Temper's mouth and then swung up to ride. He wanted nothing so much as to escape the barn and everyone connected to it. He wished he were back at home and could gallop until there was nothing around him but pampas grass and sky, but he supposed hitting the ball as hard as he possibly could would have to do instead.

Temper was a revelation. He was made to play the game. He moved like a cat out on the field, stopping on a dime, doubling back, making the tightest possible turns at the highest possible speeds. But what should have been glorious fun for Alejandro felt like drudgery. He could not shake the look on Georgia's face, the sound of her voice when she had told him that last night had been a mistake. It rang in his ears on repeat.

It was ludicrous. She was absolutely right, of course. It had been a mistake. But even as she was saying it, he was imagining her wet and naked, splayed out under him. He was remembering the way her skin had burned on his, the way she had writhed against him. He couldn't understand what had overtaken him since he met her. He scarcely recognized himself. He had felt desire before, of course, and had acted upon it—he was no saint—and there had been warmth and love between himself and Olivia, especially at the beginning of his marriage, but what he felt when he was with Georgia was something altogether new. New and dangerous. Perhaps this is what obsession was. But he could not afford to have an obsession other than polo. There were already far too many unmanageable things in his life—the lost games, his brother's indolence, his mother's disapproval, his daughter's detachment. He needed more discipline in his life, more restraint, not this wild, unruly tempest that left him winded and aching.

He slammed his mallet against the ball and watched it spin across the field at a dizzying pace. It was six weeks. Surely he could find a way to control himself for six weeks. He would avoid her except when absolutely necessary, he would force himself to be as brusque and distant as possible, he would remind himself of his professional duties, and he would exhaust himself on the field. He had gone without for so long—it was practically second nature—and it was better this way. No one would get hurt.

He wheeled Temper around and headed back to the barn.

Chapter Forty

In the absence of any helpful direction from Gustavo, who seemed to spend his entire time standing around drinking the bitter green tea the Argentines called *maté* with everyone other than her, Georgia spent her time going from stall to stall, inspecting the ponies, memorizing health records, assessing temperaments, and questioning the grooms on all the details of barn procedures. She hated being more of a burden than a help but figured she had a license this first day to ask as many clueless questions as she liked and that she should take full advantage.

She did her best to avoid Alejandro, which was not too difficult since it seemed that he was trying to give her a wide berth as well. She caught a glimpse of him and Temper out on the field at one point and could not help stopping to watch them. They were so elegant in motion.

By the end of the day, despite feeling that she had not accomplished much more than familiarizing herself with the place, she was exhausted. Her feet ached from her new boots, which she quickly realized were entirely inappropriate for her work, but were the only ones she had, and her head ached from all that she had left undone, and she was more than happy to catch a quick ride back to the *hacienda* with Enzo, who was heading into town.

The pool house seemed a refreshing mirage after her hard and dusty day. Someone had been in to clean, straightening up what little mess Georgia had left behind that morning and pulling the blinds so the little house was cool and dim when she entered. There was a large vase of white lilies, accented with trailing vines of golden honeysuckle, left on the coffee table, and their scent sweetened the air.

Georgia took off her boots, poured herself a glass of wine, and stretched out on the couch for a moment, luxuriating in the novelty of having time on her hands. It was such a change to have no one to think of but herself. No animals to feed. No dad to appease. Oh, she thought, as she saw the reflected light from the pool rippling across the ceiling, a swim might be just the thing.

She pulled on her old string bikini and walked back out into the golden twilight. The turquoise water sparkled invitingly, and as she dove in, she felt all the tensions and worries of her day wash away.

She'd loved swimming in college, and it was great to feel the muscle memory kick in. These last months at the farm had been bleak, her body felt perpetually hunched and cold. Of course, tending the animals and doing her chores had been a sort of exercise—and there wasn't time for anything else—but as she felt her muscles loosen in the warm water, she sighed with pleasure. A private pool was an unbelievable opulence, and yet another thing she shouldn't get used to.

Inevitably, her mind circled back to the events of the night before. She'd done a decent job of pushing them aside during the day, fueled by the desire to prove herself after her disastrous beginnings, but here she was, after all, in the same waters where it had all began. There was no escape from the memories now.

What if she weren't working for Alejandro? It was a ridiculous line of thought, of course, because if she weren't employed by him, she would be back in New York shoveling snow. But she let her mind wander a bit, imagining that, for some reason, she was here as a guest, and that there would be a chance meeting in the pool. She would wear a simple white two-piece and a pair of vintage Wayfarer sunglasses and look unbelievably old-school glamorous, and he would wear... well, nothing at all, of course, since that was obviously how he liked to swim.

She shook her head and circled back under the water, turning for one more lap before pulling herself up the steps and toweling off.

No more of that, she thought as she walked resolutely back to the pool house. Fantasies like that were nothing but lit dynamite.

She took a long shower, enjoying the delicious-smelling shampoo and conditioner, taking time to shave her legs and groom every last inch of herself. Reveling in the luxury of not just the expensive lotions and potions, but the time to put them on. She was more aware of her body here in Wellington than she'd been in years.

She slipped into a little pink tank dress from the collection of clothing that Billy had pressed on her before he left and then checked her fridge. It had been replenished during the day. There was a poached filet of salmon, some lemon and mint-strewn couscous, and a delicious-looking endive salad. Someone had apparently decided she deserved dessert as well, because there was a dangerously appealing flourless chocolate cake just the right size for one greedy person.

She poured herself another glass of wine and took her little feast outside to eat poolside as she watched the sun make its slow and showy descent.

Just as she'd finished the last bite of cake, the back door of the main house opened and two large and handsome Rhodesian Ridgebacks bounded out, followed by Pilar, calling after them.

The dogs ran straight to Georgia, wagging their tails and sniffing at her, hoping for whatever leftovers she might be willing to spare.

"*Lo siento*," called Pilar as she hurried to catch up. "They are friendly, *Doctora*. I swear. They have no manners, but they wouldn't hurt a fly."

Georgia laughed and patted the dogs happily. "Oh, I can tell." She scratched the dogs behind their ears. "You're a couple of sweet girls, aren't you?"

Pilar smiled. "I hope you are comfortable in the pool house?"

"Yes, thank you. It's absolutely wonderful."

"I was worried," Pilar said, "that you might feel like you're in a *pecera*—a fish bowl. Jandro told me that he accidentally woke you last night?"

"Oh," said Georgia, blushing and wondering, yet again, just how close this mother and son were, "I mean, I guess I did hear him swimming..." She trailed off.

Pilar cocked her head, and Georgia thought she detected a subtle look of surprise in her eyes. "Well, we do not usually swim at two in the morning," Pilar said. "And now that he knows you're living here, I'm sure you will not be disturbed again."

Georgia smiled and nodded, trying to ignore the sharp pang of disappointment she felt.

"Oh, and will you come for dinner Sunday night? Nine? Very informal."

"I'd be happy to," Georgia stuttered, pleased she'd been made so welcome, but immediately panicked about having to face Alejandro across the table.

"*Bueno.* I will walk my dogs now. Please let me know if there is anything you need."

Georgia watched the slim, upright figure of the Del Campo matriarch walk away, flanked by her two matching, caramel-colored dogs.

Chapter Forty-one

Dr. Gustavo was there to greet Georgia the next morning when she walked into the barn. He turned to her with a big, slick smile and a show of exaggerated gallantry. "Ah, so good to have you with us, Dr. Fellowes," he said. "I'm sure that your equine experience will be invaluable. I am looking forward to hearing all about where you've been working."

He barely paused, not bothering to give Georgia time to respond.

"No? Well, experience or no, I'm sure a vet so thoughtful and lovely will enhance us in every possible way."

Georgia met his eye. He wasn't even trying to be subtle, the old goat. "I'll do my best," she said as sweetly as she could manage. "I'm sure you have much to teach me, Doctor."

And for that first week, as long as Alejandro or Hendy was within earshot, Gustavo did teach her, loudly lecturing her on the vagaries of the barn.

"The extreme heat and humidity here make it imperative that the ponies are checked over several times a day," Gus pompously instructed her as he ran a currycomb through the coat of a glossy black mare. "Even the tiniest cut can turn into a summer sore practically overnight if it's neglected."

Georgia shuddered, imagining one of these obscenely expensive animals going down with a fly-blown wound on her watch.

"The feet have to be especially tended to, as well," he said. "The sand is very hard on the hooves."

She nodded, jotting down notes as fast as he talked.

"And be alert for equine herpes," added Gus. "That's a plague in Wellington."

But when the team captain or *patrón* moved out of hearing, the curtain came down, and the show was over. Gustavo could be halfway through a sentence, but as soon as he realized it was just the two of them, he would immediately stop talking and turn his back. For all his unctuous public flirting, he clearly loathed Georgia. He did whatever he could to poison the rest of the staff against her. He was the master of a low aside in Spanish to a sycophantic groom just as Georgia entered a stall, or an undermining parting shot as she left it, and if any story could be told at her expense, he made sure it was.

Georgia was astonished by his overt hostility, but hoping to find her own solution to the problem, she didn't complain, and even if she had wanted to, she wasn't sure just whom she could complain to. Alejandro was obviously doing his best to avoid her—all but doing an about-face every time he saw her—and after that disastrous first day, she didn't want anyone else on the team to think she couldn't handle her own business.

She felt helpless to change the dynamic and completely at sea when it came to making herself useful. Gustavo was determined to exclude her from all veterinary work, and with the army of grooms and students, she couldn't even keep herself busy in other, nonmedical ways around the barn.

Her only solace was Sugar. Gustavo felt the little pony was nothing but an embarrassing mongrel, a stain on the honor of the barn. He made it quite clear he wanted nothing to do with her foaling when the time came and left all her care to Georgia. Anytime Georgia had a spare second or felt in danger of Gustavo getting her down, she'd pop in to see the mare with an apple or a fistful of hay. Sugar turned out to be the smartest pony Georgia had ever known, uncannily aware of Georgia's moods, and always had a trick or a nuzzle for her whenever she felt low. There was more than one day that first week when Georgia felt the only friend she had was the little horse, and if it hadn't been for Sugar, she would have been entirely alone in the barn.

* * *

Alejandro noticed that Georgia was struggling, and though he couldn't prove it, he suspected that Gustavo was somehow undercutting her behind the scenes. But every time he turned her way, determined to discuss it, he would stop himself, alarmed by the feeling of his heart beating triple time, certain that he could not be trusted to talk to her in an intimate way and not find himself wanting more.

Still, one day when he passed by Sugar's stall and saw Georgia inside, her curly head bent as she combed the little pony, he could not resist the chance to connect.

"We should see that foal any day now, eh?" he said as he attempted to casually lean against the stall door.

Georgia looked up, startled. Her hazel eyes were red and

swollen, the long lashes tangled and wet. Alejandro felt a jolt of alarm.

"*Que te pasa?*" he spoke urgently, "what happened? What's wrong?"

She smiled a watery little half smile and quickly looked away. "Nothing," she said. "I'm fine."

"You're obviously not fine." He felt a welling of fierce anger at whoever had made her this unhappy. "Did Gustavo—"

"No, no, no," she interrupted. "Please, I'm fine, Alejandro. Just tired, maybe a little homesick, you know?"

He tried to read her eyes, not trusting her assurances, needing to wipe the look of distress off her face. "Come with me," he said abruptly. "I have something to show you."

She looked at him a moment and then nodded, storing the grooming tools and following him to a corner of the barn, where he showed her the ladder to the hayloft.

"Have you been up yet?" he asked.

She shook her head, puzzled. "The hayloft? No, why would I?"

He motioned for her to go up, and after a second of hesitation, she ascended the ladder. He felt a rush of heat to his groin as he watched her luscious rear, clad in tight jeans, climbing ahead of him, remembering the moment when he had pressed himself against her naked back. He tried to push the image away as he started to climb after her, but when he saw her foot slip slightly on the rung, he automatically reached up and put his hand to the small of her back— steadying her.

She stopped climbing and went very still. She clearly had regained her footing, but he left his hand where it was, unable to break the contact between them. He could not see her face, but he felt her breathing grow ragged, was keenly aware of the pulse of energy that rocketed between him, felt his entire body go rigid with desire.

"Thank you. I'm okay," she whispered hoarsely.

He squeezed his eyes shut and pulled his hand away as if he'd been burned. When he opened them again, she had slipped up through a hole to the loft, into the light-filled space above him.

Chapter Forty-two

The loft was much bigger than Georgia had expected. Instead of the cramped little crawl space in her own barn back at home, this was an entire second floor to the building, with matching floor-to-ceiling windows on either end of the room and beautiful dark wood rafters set against the bright, white ceiling. Golden bales of hay were stacked five deep and high against the wall, and the air was filled with their sweet, warm scent.

"I used to come up here as a teenager," said Alejandro.

Georgia tried not to stare at the way his biceps bulged as he pulled himself up through the hatch. She could still feel the warm imprint of his hand on her back.

"This was my hiding spot whenever I needed to get away," he said.

"Away from what?"

Alejandro gave her a twisted smile. "My father mostly. He could be...difficult. If he wasn't pushing me about our riding, he was usually messing around with some pretty student or another. There really wasn't a version of him that I could tolerate when we were in the barn. So, whenever things became especially bad between us, I would disappear up here. He never figured it out."

Georgia drifted toward a window to look out over the fields. "This place feels like a world away from the rest of the barn."

He followed her, but stopped before he was too close. "Yes, that is exactly it. A world away. I thought...I thought you might like to know about it, just in case Sugar's stall isn't always private enough."

She smiled ruefully and rolled her eyes. "That obvious, huh?"

He shrugged. "Maybe only to me."

He took a step closer then, and her breath caught in her throat as he reached toward her, but instead of touching her, he pulled something out from under the windowsill and smiled.

"I can't believe they're still here." He showed her the deck of cards in his hand. "Sometimes Sebastian would come up as well, and we would play *Truco*—Trick—an Argentine card game, you know?" He laughed. "Sebastian always won. It drove me crazy. I knew he was cheating but I could never prove it."

She smiled, thinking that she had never seen him look so relaxed and happy.

"Georgia," he said, "I'm sorry I have not been more available to you. I think that maybe you have been struggling a bit with Gustavo?"

She shrugged. "I don't need you to fix it. It's my problem to figure out."

"But it's my barn. I can step in."

She shook her head. "No. I can do it."

"Okay," he said, "but if you change your mind—"

"I won't."

He laughed. "Fine. You win. Do it your way."

She raised her chin. "I will."

He smiled at her and then reached out and pushed a lock of her hair off her forehead. His eyes were so warm. For a moment, she thought he would kiss her. She felt herself blush from head to toe. But his hand just lingered on her cheek, his soft touch almost more provoking than a kiss. The air around them turned electric.

He took a deep breath and dropped his hand. "I should get back to the horses."

She nodded. "Me, too."

He turned away from her, walking over to the hatch in the floor.

"Alejandro?"

He turned back.

"Thank you for bringing me up here."

He held her gaze for a moment. "*De nada,*" he said softly. And then he lowered himself back down the ladder and disappeared.

Chapter Forty-three

Monday was the horse world's day off, which meant Sunday was supposed to be the town's big night out. Personally, Georgia planned to collapse.

She was shattered. Her feet were painfully blistered from a long week on her feet in new boots, and she made a note to herself that she needed to get something less fancy and more useful as soon as possible. Her jaw actually ached from all the smiling she'd done in an attempt to cover up just how frustrated she actually felt.

The rituals of Sunday evening tuck were really something to see: the students already showered and dressed, the boys wearing dress shirts and slacks, the girls in heels and skimpy sequined dresses as they raced through the stalls, checking that each horse was properly bedded down for the night before they could go out and party. Enzo followed up like some benevolent overlord, tactfully confirming that everything was as it should be. When the last horse was put to bed, he told Georgia it was time for her to go home.

She couldn't help feeling a little lonely as she limped back to the pool house, hearing the laughter and chatter and car doors slamming as the grooms and students all set off in anticipation of serious fun.

She wondered what Alejandro was doing that night, whether he would go out or just stay in. She liked to think of him so near. She looked over at the main house, wondering which window was his bedroom.

She opened the gate to the pool, startled out of her wholly inappropriate reverie to find Valentina and a friend goofing in the water. Diving and splashing, they looked as sleek and privileged as a pair of Alejandro's best ponies.

The gate clicked behind Georgia, and both girls turned. Valentina gave an exaggerated eye roll and hauled herself out of the pool.

"*Vamonos*, Marcela," she said to her friend, a study in bored glamour, who climbed out after her.

"Oh, you guys don't have to go," said Georgia. "Really! I'm just going to—"

Valentina shook her head and shuffled her feet into flip-flops. "It's fine," she said petulantly. She half sneered at her friend as they pushed past Georgia. "*Abuela* says we have to make sure *la doctora* gets her privacy."

Georgia sighed as she let herself into the pool house. She really couldn't win. She didn't belong with the barn staff or the family. In fact, as far as she could tell, she didn't belong in Wellington at all. But that was fine, she reminded herself, she didn't need to belong. Really, all she needed right now was to get off her feet.

She was in her sweats, with an open bottle of wine in her hand, before she remembered Pilar's dinner invitation. She groaned. She was bone tired and would have liked nothing better than to drink wine, eat pizza, and sleep.

Still, she couldn't very well back out now. What kind of

excuse could she possibly make, with the entire Del Campo family a two-minute walk up the path?

She put down the wine, peeled the sweats back off, and hit the shower. At least the evening might give her the chance to tell Pilar how grateful she was for all she had done. The barn might be a challenge, but coming home to her little house each night was heaven. Flowers, food, all sorts of thoughtful touches. She always felt like a treasured guest rather than just an employee. And, she reflected, it wouldn't hurt to show Valentina she was something more than an irritating invading species spoiling her fun at the pool house.

Her blistered feet stung as the hot water pooled around her toes. She stroked the bar of soap over her chest—it smelled sweet—like lavender and honey—and she worked up a luxurious lather. Her finger trailed through the bubbles, soaping her lower back, remembering the way Alejandro's hand had lingered there. His hand on her back, his touch on her cheek—they somehow burned even hotter in her memory than the night they had spent together. She closed her eyes and skimmed her hand down over her stomach, thinking of that one last dark look he had given her before he'd descended the ladder...

For God's sake, she was like a woman possessed. She turned the water all the way over to cold, and forced herself under the frigid blast before wandering back into her room to get dressed.

Even with Billy's recent contributions, the contents of her suitcase took up only a few short inches on one rail. Georgia found yesterday's jeans had been put away, and she cringed a bit to think of the maid going through her ratty old things and hanging them up as if they were priceless designer wear.

She sifted through the hangers, past all the shimmery little shifts Billy had given her. They all seemed too flimsy for a family dinner, and of course, most of the things she had brought from home were hopelessly worn or altogether too casual. But then, there was her mother's red dress...

She slipped it off the hanger and looked at it, running her fingers over the bright silk. It had seemed magical to her as a child—the way this dress had turned her mother into something out of a fairy tale. When she had tried it on in the cold and dim attic at home, she had felt like an impostor, but tonight, standing in this beautiful little house, the golden sunset light streaming through her windows, the scent of roses wafting in on the soft breeze, it seemed the dress's magic might belong to her after all.

* * *

Alejandro rode late that evening, exercising Temper under the covered ring in the lingering twilight. The new pony continued to perform like a dream—anticipating Alejandro's every whim—but whenever he glanced at the lights of the pool house, Jandro felt himself unsettled.

He brushed Temper down and handed him off to a groom. Try as he might, he thought, he couldn't stay away from her. Their time in the loft had been almost more unendurably intimate than anything that had come before. He felt as if he had shown her some small part of himself that he'd never laid bare to anyone.

What, exactly, was he doing? he wondered as he strode back to the *hacienda*. There was no good ending to this story. Even if he could find a way to have Georgia, his new unbelievably insistent object of desire, it could only ever be temporary. She had a home to return to, a job, and a life he knew nothing about. And beyond that, what could he really offer? It would surely turn out to be just like every other relationship he'd ever had. He'd never be able to give her enough of his time, his attention, his affection. She'd feel cheated and tricked and jealous of the team—just like Olivia had—and Georgia didn't deserve to be hurt that way.

He stopped before going into the house, closing his eyes and frantically running his hand through his hair. Why was he even thinking about this? This would not do. She was his employee. And really, how much did he actually know about this woman? She could have a boyfriend, for God's sake. But no ring, he automatically thought—realizing that he had actually looked for one— remembering her long, tapered fingers, the unpolished nails, so pleasurably incongruous among all the shellacked talons here in Welly World. He shook his head forcefully. *Enough of this.*

His mother was on the terrace, looking unusually distracted in front of a table setting that, for all its apparently effortless elegance, he knew would have taken her a good hour to get absolutely right.

"Sorry I'm late, *Mamá*," he said, misreading her frown.

"*Está bien*," she murmured. "You're fine. But I think I made a mistake. I thought it would be the right thing to make Georgia feel welcome. She ought to meet some people her own age while she's down here. I thought after being in the barn all week, Cricket might be a nice change."

Alejandro felt an uneasy sense of competing commitments, but gave his mother the smile of approval she'd expected.

"And Rory, Valentina, and Sebastian will be here, of course, but I did not think to include Gustavo, and then he just dropped by and saw the whole setup. It was very awkward..."

"He'll get over it." Alejandro shrugged irritably. "We can't nanny that man any longer."

Pilar raised her eyebrows, but Alejandro turned away, heading upstairs to change, and wondering what the rest of the night would bring.

* * *

Georgia picked her way up the path, heading toward the *hacienda*, and tried to hold her nerve. The back of the dress was too low for a bra, and her mother had never worn one with it. But, of course, her mother had been small chested like a runway model, whereas Georgia was definitely more endowed. *Just stand up straight*, her imaginary mother instructed her, *and work with what you have.*

She'd slid on a pair of flat gold sandals that Billy had pressed upon her, and a chunky gold bracelet—her own take on the stack of tinkling bangles her mother had worn. She left her hair down, and air-dried it so that her curls were loose and a little wild.

Her mother would have worn more makeup, of course. One of the great pleasures of Georgia's early childhood had been to watch her mother sitting at her mirrored dressing table, smoothing on cream, patting on powder, drawing on her lips and eyebrows. It seemed to Georgia that her mother had been able to create a different face every day—pink lipstick one time, gold eyeshadow the next—she'd been a chameleon with her delicate pots and paints.

Georgia did not have anything remotely resembling her mother's skill, but she did apply some sheer red lipstick and a dash of mascara and was pleased with the results. *Very nice*, she heard her mother say. *Every woman needs a little color, Georgie.*

Georgia smiled to herself as she walked up the path. She felt bold and chic now, as if she had a delicious secret. She wondered if this was the way her mother had felt every day, so at ease in her own skin.

She didn't know whether she should use the front door so she walked around to the back and saw everyone seated on the terrace.

"Right this way, *señorita*," the housekeeper said.

Chapter Forty-four

Christ, she was gorgeous, Alejandro thought. The red dress skimmed Georgia's body in a way that begged speculation about what was underneath. Her hair was loose and curly, dark gold waves plummeting down her back as if she had just tumbled out of bed, her lips matched the dress, a luscious crimson he immediately imagined kissing in one hundred different ways. He couldn't take his eyes off her as she greeted his mother—and then Sebastian, Hendy, and Rory—with a peck on the cheek. But when she came to him, he was both disappointed and relieved when she kept her eyes down and raised her hand in a shy, little wave instead.

"*Doctora*, I believe you've met *mi nieta*, Valentina?" said Pilar.

Alejandro had to curb his impulse to snatch away his daughter's phone and throw it into the pool as he watched Valentina barely bother to look up from her device.

"And you remember Cricket? You met at *la fiesta*?"

Cricket strolled over in her short shorts to give Georgia a bright smile and a double kiss on the cheeks. "But of course she remembers me," she said. "We were on our way to becoming the best of friends. I love your dress, by the way. So festive. Is it vintage?"

Georgia flushed. "It was my mother's."

Cricket pursed her lips. "Oh, lucky you that you're the same size as your mum. I couldn't get more than one leg into one of my mother's frocks. But then, she's basically anorexic."

Pilar led Georgia over to one of the patio chairs. "Jandro, get *la doctora* a drink, *por favor?*"

"Of course, *Mamá.*" Alejandro looked at Georgia. "Wine? Champagne? A cocktail?"

She looked flustered. "Wine is good, thank you."

He poured her some pinot gris. As he handed her the glass, his eyes met hers and their fingers touched, and she pulled her hand away so fast that the entire cup of wine spilled down the front of her dress and then smashed on the floor. Georgia leaped up, dripping.

"Oh shit!" she said. Then she looked at Pilar, red faced. "Oh gosh, I mean, I'm sorry. Here, let me help clean up." She bent to pick up the broken glass.

"*Ay!*" said Pilar, "Jandro, *tan torpe*! So clumsy! No, no, *Doctora*, don't touch the glass. You might cut yourself."

Valentina giggled and took a picture with her cell. Alejandro made a furious note to take the phone from her permanently.

"I'm so sorry, *querida*," he said. "Here, let me help you." He pulled her up, reached for a cloth napkin from the table, and started to wipe at her dress. Cricket immediately intercepted, taking the napkin from his hand.

"Don't be ridiculous, Jandro. She doesn't want you pawing at her like that. She needs to get that dress off."

"*Sí*," said Pilar. "Lucky that you live so close. Go change, quick, and then bring me back the dress. We will take care of it before the stain sets."

Georgia, looking absolutely mortified, stumbled out the door.

Alejandro turned to his mother. "I feel so terrible. Maybe I should go help somehow?"

Sebastian laughed. "Help *'querida'* out of her dress?"

Alejandro felt himself flush. "No, I just meant—"

Rory waggled his eyebrows. "I could be useful there, too!"

"Shut up, Rory," Alejandro snapped.

Rory grinned. "Hey, just saying I'm happy to help."

"I said, *cállate!*"

Rory raised his hands in mock surrender, and Alejandro started toward him, but Cricket hooked his arm in her own. "Oh for God's sake, Jandro, it's just spilled wine, not a gunshot wound. She's perfectly okay. Come and have a drink."

* * *

Georgia pulled her dress over her head and tried very hard not to cry. As soon as she'd seen Cricket—wearing her perfectly cool, sexy, effortlessly now outfit and looking like a million bucks—she'd felt like an outdated joke in her mother's old clothes. What had she been thinking? She must have looked like she was dressing up as a gypsy.

And then she'd touched Alejandro's hand, and even that tiny little brush of his fingers against hers was like an electrical shock. She'd been so afraid that everyone would somehow know—see what was between them—that she had yanked her hand away without thinking.

So ridiculously stupid.

She stood in her panties, searching the closet. Now what to

wear? She didn't even want to go back. She was certain she'd already spoiled everyone's evening, but what possible excuse could she come up with not to return? And surely they were all waiting for her. She put on a bra and then threw on a little T-shirt dress that Billy had given her. Peach. Not too fitted. It would be fine with her sandals. She checked her look in the mirror and then twisted up her hair into a loose topknot and wiped off her lipstick. There. She looked perfectly presentable, no longer trying to be someone she was not.

* * *

The rest of the evening passed in a blur.

The table was beautiful, with roses and candles and course after course of exquisite food. Georgia's wineglass was kept filled; there was laughter and lively conversation and funny stories. Everyone was friendly and warm—they obviously went out of their way to include her. It was all elegant, and gracious, and simply lovely. But Georgia felt like a miserable outsider for the entire time.

She could only seem to notice the things that went awry. She used the wrong spoon for the soup course, managed to confuse the team name Victoria with Alejandro's daughter's name (a mistake Valentina snarkily relayed to the entire table), she didn't know enough about polo to join in any discussion of the game, and worst of all, she was forced to watch Cricket, who was seated next to Alejandro, her platinum blond head a perfect contrast to his strong, dark profile, smiling up at him, making him laugh, placing a proprietary hand upon his arm more times than Georgia could count.

By the time they served dessert, she was absolutely awash with jealousy.

"*Doctora*," Pilar said, touching her hand, "have you seen much of the town yet?"

"Oh," said Georgia, tearing her eyes away from the way Cricket was leaning ever closer to Alejandro, "not yet. I haven't really had time, and honestly, I feel rather awkward about taking your car and driver."

Immediately upon seeing Pilar's face, she regretted the bluntness of her words. Yet another mistake.

"I just meant—" she tried to backtrack.

"No, *entiendo*, I understand." Pilar thinned her lips and gave her attention to the cheese and fruit on her plate.

"*Mamá*," said Sebastian, "not everyone likes to be dependent on a chauffeur. I'm sure Georgia just likes to drive herself around. You should give her your Vespa to use." He smiled at Georgia. "It was her birthday present last year, but she won't wear a helmet because of her hair."

"That's not true," protested Pilar. "I am simply too old for such a young thing. That is an excellent idea. I will have it ready for you tomorrow, *Doctora*."

"Oh, thank you, but that's not—"

"And Cricket," said Pilar, interrupting the pretty blonde just as she was reaching up to brush a crumb off Alejandro's face, "perhaps you could show Dr. Fellowes around Wellington a bit if you have some time?"

Cricket smiled warmly. "Of course, Pilar. How fun." She looked at Georgia. "Anything special you'd like to do?"

"Oh," said Georgia, "I'm so awfully busy that I—"

"She needs a new bathing suit," said Valentina flatly.

Everyone turned to her in surprise.

"What? She does. Have you seen the one she uses? It looks like it's been chewed by *Abuela*'s dogs."

"Valentina!" said Alejandro sharply.

Valentina rolled her eyes. "Well, it's true!"

"Perfect, then," Cricket smoothly interrupted. "Pool wear is my specialty." She looked at Alejandro. "Of course, if she's working for you, darling, she probably doesn't have a minute off. I know you're driving her like a slave."

Valentina snorted. "*Papá* thinks everyone should work as hard as he does."

Alejandro shook his head. "Of course, Dr. Fellowes is free to take off any time she likes," he said.

"Really?" said Cricket. "Now I'm worried. If you're that casual about her time off, I can't imagine you're paying her enough, darling."

"What would you know about wages, Cricket?" Rory asked.

"The wages of sin, angel, those I know." She laughed. She turned back to Georgia. "Anyway, I'm more than happy to take you out. Let's definitely make a proper date."

Georgia smiled weakly and then had another sip of wine, fervently wishing for the night to end.

Chapter Forty-five

Georgia lay in her bed, listening to the wind blowing through the trees outside, her mind churning miserably over the entire disastrous evening. Image after embarrassing image flew through her brain. She flipped over and violently buried her face in her pillow, screwing her eyes shut. *Just stop.* She wasn't going to do this anymore. Maybe she'd messed up, maybe she'd made a fool of herself—and she'd definitely realized that even if Alejandro and Cricket were not yet together, it was absolutely inevitable that they would be—but the whole thing was over now, and there was nothing she could do about any of it.

This was actually good, she told herself. This was exactly what she needed. A reminder that she was not here to socialize. Not here to make friends. Certainly not here to have a romance. She was here to work. She had her issues with Gustavo, she had an entire barn full of ponies to watch out for, she had Sugar's foaling coming up, she had things to take care of. And so far, she'd been weak and distracted and not half the vet she knew she could be. This was her chance to renew her commitment, figure out her problems, and get back on track. And she wasn't going to let anyone stand in her way. Not Gustavo, not Alejandro—not anyone. Nothing but work from here on out, she told herself, nothing but the ponies and the barn.

✢ ✢ ✢

Alejandro lay in his own bed, watching the shadows of the oak tree outside his window chase across the ceiling. Jesus, what a night. He'd spent the evening in absolute agony, wanting nothing so much as to be alone with Georgia. Having her in his home was even worse than the barn. He'd spent most of his time trying to pretend he was listening to Cricket's incessant chatter while fantasizing about pulling Georgia aside, taking her to the library, to the sunroom, to his bed—anywhere he could have her alone—but between his mother, his daughter, and Cricket all demanding his attention in their various ways, he'd hardly had a chance to even speak to Georgia.

She'd looked so beautiful. First in the red dress, sexy and delicious and wild. It had been a whole new side of her—one that took all his will to resist—and then in her demure little peach-colored dress, her lips wiped clean of the lipstick, her curls pinned up—which had driven him even wilder. His fingers itching to take her hair down, he had forgotten to eat his soup, imagining how he would slide his hands up under that little dress, finding all the pleasures she was hiding underneath.

He twisted under the sheets, unable to settle. She unleashed feelings in him he'd never had before. He wanted her in a way that he didn't understand. He'd disappointed Olivia so much during their marriage, never quite loving her in the way she wanted and then losing her before he could make amends, he had sworn that he would never put another woman through that. But when it came to Georgia, he was selfish. He knew what the right thing to do was, he knew that he should keep away for both of their sakes, but his desire burned so fever bright that it all felt squarely out of his hands.

What a mess of things he'd made. How much less complicated it would have been to just let her return to New York, go back to her own life, cut all this off before it took hold of him. But now, the thought of her leaving—of returning to the north—made him clench in torment. What to do with a woman whom he wanted so badly, but knew that he could not have?

Chapter Forty-six

All that next week, Georgia kept to her new plan and threw herself into her work. She arrived early and left late. She asked Enzo and Noni as many questions as she thought they could tolerate. She changed her strategy with Gustavo, no longer waiting to work with him or giving him the chance to tell her what to do. Instead, she flat-out avoided him, spending time in whatever stalls he was not occupying. She gave each pony her steady, hovering attention, scanning them for conditions and getting to know their different personalities: the shy and studious pony, the high-strung, the adolescent hotshot, trusty old-timers, impossible neurotics, and all.

She learned to zig when Gustavo zagged. If he wouldn't let her do any medical work, she'd think of other ways to help in the barn. She got to know the students and grooms better. She pitched in on all sorts of work—grooming, mucking stalls, leading the ponies out for exercise. She refused to listen when anyone told her that she wasn't needed. She made plans, big and small. When she saw Alejandro, she made it a point to stand at least an arm's length away, never look him in the eye, and talk about nothing but work. She was the consummate professional, and soon enough, almost everyone in the barn (excluding Gustavo, of course) began to show signs of developing a healthy respect for her.

Still, even if work was better, most days she went home and sat in her house alone, reading and trying to ignore the fact that she was flat-out lonely. It was nice that she was building up some measure of respect, of course, but respect was not companionship. So, she was not entirely surprised by just how happy she felt late one Friday afternoon when she heard Cricket's husky voice making her way down the stalls.

As always, Cricket made an entrance—simultaneously on the phone, drinking a large iced coffee, petting a barn dog, and calling in a familiar way to Enzo and all the crew.

"Where have you buried Georgia?" she asked, and Georgia came to the door of the stall.

"Hey, Cricket," Georgia said, a little dismayed to realize she hadn't looked in a mirror all day, while Cricket looked as if she'd spent the hours at the spa and salon.

"Darling," came the husky drawl, "I've been hoping you'd get in touch."

"I've just been so busy," Georgia lied.

"How's now for hitting the mall?" Cricket asked, snapping shut her phone with the air of a woman who was never refused.

"Oh, I'm not off for another couple of hours," said Georgia.

"Nonsense," said Cricket. "Jandro said you could leave any time."

"I'd feel a little guilty, knocking off early," Georgia said, passing the grooms still mucking out. "I'm usually the last to leave."

"Really?" Cricket drawled, handing off her empty paper

coffee cup to a passing groom with a mouthed "Thanks."
"How very industrious. But you need a swimsuit and I don't
think anyone will miss you. Don't you think it's all right?"
she said to Enzo as he passed by.

"Of course," said Enzo, smiling at Georgia. "We're fine
here. Go."

Cricket linked arms with Georgia and walked her back to
the pool house, where she'd loudly insisted she'd wait while
Georgia changed out of her work clothes.

"You hop in the shower, and I'll just sit tight."

Georgia showered and dressed as fast as she could and
came out of the bedroom to find Cricket flicking through her
pathetically small collection of clothes.

"Oh, honey, it's worse than I thought." Cricket laughed.
"Let's go get you Wellied Out."

With her sunglasses perched on her head and snappy chatter and running commentary on everything they passed,
Cricket reminded Georgia a bit of Billy. Despite some lurking
misgivings, she told herself that she could use a friend down
here. She couldn't go on just talking to horses, after all.

They drove past panoramic shopping centers and condo
blocks, gated communities and mini-malls.

"Everything is absolutely perfect," Georgia marveled.

"Oh my God," Cricket said. "You have no idea. They'll
fine you for having a dirty car here."

"No!" Georgia exclaimed.

"Oh yes," Cricket said. "And for failing to whitewash your
mailbox. You're not in the Catskills anymore, Georgia."

Georgia laughed. "No kidding," she said. "Where do the
people in all the service industries live?" None of the homes
they'd passed could be attainable by anyone earning under a
million a year.

"I have no idea," Cricket said vaguely. Clearly the notion had never occurred to her. "Not Palm Beach anyway."

They buzzed down the five-lane highway, looping between endless top-of-the-line pickups, passing feed supply trucks and loaded horse trailers.

The enormous mall was full of pristine people and piped music. Hurrying to match Cricket's brisk pace, Georgia tried not to stare at the repeating theme of plastic surgery and pearls.

"You can buy anything you need for horseback riding here," Cricket told her over her shoulder. "Kentucky and Pikeur britches are the best, of course. Oh, and Super International."

Georgia tried discreetly to turn a price tag.

"It's not worth skimping," Cricket said. "The point here is fitting in. Even middle-class people wear these britches."

Georgia's eyes widened. "Maybe later," she said. "I really just need a swimsuit right now."

"Quick stop at Sephora?" Cricket asked as they passed.

Georgia shook her head. "I don't really wear much makeup. And what I really need are some work boots."

Cricket pretended to yawn. "Work boots? Boring. You can get those online when you're on your own. Makeup is priority number one and much more fun. Everyone wears a full face here, even when riding. It's expected."

"But that's ridiculous. It must all melt off, riding in this heat."

Cricket shrugged. "Well, they reapply after, of course."

Georgia eyed a trio of women who marched by them. They all wore the same riding breeches and boots, their hair pulled back into elaborate braids. To Georgia's eye, the only difference among them was the color of their polo shirts.

"What do they do all day, these women?" Georgia marveled.

"Oh, well," said Cricket airily, "the usual. Get up, head to the gym, and then over to Starbucks, grab a latte. Change into your riding clothes, take your riding lesson with the trainer, then go out for lunch—get a little sloshed. Maybe head over to the Pool House and Spa—nails, massages, facials—or visit with another woman's husband, whatever works. And then get dressed up to the nines and go out for dinner and clubbing. Lather, rinse, repeat."

Georgia shook her head as she looked around at the endless displays of creams and powders and potions. She felt out of her depth in every way. "I really don't need anything," she tried again.

Cricket rolled her eyes. "Oh, cut it out. Let's get you a makeover." She dragged Georgia over to one of the sales reps and plunked her at the counter. "Go all out," she told the woman. "Beginning with her brows."

The woman nodded and quickly picked up a pair of tweezers and started plucking away.

"Ow!" said Georgia. "I don't think I want—"

"It's not a question of want as much as need, darling," said Cricket. "Trust me on this."

Georgia tried to relax as the woman continued to groom her face with microscopic scrutiny, but Cricket was peppering her with questions about where she came from and how big the house was and she started to feel like she ought to just hand over a family tree and a bank statement and call it a day.

"There," said Cricket, a look of satisfaction on her face as the shop girl tilted the mirror in Georgia's direction and gave her a peek.

Georgia tried to stifle a gasp. She looked ridiculous. Not at all herself. Admittedly, the brows were better. Even she had noticed that they were getting a bit untamed. But the base and the concealer and the blush and contouring... She felt as if she were wearing a thousand-layer mask. She blinked, and the fringe of auxiliary lashes the shop girl had so carefully applied at Cricket's insistence tickled against her cheek.

"Do you like it?" asked the sales clerk, and Georgia did her best to look pleased.

"Oh yes, thank you," she said, longing to grab a jar of makeup remover and make her escape.

"She'll take the foundation, and the Nars blush, and the eyeshadow collection, oh, and that moisturizer. She needs it on the neck," said Cricket.

"Cricket," admonished Georgia.

"What?" said Cricket. "Listen, darling, I am merely taking Pilar's instructions and getting you properly kitted out. This is Wellington, not Poughkeepsie, for Pete's sake. You have to blend in."

Georgia flinched as the numbers added up at the register, but after a sidelong look from Cricket, she reluctantly handed over her credit card.

"Good," said Cricket. "Now let's go get a swimsuit."

Shopping for a suit was another tug-of-war, with Cricket picking out skimpy and impractical micro bikinis. ("Can you even get this wet?" said Georgia when she was handed something made of leather and velvet. "Well, no," said Cricket, "but it will look spectacular poolside.") And Georgia casting longing gazes at the simple maillots and boy-cut tankinis.

Cricket filled Georgia's arms with a random selection of swimwear, shoved her into a dressing room, and then established herself in a heavily upholstered armchair just outside, insisting that Georgia model every last thing for her.

Georgia gasped to see how expensive three tiny triangles could be and felt more than a little exposed letting Cricket's critical gaze rake over her barely dressed figure—but she managed to find at least one thing she liked in the pile—a simple red two-piece, not too daringly cut, with the minimum diamanté—just one tiny heart on the rear.

As she changed and then paid, Cricket kept up a constant stream of questions about how it was going at the barn.

Georgia answered freely about some of the little changes she'd made: the swap shop for riding gear, the sponsorship brainstorming session, and the initiative to bring local kids in to work in the barns to do something to break down the divide between town and riders.

"Oh my. And here I thought you were just brought on to write scripts and check for bug bites. You must be ruffling some feathers," Cricket said. "I hope you know what you're contending with."

"Do you think I'm overstepping?"

"Oh, who knows?" Cricket said. "I'm sure they're thrilled. Come on now, let's get some lunch."

The restaurant, the "crab shack" which Cricket had described, was no simple shellfish hut, and even in early evening, it hosted an amazingly elegant crowd. Rider casual, but the jeans, the fitted polo shirts, the thousand-dollar accessories, the blowouts, the perfect skin, with diamond studs and tennis bracelets glittering in the bright Florida sun...

Well, at least I'm properly made up, thought Georgia ruefully.

They settled in, and Cricket ordered a bottle for the table. They scanned the menu (*Forty-five dollars for a salad!* thought

Georgia. *Holy shit!*), and Georgia thought it might be good to ask a few questions of her own. Cricket had applied makeup close enough to look up her nose, seen her in a bikini, and managed to extract the entire financial circumstances of her family without revealing a thing about herself. Georgia put down her menu.

"So, obviously you know Wellington from top to bottom. Have you been coming here long?"

"What can I tell you? The family's had horses forever. I was on horseback from the day I was born. Pony and trap at seven. Jumped competitively since I was eleven. I get colds in winter so it really suits me to come to the sun. But enough of all that—the subject of myself is boring—what I really want to know is how are you finding Alejandro?"

Georgia blinked at the sudden non sequitur.

"What do you mean by 'finding' him?"

"I meant how does he seem to you, his stress level? He's been under so much pressure, poor darling."

"I'm not sure I really know him well enough to—"

"He's just gone through so much, you know. Olivia and his father—and then the whole craziness with Noni, of course."

Georgia cocked her head. "I'm sorry, what craziness?"

"Oh, surely you've heard, darling. Noni is the bastard daughter of Carlos. Nobody knew a thing about her until after he died, and then suddenly, there she was—in the will. Alejandro had to go hunt her down. She was living in Germany and had some rather messy history with some terrible man. It's all very sordid and mysterious. Anyway, not surprising, she was a horsey person—that Del Campo blood will out, of course—and so Jandro brought her back here to work. Pilar almost shit a brick."

Georgia opened her mouth, trying to wrap her mind around all this information.

"Anyway, Jandro's been to hell and back, but a little tragedy can sometimes season a man, I think. He's still awfully attractive, no? But then, so is Sebastian. Which brother is it does it for you?"

Though Cricket had already emptied half the bottle while Georgia merely sipped at her wine, she felt her head spin. These rapid changes in conversation—she couldn't help feeling that she was being led into a trap.

"Um, they're both very handsome, of course. And Sebastian is fun—" She blushed.

"Right?" Cricket smiled. "Oh, and Jandro, he's your boss, so you really can't think of him that way, right? I mean, even though you're working in such close quarters?"

"He's so busy, I hardly see him," Georgia said carefully. She took a sip of her drink, trying to turn the conversation. "What about you two? Have you been close awhile?"

"Friends forever. And the benefits as well," Cricket said, looking at her with those lovely, languid eyes. "I was Olivia's great friend. I always felt she would have wanted me with him."

Georgia took a large bite of bread to hide her surprise. *What about Alejandro?* she wondered. Did he get an opinion on these things?

"I mean, actually, everyone wants me and Jandro together for good," continued Cricket casually once the waiter had left. "Our families have known each other forever. And you can see there'd be a certain symmetry. My show jumping profile. His polo. We're just like bread and butter, really. So, probably," she concluded. "Eventually. Once he comes out of mourning."

"Oh," said Georgia, her heart sinking a little, though she hadn't realized it had farther to go.

She tried to pull herself together. It was ridiculous to think she had the right to feel anything approaching disappointment about any of this. She'd had her little fling. It was over. And now she should be having the time of her life. It was all so outlandish, lunch with a famous show jumper gossiping about men from a legendary sporting dynasty. If she were home, she'd be splitting an eggplant parm with the receptionist at the clinic and making sure they were stocked up on flea spray.

They ordered their meals. Cricket insisted that Georgia try the soft-shell crab, even though Georgia assured her she was not a fan of shellfish.

"He needs a first lady," Cricket said as Georgia stared at the alarming bottom feeders now on her plate. "All these high-level polo players do. He can't stand the buttering up of the sponsors he has to do. He's much more old school, to the manor born. That was why Olivia was such good news. Enough money so he didn't really have to engage with all that."

"Oh," Georgia said. "I hadn't realized she had money."

Cricket shrugged like rich was a given. "It's all in trust for Valentina now. Overhead like his, he'll have to take all the rich wives he can get and still keep winning. Anyway, enough about my love life. What about you? Anyone special back home, Georgia?"

Georgia hesitated. She felt like she had to come up with something to avoid total humiliation.

"I mean, kind of. There's an ex who wants to go into business with me. We'll see when I get back..."

Georgia turned her attention to dismantling her meal,

trying to hide the faint tug of depression that crept down her spine. She chided herself. They had both agreed. He was her boss. Nothing more. And she'd better make that her mantra.

Cricket drained the last of the wine. "I have to get ready for a party. And you probably have to be ready for work in the morning, right? Don't want to be out too late." She snapped her fingers for the check.

"I think Pilar will be pleased with what we achieved here," she said.

The check came, and Georgia reached for her purse, expecting they'd split. Cricket didn't move. Seeing Georgia open her wallet, she said, "Thank you! My treat next time."

That, Georgia thought wryly, was how the rich stayed rich.

She felt depleted as Cricket finally dropped her off and drove away, and not just financially.

Chapter Forty-seven

Alejandro saw Cricket out that night at the club. He'd had dinner with Hendy and lingered to avoid his sleepless bed. She looked ravishing in an ivory shift, all cream and gold.

She had a habit of materializing just as he was feeling dangerously susceptible. He'd succumbed to her once, too soon after Olivia's accident, something he had immediately regretted. And now he always had the feeling she'd been waiting ever since.

She would run his life for him if he'd let her, he knew. The parties, the people, the staff. She'd relieve him of at least fifty percent of his current load and allow him to give Valentina the sort of household he'd been raised in himself. Plus, neither of them would have any illusions about it being a love match. She would understand that polo always came first.

And she was discreet. Even though he'd declared any liaison among the staff out of bounds, being seen with Cricket wouldn't break any rules.

Cricket bought him a drink.

"I had a fun time with your new hire earlier," she said casually.

"Who, Georgia?"

"Yes, she played a little hooky from work and joined me for a girls' afternoon out at the mall."

He frowned. "And so, what did you make of her?"

Cricket put her head to one side. "She seems lovely. A little bit of a fish out of water, homesick, I think. She's very inquisitive. Wanted to know all about Noni. Awfully interested in how much money everyone else has got. Asked about Olivia, too—how much she'd brought to the marriage."

Alejandro shook his head. This didn't sound like Georgia.

"I know, right? Felt kind of impertinent. She admitted to a flirtation with Sebastian. Reading between the lines, she seemed to feel a bit bad about it because there's a guy waiting back home. Otherwise, the usual. It was all about wanting to pick up makeup and clothes—make the most of her time here before she's gone."

Alejandro nodded, circumspect. He was quite aware that Cricket was capable of being malicious, but still, he almost wished he could believe her. He needed reasons to stay on the straight and narrow, to banish Georgia from his dreams. How nice it would be if she was actually not the woman he thought she was.

Cricket got a text. "Have to be going, darling." She kissed his cheek, brushing her breasts against his arms as she leaned over.

He watched her as she winked and sashayed to the exit, tight little ass twitching in sheer silk, turning heads all the way.

* * *

Most nights since arriving, Georgia had fallen into bed, half comatose with exhaustion, and slept all the way through.

After the dinner with Cricket, though, Georgia couldn't relax. Her head swam with restless thoughts. Billy had not been wrong—this family was complicated and difficult and apparently had so many secrets that she'd probably never understand the relationships between them all.

She flung herself over, willing herself to think of something simpler. She tried going over the rules of polo that she could remember, hoping that trying to learn them by heart might work like counting sheep.

But if she wasn't thinking of the Del Campo family, that just gave her mind the chance to revert to the same old grooves of worry and loss. Her father. The house in New York. Sam. Her mother. She felt something tighten in her chest. Being here in Wellington brought her back to Georgia so vividly.

It was strange to feel herself pulled by the same forces that had played on her mother. Strange that for all she felt out of her league in Florida, and in many ways longed to go home, there was no avoiding the fact that professionally she was excited by Wellington, and it was hard to think of returning to regular rural practice having worked with the fine specimens and high stakes she was dealing with here. In a way, Georgia thought, getting the picture about Cricket and Alejandro, however hurtful, had been liberating. Because now she knew she didn't have a hope in hell of ever winning the man and she was free to be her best professional self.

She turned her mind determinedly back to her duties at the stables. There was so much to learn and perfect, so many accidents to prevent, and it felt as if her responsibilities needed round-the-clock watch.

Finally around four, she figured she'd do more good getting up than stewing. If she was awake, she might as well enjoy the balmy Florida temperatures while she could. She decided she'd go see the horses in person, maybe get an early start on her day. Slipping on her boots and jeans, she wandered down to the stables.

She was startled to realize that there was someone riding in the covered ring with the lights off. Another insomniac, she figured, as she stole closer to see who was there. Georgia felt her breath catch in her throat as she saw the elegant figure wheeling around in the dark, bareback on a pony, mallet aloft in her arms. There was something about her father in the way she rode, but Valentina had an unmistakable style all her own.

Georgia had a strong sense she was trespassing on the girl's secret dance, but she couldn't tear her eyes away. The performance was so balletic that, when it finally ended, Georgia was tempted to clap, but as Valentina leaned over her pony and hugged its neck, Georgia clasped her hands in silence and backed away. The moment felt too intimate to intrude upon.

* * *

Alejandro was in the tack room cleaning his bridle. Though he could easily push this kind of work off on the grooms, he enjoyed the mindless ritual of it. Brushing down his pony, taking care of his own gear—it was pretty much the only meditation he was patient enough to attempt.

The door opened, and Georgia stuck her head in. He smiled at the way she blew a haphazard curl out of her eyes before speaking to him.

"Hey there, boss, you got a minute?"

He raised an eyebrow, still smiling. "Let me guess, you have another radical change you want to make in my barn."

At first, he had been surprised by the way she had taken a running dive into things these past couple of weeks. Of course, he had trusted and assumed that she would be a good, competent vet, but the way she immediately set to task questioning the reasons behind policy and looking for better solutions to old problems had been a bit of a shock.

She had started with simple health-related areas. She made several suggestions for diet and exercise and advocated for acupuncture for an old horse where it would never have occurred to him.

Wanting to show that he had full confidence in her, he'd given her the go-ahead. And more often than not, she'd returned with the results she had promised and then some.

So when she branched out a bit, making suggestions to help get the grooms to feel more invested in the team or ways to get the local townies more involved in the sport, he felt it worth his while to listen. She had shown herself to be both thoughtful and realistic, and had yet to overreach.

"Not so very radical," she said with a laugh. "But I just heard about this program in Philadelphia. There's a polo club that targets at-risk youth..."

He nodded as he listened to her newest idea, loving her infectious enthusiasm and open, easy curiosity. Cricket had been lying, he realized. The woman she had described was in no way related to the woman standing in front of him. This woman was smart, and kind, and caring. This woman, he thought, as he found himself watching her more than listening, was also ridiculously beautiful. He became distracted by her animated face and expressive hands—the way that same honey-touched curl kept creeping back into her eyes, no matter how many times she impatiently pushed it away...It was all he could do not to reach over and brush it back himself.

It was like some terrible cosmic joke, the way that she'd come into his life. She worked for him, she had a life elsewhere to return to, and he realized that he couldn't stand the idea of hurting another woman the same way he had hurt Olivia. He told himself it was better this way. Better to keep it on the up-and-up, and reap the rewards of her professionalism and knowledge rather than muddy it with anything more complicated.

Still, having given her the go-ahead to pursue her latest project, he couldn't help allowing himself a quick, greedy look as she turned and left the room. If any woman had ever looked better in jeans, he had yet to meet her.

* * *

Later, as he and Hendy were standing in the covered arena watching Enzo and some grooms put a string of ponies through their paces, Gustavo came huffing up to them, a look of annoyance on his florid face. He didn't bother with formalities. "Do you two know what that girl is up to now?"

Hendy shot a look at Alejandro. With every new suggestion of Georgia's that had been implemented, Gustavo had become increasingly resentful and belligerent.

"I assume that by 'that girl,' you are referring to Dr. Fellowes?" Alejandro asked.

"She's planning on bringing some hoodlum teenagers to our barn. Let them work and be trained, she said. Can you imagine?"

"Yes," said Hendy. "Alejandro was just telling me about that. A rather successful program, apparently."

Gustavo turned to Alejandro. "Surely you didn't sign off on this? It's pure idealistic nonsense. These *ladrones* will rob us blind!"

"Oh, come now, Gus," said Hendy. "That's quite a broad assumption."

"No, it's common sense. This girl—she knows nothing about our customs, our history. She charges in here, insists on upturning generations of strategic thinking based on her random whims—"

"Gustavo, she's just trying to help," said Alejandro.

"She has no sense of hierarchy! She's been treating grooms like equals! She needs to understand here we have low staff, and we have high staff..." He was ranting now, a film of sweat forming on his upper lip, his face getting redder and redder.

"Stop, please. You're being ridiculous. This is not a serfdom," said Alejandro. "Dr. Fellowes is acting perfectly within the bounds of the team."

"Oh, you'll always land on her side, won't you?" sneered Gustavo. "She's nothing but your *compañera*, your pretty little *novia*. You're just like your father with his playthings—bringing your *putas sucias* to the barn."

Alejandro lunged forward, ready to strike the man, but Hendy was faster, grabbing Alejandro around the shoulders and forcefully holding him back.

"I'd leave right now if I were you, Gus," gritted Hendy, struggling to keep Alejandro away.

Gus looked at them for a moment. "I am simply speaking the truth," he said. "What a pity that you two won't hear it."

Chapter Forty-eight

As much as he hated to do it, Alejandro knew that he had to let things slide with Gustavo for the moment. The final and most important game of the season, one particularly personal for Alejandro and Sebastian—the Carlos Del Campo Memorial Cup—was rapidly approaching.

Alejandro knew that they needed to throw all their concentration toward preparation. This was not a game they could afford to lose if they wanted to hold their heads up in the polo world. Apart from the time that would be lost replacing their lead vet this late, it felt impossible to fire the man his father had anointed before the cup being given in his name.

And their luck had shifted on the fields lately. Something had changed. They had been winning. Alejandro—for all his missed practices, his occasional glasses of wine, his mind on a woman's body instead of the ball—was playing better than he'd ever played in his life. And unlike his prior relentless perfectionism, this new joy on the field was contagious. His teammates were playing at his level, and they could not be stopped. Alejandro loved to glance at the sidelines and see Georgia there, tending the horses, cheering the team on, the pride on her face when they brought in another victory. He had to admit to himself that he was starting to play for different reasons now, not just to win, but to win for her.

Tonight, they had pulled out ahead at the very last second, and the game had been so exciting, so filled with adrenaline, that when he had swung off Temper after the last goal, he had wanted nothing so much as to sweep Georgia up into his arms and ride away with her, but Sebastian had ridden in between them and asked Georgia to take a look at his mount's back hoof, which the horse had been favoring.

After they unloaded the ponies, Georgia and Sebastian's horse followed Alejandro and Temper to the barn. They tied up the horses in side-by-side grooming stalls.

"You make it seem so easy," she said as she lifted the saddle onto her arm. "Does it feel easy?"

Alejandro slipped the halter from his horse. "What, polo? No." He smiled. "Though I'm glad to hear that's not too obvious."

"I hope this doesn't sound ignorant but are players trained differently in Argentina than here or England? I just mean, you and Sebastian seem to ride in a way that's more...elegant maybe?"

Alejandro laughed. "We were put on horses before we could walk."

"So early exposure, and perhaps some genetics, at play. How about something in the water there?" she teased.

He shook his head. "They're just different kinds of players. The others have strengths I don't." He scratched Temper behind the ears. "Training, luck, hard work...I suppose it helps if you have an innate bloodthirsty competitiveness."

"But you guys just seem like you're in your element in a way that Hendy and Rory don't."

"The only time I feel in my element is when I'm home—in Argentina."

"I'd like to see that," she said, and blushed. "I only mean, you already ride so wonderfully. I can't imagine what you must be like back home, on the *pampas*, isn't that what they're called?"

Alejandro smiled, amused. "Yes, *las pampas* is the correct word, but riding those grassy plains is more about *gauchos*—our cowboys—than polo."

Georgia ducked to examine her horse's hoof. "That's what I get for trying to sound like I have any idea what I'm talking about," she said laughingly. "Well, Valentina certainly looked like she's got all the Del Campo talent and then some. I mean, no offense to her old man, but from what I saw, she might just give you a run for your money on the field."

Alejandro suddenly went cold. He stopped brushing his horse and turned to look at her. "What do you mean?"

"The other night, I saw her riding—"

"Valentina hasn't ridden since her mother's death," he said quietly.

Georgia looked taken aback. "Oh, I—" she stuttered.

Alejandro clenched his fists. "How many times?" he asked.

"Only once that I've seen—"

"Which horse?" He felt sick.

She bit her lip. "Well, perhaps there was some mistake. I mean, I can't be sure—"

"Which horse?" he repeated in a cracked voice.

"Storm. I'm sorry. I didn't know it was a secret. Honestly. I mean, everyone rides here. And Valentina—she rides so well, it never occurred to me anything might be wrong."

Alejandro felt the moment grow very still. "Georgia, I'm

sorry, but you don't know what the hell you are talking about."

"Don't punish her." She stepped in front of him.

"Please excuse me," he said, forcing himself to keep his voice low. Georgia looked at him and then moved aside.

He stormed from the stall and left her to settle the horses.

Chapter Forty-nine

Waiting for his daughter outside the school, Alejandro reflected that it was about as far from the simple little *escuela* he had attended as a child as one could get. The building had a vast Palladian design; it looked more like a mansion than a school. Like so many of these developments, it had been named for the trees cut down to build it—Oakwood.

God, he had hoped that Valentina had permanently lost interest in riding. She had naturally recoiled in the immediate months after her mother's death, staying away from the barn, and that had made it easy for him to declare that she should take a break from the horses.

It had been one of their favorite things to do together, before Olivia was gone. He had loved being out on the field with his talented daughter, teaching her every trick he knew. But after Olivia died in her jumping accident, it made him physically ill to see Valentina anywhere near a horse. And she was too numb to care. She holed herself up in her room, listening to music, surfing the Web, avoiding as much human connection as she possibly could.

Afraid that she'd eventually want to ride again, and yet, not wanting her to be shut away, he had booked her solid with extracurriculars the following year. He'd steered her toward dance, and music, the endless ballet lessons and reluctant clarinet recitals. He'd hoped to wear her out on other fronts while all passion for riding expired.

And now—despite all his distractions, despite him outright forbidding her—she was riding again. He shuddered, imagining it. On Storm, no less—a horse as bold as she was.

He knew he was being hypocritical. Of course, he put himself in the same danger every day. But he was the adult. Polo was his job. There was no reason that Valentina should have to ride. She did not have to follow in his footsteps.

He closed his eyes, willing away the vision of his daughter getting thrown, of her lying in a crumpled heap on the ground. If he lost his daughter, there would be nothing left.

* * *

Valentina seemed surprised to find her father waiting for her after class, something he hadn't done in the longest time. For a moment, she smiled—and Alejandro remembered how he used to show up unannounced and take her for ice cream when she was younger.

She climbed in the car and fastened her seatbelt and then looked at him questioningly when he didn't start the car right away.

Alejandro smoothed his daughter's hair from her brow. "You've been seen riding, Valentina," he said quietly. "You endangered your life, the life of the horse—and you lied to me. Tell me what you think I should do."

She jerked back beyond the reach of his hand. "How did you find out?"

He shook his head. "Does it matter? Someone saw you.

Night riding, no less. In the covered arena with no light. And on Storm, of all horses."

"You ride at night all the time."

This stopped him for a moment. He hadn't realized she knew. "This isn't about what I do, Valentina. This is about what you've been doing. It's too dangerous. You know that."

She stared out the window, refusing to meet his eyes. "If riding is so dangerous, why do you keep going?"

"To pay the bills," Alejandro said. "Who else is going to keep you in shoes?" He regretted the facetiousness as soon as he'd spoken.

She finally looked at him. "So it's my fault you're out there risking your life every week? Polo players die on the field all the time, even the best. Is it on me if you get hurt?"

"*Hija, por favor*, of course not. I make that choice. It's on me. But we're not talking about me, we're talking about you."

"And you think if you get hurt or"—she wiped away a rogue tear, her voice shaking—"something happened to you, that it wouldn't matter to me?"

"You're purposefully changing the subject."

"I'm not, actually. I'm just trying to understand why your life is somehow worth less than mine—or maybe why your need to ride is somehow more important than mine. I love riding, *Papá*. And I'm good. You know that I am."

"You have some talent, but that's not the point."

"The point is, you don't get to decide. I'm not some pony you can control. Or employee you can fire at will. You might have missed this, *Papá*, but I'm pretty much grown-up."

"You are growing up, *niña*, there's a difference. You're still under my roof, still under my care. Anything happens to you, that's my responsibility."

"But you know that you weren't responsible for what happened to *Mamá*," she whispered.

There was a long silence while Alejandro rubbed his hand rapidly over his eyes. "I wish that were true," he finally said. "I desperately wish I could believe that. But if I had been paying more attention, if I had given your mother more of my time...maybe, it all could have been avoided."

"That's ridiculous, *Papá*. It was a freak accident!"

He looked away. She couldn't understand. And in the emotion that threatened to overwhelm him, he had to draw a line. "You're grounded, Valentina. I want you on the property and out of the barn for the next month. If I hear about you riding again, we will be talking about boarding school."

He started up the car and drove her home, unnerved by her silence. When he pulled up outside the house and unlocked the doors, he was devastated by her cold tone.

"You know, being hard on me doesn't mean you're paying attention. You talk about how you weren't paying attention to *Mamá*? I wish you gave me half the attention you gave her. You can take away everything but that doesn't change the fact that you haven't really been there for me, *Papá*. You haven't been there for years."

She slammed the door behind her. Alejandro wanted to run after her, turn back time, and scoop her up like the small child she'd been. But what would that do? He couldn't change his rules, and she would just push him away even further. Nothing was solved either way.

For a brief moment, he actually prayed—prayed to Olivia—asking out loud, "What should I do, Liv? What should I say?"

Nothing but silence answered him.

Chapter Fifty

Attending a practice match the next day, Georgia couldn't stop thinking about Valentina and the idea that Alejandro had unwittingly deprived the girl of yet another important thing in her life.

Why shouldn't Valentina get to ride? she wondered. Valentina had lost her mom, the man her dad had been, and the solace of horses. It was simply too much to take from someone.

Georgia thought about the months after her own mother had left. How much worse it had been that she'd taken all the horses with her. Not being able to ride had hurt Georgia almost as much as the abandonment itself. She honestly didn't know which she had mourned more—her mother or the horses.

She watched Alejandro as he wheeled around his teammates. "Hey, Rory!" he shouted. "I told you a thousand times! The golden rule in polo is go to the man first, then the ball!"

The men laughed as they rode, shouting out good-natured insults and instructions. "Hit it! Hit it!"

"Count your men!"

It didn't seem fair that Alejandro should get to play like this while his daughter stayed earthbound.

She turned as Pilar and Cricket came arm in arm to the field and leaned over the fence beside her.

Pilar greeted her warmly, and Cricket gave her a kiss without interrupting her monologue, which, as far as Georgia could gather, involved a new sponsorship opportunity with Veuve Clicquot.

Alejandro slowed to an easy canter as he passed the fence.

"I thought you'd call me," Cricket pouted.

Alejandro shrugged. "Things have been busy."

Pilar shaded her eyes as she looked up at her son. "Cricket's come to invite us all to a party being given in her honor next week."

"So unnecessary, but sweet of them," Cricket said. "But it's Veuve Clicquot, and I heard they're looking for a new team. So I thought we best get you boys in there."

"That's very good of you," said Alejandro. "Can I send Rory?"

"You should at least make an appearance, *querido*," Pilar said.

"Yes! Thank you!" Cricket laughed, and Georgia had the feeling that she and Pilar were pretty much in cahoots.

"Georgia, you could come, too," Cricket said, as if the idea were a blast.

"That's okay," Georgia said. "Really. I'm so worn out at the end of the day. Bed is all I ever want."

"No way. I'll get you on the list," Cricket said.

"The opportunity does sound wonderful, Jandro," Pilar said. "There certainly can't be any harm in meeting them. See what Hendy thinks."

Alejandro looked down at them and met Georgia's eyes.

"I'll go if you go," he said and then galloped back onto the field.

Georgia blinked. "Oh."

Cricket looked at Georgia, a strange little half smile on her face.

Chapter Fifty-one

Late that night, Georgia was going over some medical records for one of the ponies when a sharp knock came on her door. She looked up to see Valentina standing there, looking extremely pissed off.

Georgia opened the door, puzzled. "Valentina?"

"It was you, wasn't it?" said Valentina, entering the pool house without waiting for permission. "You're the bitch that told him."

Georgia shook her head. "I'm so sorry. I had no idea you weren't supposed to be—"

"I knew it!" said Valentina, furiously flinging herself onto Georgia's couch. "You got me into the worst kind of trouble! Why not just say something to me instead of sneaking off to my dad?"

"I wasn't sneaking," Georgia insisted. "I was raving about how much I liked watching you ride. I was saying you ought to get on the polo field with him."

"Well, maybe you should have asked me before you said anything to anyone!"

"How was I supposed to know you were banned from riding? I just thought you didn't like horses."

Valentina looked at her for a second, and tears welled up in her eyes. She sighed. "I love them."

"Of course you do . . . Do you want a cup of tea?"

"Can I have wine?"

"No."

"Okay, then tea. With five sugars and milk."

Georgia smiled as she put on the kettle. More sugar than tea. Despite all appearances, Valentina was still a child.

"So, what happened?" Georgia asked, after handing Valentina a steaming mug.

"I'm grounded," said Valentina glumly. "And he says that if he catches me riding again, he'll send me to boarding school."

Georgia blinked in surprise, "Oh, surely he wouldn't do that."

"Who knows what he'd do? He's completely unreasonable when it comes to this kind of thing."

"But if he knew how important it was to you—"

"He's not going to listen to me. He's got like, PTSD. It's because of my mom. He's freaked out that I'll die, too."

Georgia sipped her tea and nodded, not wanting to spook her by saying too much.

"And you know what the stupid thing is? I feel pissed at Mom as if it was her fault," Valentina admitted. "Like, you know, I miss her—I miss her a lot—but sometimes I just think, you bitch, if you hadn't died, I would still be riding. And *Papá* wouldn't be so crazy."

"Huh." Georgia smiled gently. "I guess it doesn't make a difference, whether it's death or desertion. Feels like abandonment either way."

"Aren't you still mad that your mom left you?" Valentina said.

"Oh," said Georgia, "how did you—"

"I was bitching to Cricket after she told me it was probably you who told Dad about my riding. She filled me in."

Georgia tried to ignore her annoyance at the idea of Cricket sharing her personal situation with Valentina and considered. "I don't think my mom could be who she needed to be at home. And we managed." She straightened her back. "I'm grateful she didn't take me with her. She knew that my dad needed me, I think. And I'm glad I was there for him."

She topped up the cup Valentina held out. "So what are you going to do with this time now that you're grounded?"

"I dunno," Valentina moaned. "I'm not even allowed in the barn, which is actually fine since it would totally suck to be around the horses and know I couldn't ride anyway. But it's shitty because, with all the staff at the house, and Wellington being so small, I just feel like there's no place I can go, you know? Even when I'm in my bedroom, the maids wander in and out and *Abuela* is in there every ten minutes wondering what I'm doing." She looked around the room. "I actually used to come here when I needed some space. You know, before you moved in."

"Oh, Valentina, you can come here anytime," Georgia said. "Whether I'm here or not. It's your place. And your pool, too. Don't run for the hills every time you see me. Really. You'd be doing me a favor."

Valentina smiled shyly at her. "Thanks," she said. She snuggled back on the couch. "I'm sorry I called you a bitch, *Doctora*."

Georgia smiled ruefully back. "That's okay, Valentina. Just don't do it again."

Chapter Fifty-two

When she learned by text that Billy and Beau were back in town for Cricket's Veuve Clicquot party, Georgia didn't stop grinning all day.

She was dressed and ready to go by the time they came by for her, and she greeted her friends with warm hugs. They were full of exclamations about how fantastic she looked.

"Peaches, I barely recognize you!" Billy cried. "Are you actually wearing blush?"

Beau cooed over how toned she was from the swimming and how her hair was streaked gold from the sun.

They insisted she take them on a tour of the barn, and it was fun to see it all through their eyes. Of course, they were used to the lux accommodations for horses. So the opulence was no surprise, but they admired the ponies and were properly impressed by all the little methods and ideas that Georgia had brought to the place. And they were especially delighted to see several of Beau's saddles proudly displayed among the richly polished tack.

And Beau and Billy were clearly going great guns with their new business. Georgia teased them that they were like an old married couple already, but she was happy to see the partnership was really kicking in.

They, in turn, were amazed by Georgia, seeing how easy and friendly she was with everyone and how comfortable she was in the barn.

"Look at the way they follow your beck and call," Billy stage-whispered after Georgia instructed a couple of grooms to take some ponies out to the paddock. "You've got it going on, Fellowes!"

* * *

They arrived at Cricket's Palm Beach party around nine. Georgia was stunned by the incredibly sleek and modern space with its gorgeous view of the water.

The vibe was cool and edgier than the Wellington club scene. A beautiful female DJ spun disks, and Veuve Clicquot ran like rain. The guests looked different. No farmer tans on display, not so very young and drunk. They weren't competitors, Billy explained, so much as investors and financiers. People, he said, who thought nothing of dropping a million dollars on a Wellington season.

There was a celebrity set, too. Georgia had to avoid whiplash a couple of times when she spotted famous actors and musicians in the mix.

Sebastian and Rory showed up to complete the gang's reunion, and when Cricket made a spectacular entrance around ten, wearing a draped white mini-dress and six-inch heels that showed her long, tan legs off to perfection, there was only one person still missing.

"Where's Alejandro?" Cricket pouted, looking around.

"It's fine if he's late," Rory assured her. "Good if he only materializes for five minutes, actually. Kind of cool. Rarity gets the sponsors begging."

Georgia retreated with Beau and Billy to the balcony, where they could lean down and take everything in. The guys shared a joint like teenagers—Georgia sticking to her wine—and they all giggled as they people-watched from afar.

They observed Cricket spending a lot of time flirting with some kind of balding financier. She'd let him nibble her ear but then do a quick sidestep to avoid a hand on her ass. She obviously wanted him close, but not too close, and had one eye permanently on the door.

Georgia could see this was an occasion where Rory came into his element. He worked the room brilliantly, showcasing Sebastian and Lord Henderson. He looked as if he was somehow making the champagne marketing people feel they'd entered a fabulous rarefied world.

Everyone was talking about the team's recent wins, and Rory confidently assured them all that La Victoria were building to a glorious season finale.

Sebastian, too, was in good form. He looked conspicuously happier, Georgia thought, when away from the barn. He was telling great stories about the early days of polo and the lineage of the team—and talking persuasively about the synergies and strategies the players were achieving.

Hendy was talking statistics with sports reporters; it was all hitting ratios and spread bets, and which ponies would be in the line, and Georgia was thrilled to discover that she understood almost all of the lingo at last.

The only one who looked actively unhappy was Gus. The man's forehead was beaded with sweat, and his eyes were staring wildly at everything other than the person he was talking to. After politely introducing him to Beau and Billy, Georgia watched him tip back a glass of whiskey and drain it.

"That's my nemesis," she whispered to Billy.

"He doesn't look very happy," Billy said.

"Well, he's the only one here who's not," said Beau in his soft Southern drawl. "Cricket really knows how to throw a bash."

Finally, Georgia felt her stomach leap as Alejandro himself entered, turning every head with his long stride and broad shoulders. He already looked bored out of his mind, but it seemed to Georgia that every woman in the room, and quite a few men, went into high alert at his appearance.

Cricket immediately moved in to tour him round the room to meet the Veuve Clicquot team.

"He looks different," said Billy. "Not as miserable."

"Grief's lifting," Beau said. "Maybe he's getting laid on the regular. Do you have something to do with that, Fellowes?"

"Beau!" Georgia said.

"Oh, don't act all innocent, Peaches," said Billy. "We know what you've been up to."

Georgia saw Alejandro glance their way before heading over in their direction. He warmly greeted Billy and Beau and then turned to her. *That's the first genuine smile I've seen from him tonight*, thought Georgia. He leaned in close to make himself heard over the music.

"So, you came, after all."

"Well, you said you would if I would. And it's for the good of the team, after all."

He nodded. "Listen, I'm sorry I was such a prick to you about Valentina riding."

"That's okay," she said. "You were worried. I understand."

He leaned in even closer. She could smell his warm, spicy scent. A little shiver shot down her back. "This is my idea of hell," he admitted, gesturing at the party.

Georgia laughed. "A very well-catered hell. It's not so bad. The sponsors seem interested."

"God knows. It probably won't come to anything," Alejandro said. "Listen, maybe later we can—"

He was interrupted when, out of nowhere, Cricket descended on him, insisting that there were at least a dozen more people he just had to meet. She swept him away with a passing air kiss for Georgia.

"Oh my God, Georgia," Billy teased her, "you must be a good influence! He's still ridiculously serious, but at least it's like he's enjoying being gloomy these days."

"And what about that wattage when his eyes met yours?" Beau shouted.

They waved away all of Georgia's protests about his history with Cricket.

"She might as well be his sister for all the interest he's showing in her," Beau insisted as they watched Cricket help him work the room. "He looks like he wants to throw himself out the nearest window."

"Not like when he was over here," said Billy, elbowing Georgia in the ribs, "when all he wanted was to throw himself at you. You know it, and I know it. Don't play dumb with us, G."

"Fine. Maybe some stuff happened at the very beginning. But we've been total professionals ever since, and anyway, he likes his women rich. For his team's sake, if nothing else."

"Humph. We'll see." Billy winked. She gave him an exasperated look and excused herself.

In the line for the restroom, she found Gus clearly in trouble, arguing with the cloak room attendant about his jacket. He seemed to be accusing her of stealing but he was only semi-coherent and staggering about as if he were navigating a listing ship.

For a moment, Georgia considered catching Alejandro's attention—and letting him see his head vet falling to pieces—but then she couldn't help feeling sorry for the old goat.

She rapidly summoned Beau and Billy and asked them to convince Gus to let them give him a ride home. As they solved the coat mystery (Gus had been wearing it all along without realizing), Georgia found Cricket to say thanks and good-bye.

"So soon, darling?" asked Cricket as she posed for a selfie with a young pop star.

"Something's come up," said Georgia, hoping that Gustavo wouldn't stagger back in.

Alejandro frowned to see she was leaving and raised his arm good-bye.

Outside, Beau and Billy helped her manhandle a very drunk Gus into the car despite the vet's best efforts to pick a fight with everyone they encountered.

Georgia was worried he might vomit in Beau's pristine interior so they kept the windows down and a bag handy.

Gus was just coherent enough to direct them to his address—an apartment not too far from the hacienda—and between the three of them, they got him upstairs and through the door. Georgia went to bring him water and found a bare fridge, a hell of a lot of empties, and a sink full of dirty dishes.

She hesitated a minute to look around at the sadly empty interior of his traveling bachelor pad—it was odd to see how few possessions such an accomplished vet would have—and to consider just how lonely and unhappy he really seemed to be.

She and the boys guided Gustavo into his bedroom, and she wondered out loud whether they should go so far as getting him at least partially undressed.

"Ugh," said Billy. "I'm sorry, but there is no version of this where I take off this guy's pants."

"Just the shoes then," said Georgia, and knelt to untie the laces.

"You," Gustavo slurred, watching her through eyes he could barely keep open, "you think you're so *importante*—"

"Okay then," said Georgia, tugging his shoes off and deciding she didn't want to touch the socks, "you're ready for bed now, Gus."

He jerked his foot away, almost kicking her in the face. "I can do it!" he said. "I don't need your help in any way!"

"Yes, you've made that abundantly clear many times, both here and at work," she muttered to herself.

Beau and Billy were all for returning to the party, but Georgia, with work the next morning and the match so soon, was ready to turn in. They made plans to meet up tomorrow. She thanked them for helping with Gus and kissed them good night after they dropped her off at home.

* * *

Approaching the pool house, Georgia saw the lights blazing and music on. Outside, fast asleep and fully dressed on adjacent sun beds by the pool, she found Valentina and Javier, one of the grooms, a sweet kid from Mexico.

Javier was a good-looking eighteen-year-old with skin like

polished mahogany. When Georgia could get him to stop shoveling muck for five minutes, he'd revealed that most of his family were back in Mexico. His father was a bus driver there, which, given the gang activity, was much more dangerous than it seemed, and Javier sent most of his check to his parents on a monthly basis. His diligence had caught the eye of a local riding instructor, and he'd worked his way up from a local stable. He always wore a look of happy surprise, as if he couldn't believe his luck.

Georgia shook him gently awake and, seeing his panic on being discovered out with the boss's daughter, grilled him gently on what Valentina had had to drink. He admitted they had each had a bottle of wine to themselves.

She sent him back to his digs—a trailer on the far side of the property he shared with four others—and promised she'd take care of Valentina.

As soon as Valentina sat up, it was clear she was going to vomit. Georgia held her hair while the girl was sick and thanked her stars that it was Valentina she was helping this way, and not Gus.

She led Valentina to her own bed, not wanting to wake up Pilar in the big house, and tucked her in for the moment.

Valentina was fixated on her worry for Javier's job and insistent Georgia understand the evening's sneaky drinking had been all her idea.

Georgia reassured her over and over she'd make that clear and finally settled her down. And then she picked up her phone and called Alejandro.

"I'm so sorry to drag you away from the party," she said, "but there's a little situation with Valentina."

Instantly, she could hear the alarm in Alejandro's voice. "Is she all right?"

"Yes, yes, I should have led with that. She's fine. She's just...well, drunk as a skunk, actually. And pretty much passed out in my bed. She got into the pool house wine, I'm afraid. And now she seems to be paying the price."

"Ah, no," groaned Alejandro, the worry instantly switching over to annoyance. "*Lo siento.* I'm so sorry, Georgia. You shouldn't have to deal with that."

"It's fine. I think the worst is over. And of course, she's welcome to stay the night. I can sleep on the couch. But I just thought you should know what's going on."

"Absolutely. Thank you. And of course she will not stay over. I will be there."

After checking Valentina one more time and establishing that the girl was sleeping deeply and breathing evenly, Georgia collapsed, fully dressed, on the sofa.

* * *

Georgia woke as Alejandro's headlights swept up outside.

She approached the door in sleepy confusion and stood back to let him in as if in a dream.

"I'm sorry to disturb you so late," he said.

"*Mi casa es tú casa,*" Georgia said. "Literally actually—" She immediately wanted to kick herself for speaking so foolishly, but instead, she opened the door to the bedroom. "She's in here."

Valentina was groaning but asleep. Alejandro went to lift her, but then hesitated a moment. "You know, my wife, she once told me never to wake a sleeping baby. Let's leave it a minute, if you don't mind," he said. "See if she wakes on her own?"

"Good idea," Georgia said, and went to make some tea.

After a few minutes, Alejandro came in and pulled up a stool at the counter. "I don't know how angry to be, honestly," he said to Georgia. "I'm just relieved she's okay."

Georgia shrugged. "Well, she's sixteen. Time for this kind of thing to start happening, right? Not that she shouldn't have consequences—I wouldn't worry too much just yet."

"Who was she with?"

Georgia hesitated, not wanting to betray Valentina's trust. She figured honesty, though, was her only option.

"Javier."

Alejandro's face fell. "The groom? This doesn't seem like him at all."

"From what I gathered, most of this was Valentina's idea. I believe he just kind of followed her like a love-struck sheep."

Alejandro smiled ruefully.

"I know this doesn't look good for either of them," said Georgia, "but I will say that it could have been much worse. At least she was out with someone who I don't think would ever dream of taking advantage of her in her inebriated state."

Alejandro made a small huff with his breath, as if the possibility had knocked the wind right out of him.

"Sometimes I feel like there is nothing—nothing at all I can do—to keep this girl safe," he said miserably. "If it's not drinking, it's the drugs around here. This place is riddled with overprivileged trustafarians. There are temptations in every restroom, E and molly at every club. It seems like every time I talk to the other parents, their kids are in rehab."

Georgia thought about the bleak scene she'd found at Gustavo's, but decided against bringing it up. "My mother used to say," she said hesitantly, "girls who ride horses don't have time to get in trouble."

He looked at her, quiet for a moment. "I can't risk losing her, Georgia."

"There are other ways of losing a daughter."

"I know," he said, "I know." He ran his hands rapidly through the thick silk of his hair. "But she's sixteen and drinking, I can't just let that go."

"There might be some more constructive punishment than grounding, though," Georgia said.

"Uh-oh." He smiled. "Another new initiative?"

She felt herself blush, but forged on. "Valentina herself got me thinking. I'd really like to refresh my own riding. I quit when I was Valentina's age, when my mother left, and down here I've been so conscious of what a waste that was...And I know we're all super busy, and Enzo may have been humoring me, but he did say it would do him a favor if I'd exercise Tango. So I was thinking..."

"Tango loves to teach," Alejandro said.

"Maybe Valentina could help him teach me? Strictly on my off-time," she hastened to say. "I won't do anything that interferes with my responsibilities or practice for the match. But if Valentina teaches me, that way she'll be paying a little penalty for tonight's behavior and helping me, but also, she'll get to be with the horses again. Perhaps it will keep her out of trouble. Do her some good?"

Alejandro looked thoughtful. "There is a quotation that my father always used to say: 'There is something about the outside of the horse that's good for the inside of a man.'"

"Winston Churchill." Georgia smiled in recognition. "He also said, 'No hour of life is wasted that is spent in the saddle.'" Alejandro's eyes lit up with delight before the shadow of anxiety fell again.

"It'll be safe," Georgia assured him. "And probably very

irritating for her! She'll have to go at a slow pace because I'm really rusty, but I know enough that I can keep an eye on her. She'll be holding my guide rope until I say I'm ready to do without, and you can let me know when you're ready for her to ride with me—whether she can take out Storm or another horse..."

He seemed to think about this for a moment. "I like it," he finally said. He quickly reached out and covered her hand with his. "Thank you," he said, "for giving a damn."

Georgia could hardly breathe, feeling the warmth of him on her skin.

There was a groan from next door. "*Papá? No me siento bien.*"

He laughed and released Georgia's hand. "I've got this," he said.

Georgia sat staring in wonder at the hand he'd held, telling herself sternly that this was a man who had his pick of some of the most beautiful women in the world, that he was just saying thanks.

She leaped up as he emerged from her bedroom with his daughter in his arms. He carried her like she didn't weigh any more than a tiny child. Valentina snuggled her head against her father's chest. "*Lo siento, Papi,*" she said thickly.

"*Está bien, mi corazon,*" he answered, gently depositing her into the car so he could comfortably deliver her to the door.

"You're sure there's nothing else I can do?" Georgia asked.

"No," he said, "it's late. You should rest. It's not the first time I've been up with a sick *niña*."

He turned back to her, brushed his hand over her cheek, and gently kissed her forehead. "*Muchas gracias, de verdad.*"

She only let her breath back out once he was in the car and pulling away.

Chapter Fifty-three

The day of Georgia's first lesson, Alejandro woke Valentina early, and tense with nerves about his daughter being around horses again, he walked her to the barn himself. They found Georgia brushing out Tango and getting ready to tack up.

After Georgia and Valentina led Tango down to the covered arena, Alejandro looked around rather desperately for any physical activity he could tackle. Something to keep his eyes and mind off his daughter being around a horse—he wanted hay bales to be moved, a stall to be mucked out—but as usual, his grooms and students had left the place immaculate. There was no excuse to avoid watching the lesson.

Valentina stood in the ring with the lunge rope, endearingly excited to be in a position of authority for once in her life. It reminded Alejandro of playing with Seb in the back field as kids.

He felt himself relax. His daughter looked so proud and commanding as she put Georgia and Tango through their paces; it was beautiful to see her easy authority.

And Georgia rode better than he would have guessed. She saw him watching and flashed him a quick smile.

Valentina took Tango up to a canter, and Alejandro took a few steps toward the ring, a bit alarmed the pace might be too much too soon for an amateur, but he stopped halfway there to watch a wonderfully unself-conscious Georgia. He could see the sheer joy she felt in riding. Her pretty face, laughing as she posted on a cantering Tango, was happier than he'd ever seen her.

A long braid of hair snaked from under her helmet, twitching above her bouncing breasts as she moved in time with the horse. Her muscular thighs, encased in tight black breeches, flexed and relaxed. God. She had the body jodhpurs were made for. When she adopted jumping position to go over a low pole it was more than he could do not to stare at her pretty upturned ass.

"You're actually not terrible!" shouted Valentina, and Georgia grinned proudly and gave a mock salute.

"No one could ride badly on Tango!" she said back. "He's doing it all for me."

"Go ahead," said Valentina unhooking the lead, "take him into a gallop. Have some fun!" Georgia shortened the reins and gave him a little kick. She clicked her tongue and gave Tango the signal to run.

Alejandro looked away. He had to admit that he still had a difficult time seeing a woman going full speed on a horse. He knew it was ridiculous—especially since he rode with men doing absurdly dangerous things every week—but seeing a woman ride like this, it just made him think of his wife galloping at top speed before they hit that jump. The scream of the pony as he was caught in the hedge, the horrible, deadly silence in the long, stretched-out moment when his wife's body hurtled through the air and then hit the ground with a deafening thud, her neck already twisted at an angle from which he knew she'd never recover.

Georgia's breathless laugh burst into the air, startling him out of his dark thoughts. Her laughter was so infectious. He lifted his eyes back to her—madly racing around the ring, Tango gleefully flying beneath her—and all memories of his wife's broken body evaporated. He just saw two creatures delighting in the way they seemed to break free of the bonds of gravity. He knew exactly what they were feeling—having felt it himself so many times before—the heady moment when you couldn't tell where you ended and the horse began, when you felt that you might just launch into the sky and never come back down. Georgia whooped with glee, taking one more lap around, before slowing Tango to a trot, then a walk, and finally dismounting. It was seven, time for work to begin.

Alejandro felt the air come back into his lungs with a flood, suddenly realizing that he had been holding his breath from the moment she had started to gallop.

Pulling off her helmet, Georgia looked up, startled to find him staring. She smiled hesitantly, embarrassed now by her abandon on Tango and trying with one hand to flatten the mad static in her hair.

She seemed to search his face—for an okay of some sort— a shy eagerness that maybe he had shared that transcendent moment with her in some way. He couldn't help himself; he loved that look.

He returned her smile and then walked out and took Tango's reins from her.

"That felt amazing!" Georgia laughed. "Valentina, thank you. You're a natural teacher. I never dreamed it would all come back so fast."

"We've a long way to go," Valentina said.

Alejandro laughed, "Quite the taskmaster."

"Better believe it," Valentina said. "My plan is to get her on the polo field. Same time tomorrow, Georgia?"

* * *

The only indication Gustavo had given that he remembered Georgia's help after Cricket's party was that he was even more facetiously polite and sour with her than ever.

It was hard for her to bite her tongue in the face of his dislike, hard to tolerate his snide asides and continued insistence on her doing the most demeaning portion of the work, but just when she'd think she'd had enough, she would get a little flash of his sad apartment, of the way the sheets on his bed had looked as if they hadn't been changed for months, of the dirty dishes and empty bottles of beer crowding his kitchen counter—and it would be enough to turn the other cheek, take a deep breath, and walk away yet again.

Cricket came by with Pilar in the late afternoon, trailing a cloud of scent and looking ravishing in a sky blue silk tank and skintight pants. She'd taken Pilar to a ladies' lunch at the club to celebrate the inking of the Veuve Clicquot deal and wanted to see Alejandro's newly sponsored team in action.

"Now we're talking!" she crowed as Alejandro fed Sebastian a winning goal while they practiced. "That's the way to do it, boys!"

Enzo and Noni looked at each other and then met Georgia's eyes.

"She's acting like she owns the place," Noni muttered.

"I hear she soon will," Gus remarked, taking obvious satisfaction in his superior sources and the darts of hurt and worry he left in his wake.

Cricket made a big performance of talking to Pilar about wardrobe choices for the next leg on La Victoria's journey and their plans for London in the spring.

"When does your employment terminate, Georgia?" she asked.

"End of next week," Georgia said, ruefully smiling at the endlessly heavy-handed ways Cricket enjoyed making the distinction between herself and a hired hand.

"Oh. No London?"

"No, no," Georgia said. "Home for me."

"Pity," Cricket said with a shameless lack of sincerity.

After five minutes of crazy, high-maintenance fuss requiring every available barn hand to help establish the whereabouts of her phone and her dog and her keys, Cricket finally drove off with a "*Ciaooo!*"

Georgia stood with Pilar a minute as they watched Alejandro and Sebastian turning their ponies in tight circles in the ring.

"Cricket seems very excited," Georgia said.

"She has a right to be," said Pilar. "She pretty much single-handedly got them the sponsorship."

"It was really nice of her," said Georgia.

Pilar turned to go and hesitated. "It was a good suggestion of yours," she said. "Getting Valentina back in the saddle. *Muchas gracias.* I think you must know this, but horses are such a help with loss."

"My pleasure," Georgia said. "She's really helped me, too."

"So what are you going to do with all you've learned here? Where to? After the season."

"Home," Georgia said. "It's time I got back."

"Why? Worried you'll be a runaway like your mother?"

"Oh," said Georgia, startled at the older woman's frankness. "Uh, well, not exactly." It was always a shock to find she was on the family's radar at all, and Pilar was particularly unsettling, sizing her up with a sideways glance and taking in so much more than Georgia ever realized.

"As I understand it, your mother made a commitment to you and your father that she broke. It's not your responsibility to stay there in her place. I'm sure your father wouldn't want that."

"I don't know," said Georgia, smiling. "Sometimes it sure seems like he does."

"It's none of my business," Pilar said, "but I knew your *mamá*, Georgia. And you're nothing like her."

"You did?" Georgia asked, startled but fascinated, and feeling a churn of anxiety at what felt like her mother's sudden proximity.

"*Que mujer linda*—so lovely—but totally self-involved. And restless, as you are well aware. A gypsy thing maybe. But she was all *viento*—air—no earth to her at all. Not like you. You keep your feet on the ground. You're solid. She was like a dry leaf, skittering here and there. She did know her horses, though. You two have that in common. Are you in touch?"

"No," Georgia admitted shamefully.

"No?" Pilar said. "Well. If you were to find you wanted to be, I could help. She was in Ireland last I heard. Remarried that trainer. Let's see if this time it sticks."

"Ireland?" Georgia asked, feeling rudderless, sad, and strange. "The last I'd heard, she was single in St. Moritz."

Pilar touched her arm.

"Forgive me for saying this, but your mother never should have tried to tie herself down. It just made her more restless. But you, I think you can be in one place. Just make sure it's the place you want to be, *entiendes*?"

Georgia smiled, nodding. "Yes, I understand."

Chapter Fifty-four

The day of the championship finally arrived, significant not just because it was the closing season match but because Alejandro and Sebastian would be playing in honor of their father.

Georgia had never dreamed she'd have become so invested in the team's success. She found herself feeling ridiculously superstitious, rooting out her lucky underwear before starting the day.

Checking and rechecking the ponies for play and preparing the emergency medical bag, Georgia couldn't help comparing the experience with the first polo match she'd attended.

It was much more interesting now that she knew something about the game, but also so much more nerve-racking, knowing how many things could go wrong in any moment, especially since she had come to know and care so immensely for the players and ponies themselves. As the final match of the season, today would also mean she'd pretty much reached the end of her work in Wellington, and with that realization went a whole world of feeling she couldn't even begin to admit.

Alejandro, Sebastian, Hendy, and Rory stood for a last photograph in their pristine boots, white jeans, and form-fitting team shirts. Sebastian and Rory gave interviews and flashed dazzling smiles while Hendy and Alejandro made the pony line list.

The barn was like an engine, every piece tuned and thrumming with activity. While loading the ponies, in a last-bid effort to appease the implacable Gustavo, Georgia told him she'd be needing him to take the lead since this game was so important and the match was at a new field, one that Georgia had never been to before.

"I'll go on ahead so I'm there as the ponies are unloaded," he agreed. "You stay here to see the last trailer and groom on their way and then I'll send back my car for you."

Georgia did as she was told. Standing in the barn as the last vehicle rode out, she felt oddly abandoned. Every groom who could be spared was watching from the public pavilion.

Waiting impatiently for Gustavo's car to return, Georgia straightened her clothes and retied her hair. Then she checked on Sugar, who seemed still a comfortable distance from delivery, and affectionately scratched Tango's neck. "Bet you wish you could be out there today, huh, Old Timer?"

It was ten to one before she realized Gus wasn't sending the car, that he had deliberately sabotaged her chances of making it to the match in time. She was less angry with him than herself, for being such a stupid, trusting fool and as a result failing her last test.

She had been so content to be part of the team she hadn't even found out the destination. She had no directions, let alone passes for entrance.

For a fleeting second, it occurred to her to give up, to stay right there with Sugar and Tango and let Gus take all the credit. But she'd worked all season for the high point of this match, and she wasn't going to miss it.

She searched her phone for the event, noted the address, and grabbed her little scooter. All the way down the drive, she was still waiting for Google maps to kick in and it wouldn't.

She had the Vespa on the highway, totally illegally, feed trucks blaring past, while her stupid phone kept freezing and pinwheeling and refusing to behave.

She pulled into the hard shoulder while vehicles kept rushing by. There was no one she could call at the field apart from Gus, who refused to pick up.

Finally in a panic, she tried her father, willing him to answer. It took forever to get him to understand what she needed and to spell out the name of the event. And it felt like an eternity in which he waited for his laptop to power on and the dial-up modem to kick in. He kept asking her maddening questions about how she could have managed to get herself lost today of all days. She told him she'd been deliberately undermined by her superior but realized she sounded like some demented, paranoid character and at that point just tried not to weep.

Buzzing at last in the right direction off the highway, she thought of her giddy happiness after her riding lesson, all the pride she'd taken recently in her work in the barn and wondered if this was all some big cosmic plot to instill humility. She pulled into the parking lot and ran for the match.

Gustavo, with a smug half grin on his face, greeted her loudly. "Ah, *Señorita* Fellowes, I was starting to worry about you. The game is all but over."

Georgia gritted her teeth and tried to keep her voice calm. "I thought we agreed that you'd send the car back?"

Gus shook his head and shrugged. "No, no—you said you'd take your little Vespa, I'm sure of it."

He smirked at her, insufferable with the success of his scheme.

Georgia fought down the urge to smack the man. "Fine," she said at last. "When are the next ponies going in? I'll give them the last-minute check."

"Already done," said Gus. "Really, there's nothing left for you to do but cheer the team on."

Georgia seethed as he walked away, laughing. She had tried and tried with this man but there was no getting around it; he was determined to undermine her—and humiliate her—any chance he got.

But he was right. Barring an emergency, there was little left for her to do. The team was already changing out their ponies for the last time, and when Georgia tried to enter the pen to check the spent horses, Gustavo made an ostentatious show of waving her off and making it clear that he had it under control.

Beyond frustrated, Georgia felt ridiculous tears spring to her eyes. She had just dashed them away when Cricket clapped a hand on her shoulder. "Where have you been, chick? Everyone was wondering."

Georgia shook her head. "Got lost," she muttered.

"Oh well, looks like Gus held down the fort for you anyway. Can you believe they're actually going to win this thing? It's in the bag!"

For the first time, Georgia looked out onto the field. The ponies were thundering down the turf. Alejandro looked and clearly felt magnificent—all his certainty and command were back. Galloping toward the goal, ducking and diving the defense, he was blocked on every side until suddenly in a break of brilliance he was whizzing around everyone on the pitch and powering all the way to get his goal. The crowd rose as one, and La Victoria, to the man, all had huge, glorious grins on their faces.

Cricket laughed. "I haven't seen Jandro this happy for years."

She was right, thought Georgia, as she applauded, watching Alejandro and Temper joyfully gallop across the field. Alejandro looked like he had dropped twenty years and a ton of sorrow.

The last horn blew, and the Del Campo brothers whooped and threw their arms up in victory.

"I better get over there," said Georgia as the players rode off field, their helmets raised up in the air.

Cricket followed her.

Alejandro rode over to shake the hand of the other team captain and then cantered toward the pony lines and swung off Temper, handing off the reins to a stable boy. Georgia, entering through the gate, smiled and raised a fist in victory for him. His eyes met hers, and then in one swift moment, she was off her feet and in his arms, folded into a hug as warm and joyous as anything she'd ever felt.

"We did it!" he crowed, swinging her around.

Georgia laughed out loud as her feet found the ground again, but his arms didn't let go. He looked down at her, still grinning, and their eyes locked. Suddenly his smile softened, and Georgia felt her breath catch in her throat.

"*Papá!*" Valentina yelped and crashed into him, wildly hugging him from behind. "*Ganamos!* We won!"

Alejandro turned around, laughing, and embraced his daughter. "*Sí, mi princesa! Ganamos!*"

Hendy was there to shake Georgia's hand. "I'm so sorry—" she began.

He shook his head. "Tsk. I heard you got lost. Think nothing of it. We missed you today, but you've been a wonderful asset to the team, my dear."

Georgia took a step back, trying to smile, until Valentina, too, came to hug her in delight.

Next to her, Cricket raised an eyebrow. "Poor Georgia," she drawled, "you'll miss all this."

Chapter Fifty-five

But you have to come, Georgia!" pleaded Valentina. "Everyone will be there!"

"V, you don't understand this because you are still young and nubile," said Georgia as she and Valentina sat dipping their toes in the pool, "but for most people, the prospect of spending the evening in the company of others wearing nothing but a swimsuit is not a very appealing one."

Valentina rolled her eyes. "I've seen you in your swimsuit. You look fine. Not too shabby for such an old lady."

Georgia snorted and splashed Valentina with her foot. "What a nasty child you are," she said, laughing.

"Anyway, put on a sarong and suck it up. This is a huge win for La Victoria, and we've got to celebrate!"

* * *

This is ridiculous, thought Georgia, as she stepped off her scooter wearing her bikini, a sarong, and high-heeled sandals, along with the cherry red helmet that had been given to her when she took possession of the bike. I might as well be naked with a bucket on my head.

But once she ducked through the club and found the terrace, open to the beach, she realized that she was overdressed, if anything. Women strutted by wearing nothing but mere patches of fabric, the tiniest triangles hovering over their toned and perfect asses and silicone-enhanced breasts. The men were scarcely less shameless, wearing nothing but shorts and showing off their muscled and tanned bare chests.

"Oh darling," said Cricket as she slipped in next to her, "don't you look cute? I thought that suit was just for bashing around the house, but you're totally pulling it off."

Cricket was wearing a gold lamé one-piece that plunged down past her belly button in the front and danced just above the crack of her ass in the back. And yet, thought Georgia, with her fashionably small chest and narrow hips, she still looked more classy than trashy. There really was no look this woman didn't rock.

Cricket toyed with a long, gold chain around her neck. "I'm glad you decided to come—despite the whole showing up late fiasco today. I'm sure no one really noticed, though, right?"

Georgia frowned. She didn't want to sound like a whining child and throw the blame on Gustavo, but still . . . "It wasn't my—" she began, but Cricket had already lost interest. Seeing Alejandro's approach, she made a busy display of flirting with the nearest financier.

Suddenly Alejandro was standing in front of Georgia, bare chested, with a drink in one hand and a pair of board shorts hanging below the vee of his well-defined abs. Georgia was reminded of that first night at the pool and felt her breath leave her body.

"*Buenas noches*, ladies." He smiled. "You both look lovely." His pleasure in winning today still seemed to radiate from him. He was loose and relaxed and maybe a little drunk. He seemed to be enjoying himself in a way that Georgia had never seen before.

In the background, a salsa band started playing. Alejandro's smile got even wider. *Definitely a little drunk*, she thought.

"Come on," he said, putting down his drink and grabbing Georgia's hand. "Let's dance."

Before she had time to protest, they were out on the deck, Georgia stumbling as her heel caught in a slat.

"Stay still," said Alejandro.

"What?"

He knelt down at her feet and unhooked her shoe, his hand brushing over her ankle and then lingering on her instep for a moment. Georgia felt her entire body enflame.

"Now the other."

She obediently lifted her other foot for him. He removed that shoe as well, grinning up at her devilishly.

"You can't dance in the sand in shoes," he said, leading her away from the dance floor and into the shadows of the beach.

Good God, thought Georgia, *who* is *this man?* Where was the carefully guarded and disciplined boss she thought she knew?

Alejandro tossed her heels over his shoulder and took her in his arms. "I can't remember the last time I danced," he murmured.

"Me neither," admitted Georgia, thinking to herself, actually, she couldn't ever remember dancing quite like this.

Alejandro pulled her closer. He smelled like the sea and good whiskey, with just the faintest trace of sweet hay. Georgia closed her eyes and let him lead her.

* * *

Once upon a time, thought Alejandro, he had been as comfortable dancing as he was on a horse. Why had he ever stopped?

Because there had been no one he'd wanted to dance with... Not until now.

He looked down at the top of Georgia's head, fighting the urge to lay a kiss on her sun-gilded curls. He felt the bare, warm skin at the small of her back, tightened his grip on her hand, took a step, and pressed himself against her, closing what little space remained between their bodies. He heard her gasp as their flesh met, felt himself throb in response, felt the firm softness of her breasts pressing against his chest, the silken feel of her skin, the unbelievable heat generated between them.

"I'm—I'm sorry about being late today," Georgia suddenly choked out.

He frowned and shook his head, not wanting to think about work in this moment, wanting to lay all that aside for once. The season was over. He'd had a few drinks already—everyone was always eager to buy a drink for the winners—and he figured it was okay, just tonight, to stop worrying about what everyone thought, to push away his responsibilities. To do what felt good, not necessarily what was right.

"Don't worry about it," he said. "It could happen to anyone. Gustavo took care of things."

He felt her stiffen in his arms, take a step back from him, and peer up into his face.

"That's the thing," she said. "I wouldn't want you to think I was so irresponsible as to not—"

"Jandro," came Cricket's husky voice, "I'm sorry to cut in, darlings, but you know, there's that thing we should get to."

He blinked. "What thing?"

"Oh, that pesky little party I've been telling you about. Dimitri Angelis will be there. You know, the shipping titan Hendy's been trying to fix you up with for ages?"

Georgia let go of his hand and stepped out of his arms. Alejandro suddenly felt cold and exposed. He sighed and ran his hands through his hair. Of course. Hook a sponsor while victory was warm.

"Sorry, Georgia, we'd invite you along—but it's a delicate conversation—finance at this level—and we wouldn't want to do anything to endanger the business aspect of things." Cricket fluttered her hand. "You understand, don't you? Too many hangers-on come along and we might look like amateurs."

"Yes, of course," said Georgia. "I—I was just going home anyway. It's been a long day." She smiled at Alejandro. "Thank you for the dance."

He smiled back. "My pleasure, *querida*."

"Don't forget your shoes, darling," said Cricket as she slid her arm through Alejandro's. "I'll drive, Jandro. You are obviously not quite yourself."

Georgia watched them walk back up the steps to the terrace, arm in arm, to be greeted by an impatient Hendy. They looked so right together. Cricket's silky blond head leaning against his shoulder, their skin nearly the same lovely dark gold color. You could hardly look at them without thinking, *Meant-to-be*.

Georgia sat down on a log, reaching for her discarded shoes. Cricket was right, of course. Alejandro had clearly had a few too many. She could have been anyone on that dance floor. He probably wouldn't even remember it in the morning. And all the better if he didn't. She flushed, remembering the scent of him, the way he had pressed up against her, his skin on hers...

He might not remember. But it would take more than a few drinks to make her forget.

Chapter Fifty-six

Georgia rode home barefoot. It was tempting to leave her shoes behind for good. What the hell had she been thinking? Dressing for some Miss World Pageant? But since she still had a few days left in this place and might need to dress up again, she supposed she shouldn't do anything rash.

She tried to focus on the fun of it, the warm night air whipping her sarong, the smell of the ocean and the towering palms, the beauty of pretty much every passing car. She'd had a dance with a polo legend on the sand at Palm Beach. *That was nothing to sneeze at, Fellowes.*

If she thought about it, it was perfect, really, to have had the fun of a flirtation with a man like Alejandro. Just what Billy had told her to look for in the beginning, a little romance to take the edge off winter.

Pilar was waiting in the front of the house when she pulled up, clutching her silk robe to her chest and looking mildly put out.

"Dr. Fellowes, a friend of yours has arrived."

Georgia shook her head. "I don't understand—"

"A young man, he seemed to know you quite well, but

he said you were not expecting him. He brought a suitcase with him."

Georgia thought quickly. A man? It must be Billy, of course. But why would he stay here? Unless something happened with Beau...Of course. That would be it. A breakup and he wanted to lick his wounds with Georgia. *Oh, what a shame.*

"I'm sorry he arrived so late, Pilar. Is he in the house?"

"I sent him back to the *casita*. He waits for you there."

"Okay, thank you. Sorry again for the inconvenience."

"Dr. Fellowes—Georgia—this man, he didn't seem a menace, but if you do not care to have him here, just scream very loudly and I will release *mis perritos*. My doggies can be quite effective if I tell them to be."

Georgia laughed. "I'm sure it will be fine."

Georgia hurried around the back of the house, eager to see Billy. Really, he couldn't have come at a better time. After the day she'd had, it would be a sweet relief to talk it through with her best friend.

He was standing in the shadows by the pool—his back turned toward her.

"Billy!" she called. "What in the world are you—"

He turned around and smiled that sweet, easy smile. Not Billy. Not even close.

It was Sam.

Chapter Fifty-seven

Alejandro thought he should go home first to change. He couldn't very well wear a swimsuit to a cocktail party, no matter how small and informal Cricket assured him it would be.

"Of course, darling, I've got to change, too. We'll stop at my place first. I'm sure I have something that you can wear."

Alejandro smiled, amused. Yes, he imagined Cricket had a whole closet of assorted men's discarded clothes to choose from.

He closed his eyes and leaned back in the car seat, still a little high from the drinking. Cricket was right—he was not feeling exactly like himself. But that was not necessarily a bad thing. He replayed the dance with Georgia in his head and smiled. He knew he'd broken all his own rules—fraternizing with his employee, holding her close like that—but he really couldn't muster up the energy to give a damn at the moment. Winning the game had freed him somehow. It felt like the end of a long curse.

All his constraints and rules suddenly seemed priggish and arbitrary, designed by someone who pushed away the pleasures of life with both hands. When he'd seen her at the match, eyes shining, obviously so proud and pleased by his victory, she looked like a living beacon, a sign that the worst days were over. And then, when he'd seen her again on the terrace at the party, easily the most beautiful woman in the room, that was that. He was tired of holding back. He was sick of being numb. This woman woke him up, gave him joy. What was the point of fighting that kind of feeling?

Cricket parked the car, and they took the elevator up to her loft. "I'll just be a moment," she said, climbing the stairs up to her bedroom. "There's a nice bottle of champagne in the fridge. Why don't you pop it open?"

He wandered into her kitchen. Cricket's place was immaculate as always. Vast and streamlined and modern. But he always felt just slightly chilled here. There were no soft surfaces, no warm corners to curl up in. Just polished concrete floors and vast, shiny leather couches. Metal and glass everywhere you looked.

He thought about the one time he'd stayed the night here. It had been years ago, just before they had finally taken Olivia off life support. Cricket had visited Olivia at the hospital every day, bravely acting as if her old friend would wake up and be her regular self at any moment. She did sweet and intimate things for his wife—painting Olivia's nails, applying lip balm, brushing her hair—things that Alejandro could scarcely bring himself to do. For him, Olivia had been gone since the accident. This body in the hospital bed was just a shell, and caring for it felt unnervingly like grooming a cold corpse. So he was grateful for Cricket's help, for her silent understanding.

And one day, their eyes met over the hospital bed, and he saw the same pain and loss reflected in Cricket's face that he knew was in his. And he had reached out to her, wanting to comfort her, wanting to thank her for her kindness, wanting to erase that deep, hollow sorrow he knew that she felt as keenly as he did.

They had come back to her loft, and he had spent the night. But while the first kisses had been tender in some ways, the sex had been athletic, competitive, and oddly dispiriting in the end. Before they'd even finished, it felt like a mistake.

He lay awake after, in the cold grip of guilt, as if Olivia were there with them.

Afterward, as Cricket slept curled up beside him, Alejandro's guilt had turned to panic. It was all he could do not to bolt out of the bed—out the door. He basically held his breath until morning, then went back to keep sad, angry watch over his wife's wasted body.

Cricket had talked to him later, assuring him that she knew that what had happened between them was nothing more than a moment of weakness on both their parts, that she understood it was a one-time-only thing. But now, as he took down the champagne flutes and popped open the bottle—pouring the golden liquid to the brim of each glass—he realized that he'd known for a while that Cricket had been waiting with patient confidence for much more. There was something seductive about her certainty, and he had to admit that, in the back of his mind, he'd been considering it. He must have let Cricket see that possibility, must have fed her hope, knowing how easy it would be, the relief his mother would feel if he made that match, and perhaps even Valentina would want a stepmother from her world.

"How about this shirt, darling?" said Cricket as she walked into the kitchen. He turned around, ready to offer

her the champagne, and took a deep breath when he saw
that she was wearing nothing but the shirt. And even that
was quickly removed and offered to him. "Don't you like
it?" Cricket said, her golden body naked—as sleek and lovely
as everything that surrounded her—a challenging gleam in
her eye.

* * *

"Want a robe?" said Sam, assiduously looking away from
Georgia's skimpy bathing suit as he fetched one from the
bathroom.

Georgia shrugged. It seemed beside the point now. "It's a
warm night, but oh fine," she submitted a little irritably as
he rested the robe on her shoulders.

Sam smiled nervously. "I guess you've gone native."

Georgia handed him a glass of wine, and he sat down beside her. "It's so nice to see you. But I must admit, I'm still a
little confused about just why you're here."

"Your father said you were so upset this afternoon," Sam
explained. "He said they were treating you terribly. That
you're in way over your head."

Georgia took a deep sip of her own wine and swallowed
her annoyance. "I wouldn't exactly say that," she said. "It was
just a difficult day, is all."

"He was worried. He asked me to come down and see if
there was anything I could do to help."

Georgia shook her head. "So you flew down on a moment's
notice?"

Sam smiled nervously and looked away from her. "Well,
I don't think it's any secret how I feel about you. Your dad
certainly knows." He shifted toward her. "Georgia, when we

were together, I think that was maybe the happiest I've ever been."

"That was high school, Sam. We were kids. We were completely different people. And if you remember, I wasn't quite all you wanted even then—"

He looked at her pleadingly. "See, I don't think that's true. I think I knew that you were the one I wanted to spend the rest of my life with from the very beginning of things, and that's what freaked me out. We were so young, and I'd never been in love before and I just—I panicked. I only let you go because I thought it would be easy to find what was between us again. I thought I'd fall in love a dozen times over. But I never did."

"Sam, I—"

"Please, just let me finish, Georgia. I need to get this all out. I'm sorry I hurt you—I can't tell you how much I've beaten myself up over that—but I never would again. Because I'm ready now, the same kid who fell in love with you back then, but man enough to commit. I've never gotten over you."

She looked at him for a moment. "Oh, Sam."

"Don't tell me you don't feel the same way."

She hesitated. "I—I don't know what I feel honestly."

He smiled at her and took her hand. "If you would just give me a chance, I'll show you. I know it could be amazing between us."

She pulled her hand back. "Sam, I—"

There was a knock on the door. They both looked up, startled, to see Valentina peering through the window at them. Georgia leaped to her feet, spilling her wine. "Oh!"

Sam stood up and went to the kitchen.

Valentina opened the door and stuck her head in. "Hey,"

she said, "sorry. I just came out to ask why I didn't see you at the party, but"—she looked at Sam, mopping up the spilled drink—"I guess I see why now."

"Oh," said Georgia, belting her robe. "No, I was at the party, and this—this is my friend, Sam. He just surprised me with a little visit. Sam, this is Valentina."

Sam smiled at Valentina. "Pretty name," he said.

Valentina frowned at him, her eyes narrow with suspicion. "Well, anyway, I just wanted to make sure you were okay, Georgia. But obviously, you're doing just fine."

Georgia inwardly groaned. Great. Now the entire Del Campo clan would hear about this. "Yes, thanks. I'm fine." She took a breath, but couldn't help herself. "Is—is your dad back yet?"

Valentina gave her a saccharine smile. "I doubt it. He's with Cricket."

Chapter Fifty-eight

It would be so easy, Alejandro thought as Cricket came to him on those sleek and magnificent legs; he knew his body would respond to hers like muscle memory. But he felt himself freeze. Cricket's eyes were already gleaming in victory but his heart was full of Georgia. Anything with Cricket would be a pale imitation of the feelings he had for her.

"I'm sorry, Cricket," he said as the triumph died in her eyes. "You're so beautiful, but I'm beginning to realize that I want—I need, something else. I should go."

He set the champagne flutes down on her glass side table with an icy chink, ignored her look of fury, and lightly kissed her good-bye.

* * *

Georgia felt cold now, the robe belted tightly around her.

"Where were we?" Sam said, rubbing her shoulders. "Should we go to the bedroom for more privacy?"

"No, Sam." Georgia stood up. "I'm sorry. This isn't going to work."

"Georgia, please. I told you I was sorry. I don't know how many times I can apologize for something I did when I was just a kid."

"No, I know. We both were, Sam. We were children really. And the truth is, I think it was over for me before you were unfaithful. We'd run our course. You cheated because you knew that. And I didn't let you back in for the same reason."

He took a step toward her. "Georgia, no, you—"

She pulled back. "It was nice of you to come down here and make me feel so looked after, but you deserve better than the feelings I have for you. Better than grateful. I'm sorry I couldn't tell you that sooner."

Sam put his head in his hands and, to Georgia's surprise, began to weep.

She knelt in front of him, her hands on his knees.

"I'm so sorry you flew down here. And I'm sorry if I've held you up. I've confused things by not getting out of your way. By keeping up ties that should have been cut. You'll see things clearly now, I'm sure of it. This is for the best. You'll finally be ready to move on, I promise."

* * *

Alejandro finally flagged a town car and took it straight back to the *hacienda*. He wanted to pick up that dance where they'd left off.

The *hacienda* was dark and quiet. His mother and daughter, obviously asleep. He stumbled through, out the backdoor, and down the path to the pool, eager to get to the pool house.

Her light was on. Was it too much to imagine that she was waiting for him? He stopped for a moment, smoothed his hair, took a deep breath, and walked toward the cottage.

He saw movement through the window—Georgia, her hair plummeting down her back—kneeling in her robe between the legs of a man he'd never seen before.

He stopped dead, suddenly cold and dizzy. Of course, he thought, Cricket hadn't been lying after all. She had told him Georgia had a man in New York. And tonight, when they were dancing, she had halted things—had wanted to tell him something—just before Cricket had cut in.

He closed his eyes, unable to take the sight of her with the man a moment longer. He felt as if all the joy of the day—all his triumph and optimism and forward momentum—had drained from his body.

He turned and left, not once looking back.

* * *

The next morning, Georgia came out of her bedroom to find Sam folding up the blankets from the bed she'd made for him on the couch. They exchanged strained pleasantries over a quick breakfast before she walked him out to his car and gave him a fond but subdued good-bye.

"It was really lovely of you to come," she told him. "I'll see you back up there very soon."

She waved him off with a feeling of sad relief, glad he'd be free of guilt and she of the confusion she'd felt about him so long.

* * *

All morning, Georgia kept herself busy in the barn, checking and then rechecking the ponies. Determined to make sure that not a crack in a hoof or a tiny bite to the skin went overlooked. She would leave here knowing that each of these horses was in perfect shape. And if that kept her from seeing Alejandro before she left, so be it.

She was in Sugar's stall, combing out her mane, when Gustavo blustered in, closing the gate behind him.

"So, *señorita*," he said, "how did it feel yesterday? Stings a bit, eh, to realize you're expendable after all? That you weren't even missed?"

Georgia shook her head, determined not to let him get to her. There was no point at this juncture. She was leaving, and he would remain—coming back year after year. These were his horses, after all, his team. Maybe he'd been right to be so protective.

"It wasn't great, frankly. But I'm sure I'll get over it," she said, keeping her eye on Sugar, who was rolling her eyes nervously. The mare had never taken to Gus. She was too smart not to know that he thought she was better off as glue.

"You know," Gus said, with sickening intimacy, "I knew from the minute I saw you that you were trouble. Making me look bad, and bewitching Jandro and Hendy into thinking you knew what you were doing."

Georgia stayed silent and kept brushing, breathing through her mouth to avoid the cloying stink of alcohol on Gustavo's breath. Determined not to provoke him, she'd let him finish and then just leave.

Gustavo was staring at her, swaying slightly, his eyes glazed. A little cluster of spit had settled at the corner of his mouth. "I didn't think you'd last this long. I mean, I thought I'd either have you out of here within that first week or"—he ran the backs of his fingers over her shoulder—"tamed..."

Georgia jerked away. "That's enough, Gustavo. Go get coffee. You need it. I'll be out of your way in a minute."

Sugar neighed nervously, swinging her head. Georgia turned to comfort her as she hung up the last of the tack. "It's okay, baby. Don't be scared."

"It'll be me telling you when you're free to leave, Dr. Fellowes," he hissed, cornering her in the stall.

Sugar pawed the ground anxiously as Georgia turned and faced him, furious now.

"Back off, Gustavo. I've tried to be patient with you, I've tried to be friendly, I tried to honor your experience and look forward to all you had to teach me. But you are the fraud here. You are the one who cares more about his next drink than any one of these ponies. I've watched you endanger them on the field, I've watched you neglect them in the barn. And there is nothing I am looking forward to more about leaving here, than never having to see your face ever again. Let me pass."

He stood back for a second, just enough to open a gap. And as she brushed by, with surprising swiftness, Gustavo grabbed her arm and twisted it behind her back, pressing himself against her. "You fucking little bitch!"

"Get away from me!" she snarled.

The gate to the stall swung open, Alejandro stepped in, and this time Hendy wasn't there to hold him back.

* * *

That was rash, thought Alejandro as he iced his jaw. The bruise was already starting to bloom.

He'd hit Gustavo only once before Sugar had reared and started to buck, and then they'd all been in danger and had to duck rapidly out of the stall.

Gustavo had charged him as he bolted the stall door, getting in a couple good jabs to his face before the grooms had separated them.

Still being held back by two men, Alejandro had fired Gustavo on the spot, relishing the moment even more for all the times he'd had to resist before. Gustavo had been a shit to him forever, and after hearing how the man had spoken to Georgia, telling him to clear out and never come back had been a sheer pleasure.

He'd turned instinctively to Georgia, hoping, he supposed, for some kind of approval, but instead she looked appalled. She finally asked, in an agonizingly polite way, if he minded if she slipped out a little early that night.

He'd nodded, of course, and as he watched her leave, the last of the adrenaline drained out of him and he suddenly felt empty and foolish.

The only consolation, he thought, as he tested the movement of his jaw, was having a place to put the pain.

He downed a couple of aspirin and went out to the paddock to catch a pony that hadn't been ridden hard the day before. Alejandro saddled up and rode out of the estate, determined to ride until he was comfortably numb once again.

* * *

Georgia went back to the pool house, slid off her clothes, and crawled into bed.

She was shivering badly, cold despite the reliable Florida warmth. Shaken up by Gustavo, still tender about Sam, and whether she wanted to admit it or not, absolutely heartbroken over Alejandro.

She'd been mortified by the scene she'd provoked at the

barn, couldn't forgive herself for going and blowing up the bomb she'd been working all season to diffuse.

She felt she'd lost everything. She pulled the sheets over her head and let the hot tears spill, crying until she thought she couldn't cry anymore.

Chapter Fifty-nine

Around three in the morning, Georgia was awoken by an insistent tapping sound. She pulled herself out of bed and found Alejandro at the door. For a split second, she thought it was the fulfillment of her every fantasy, but she soon saw from his look of worry and apology that it was definitely not.

"Sugar, she's in labor—"

"Give me one minute," Georgia said, and shut the door on him. She pulled her scrubs on first back to front, then rightways, tied back her hair, swished toothpaste over her teeth, and ran to join him.

They walked to the barn in silence. It was oddly intimate, having the starry night to themselves, but the silence was excruciating. Georgia's inner wheels were spinning as she tried to find an entry to conversation that might cover the lost hopes and drama of the last two days.

She picked a head of jasmine and spun it between her fingers, trying to come up with something to say. "Does Sugar seem to be having any trouble?" she finally asked.

He shook his head. "Not that I can see."

The barn was peaceful with the snuffles of sleeping animals and the steady clop of Sugar walking in circles.

Hearing their arrival, Temper stuck his head out of his stall and gave a loud huff of breath to show he was very much awake and aware things were astir with his girlfriend. Alejandro gave him a scratch to settle him down.

They both stood back a little from the foaling stall, careful not to invade the mare's privacy and risk slowing down the labor. Alejandro gestured that Georgia should take the first look.

She watched the mare turn a circle, squat down and stand again, all the while refusing, for the first time since she'd arrived, to acknowledge Georgia's presence in any way.

"Looks good." She smiled, pulling back.

"We can wait it out in the tack room. Be close in case we're needed."

Georgia looked at him in surprise. "You don't have to stay. I can always call if anything goes wrong."

"I'll stay, if you don't mind," said Alejandro, as constrained as she'd ever heard him.

The tack room was comfortably warm, but there was only one place to sit—a rather small leather couch. They eyed it warily. Alejandro gestured toward it. "Please," he said. "I'd prefer to stand."

Georgia sat down. For the first time, she saw his face in the bright light. She gasped. "Oh, I didn't realize. Are you all right?"

Alejandro dismissively touched the bruise on his cheek. "Yes, I'm afraid the old man got the better of me."

"Hardly," she said.

They smiled at each other for a moment and then looked away in unison.

"Anyway, thank you," Georgia said softly as she turned to pour some coffee. "I didn't say that before, I don't think.

Thank you for stepping in. I don't know that he was going to do anything so very terrible, but he was drunk and things were getting ugly."

Alejandro shook his head as she handed him a cup. "*De nada.*"

There was a long pause as they both took a scalding sip.

"What will happen to him, do you think?" Georgia frowned. "His career won't be over?"

Alejandro shrugged. "No, don't worry. He'll do fine back in Argentina. He can build a franchise on the back of his experience here. Despite what you've seen, he's not a bad vet. And his family back home keeps the drinking in check."

"That's good," she said.

"He was miserable in Wellington. Even when my father was alive, there was trouble. Sometimes I think Gustavo knew things, held things over my father's head."

"But what could he possibly have—" Georgia stopped herself, thinking of Noni.

Alejandro nodded. "*Sí*, Antonia. I'm sure you have heard her story by now. And of course, I didn't know I had a sister. That was a surprise. A good surprise as it turned out. Noni is my rock. But there were so many other women, too. Who knows what else my father was hiding?" He shrugged. "In any case, it's better that Gustavo find his own way now. He'll land on his feet. He always does."

Georgia thought of her own father, steadfast to a fault.

"Was that very hard," asked Georgia, "all that with your dad?"

Alejandro paused for a moment. "It just was what it was, *entiendes*? He had many wonderful qualities. He taught me to play, and of course I loved him. He was *mi papá*. But he was not an easy man, and I hated what he did to my mother, to our family. And I swore that it would never happen in my own marriage."

He was quiet for a moment and then raked his hand through his hair and took a step toward the door. "You know what? I'm going to check on Sugar."

And the door shut behind him before she could answer.

* * *

Alejandro knew he'd been abrupt. But the conversation was getting too intimate, and Georgia looked so beautiful, sitting there, her face was so trusting and understanding, her smile so warm...

She has a man, he sharply reminded himself.

He peeked into Sugar's stall. She was repeatedly lying down and then standing up again. A good sign that things were progressing. Temper was still wide awake but seemed a bit less agitated, as if he, too, sensed that things were going the way they should.

Not wanting to disturb the mare, but unwilling to go back to the tack room just yet, Alejandro walked out into the courtyard. It was a dark night, no moon at all, and wonderfully balmy, but Alejandro shivered anyway, wanting and yet not wanting to go back into the barn.

"How is she?" came Georgia's voice, and she stepped out of the barn and joined him outside. "Everything all right?"

"She's starting the next stage. Up and down, up and down," he said.

She nodded. "Good. It shouldn't be too long then."

They stood silently for a few moments. Listening to the night birds and the buzz of insects. Alejandro was achingly aware of her beside him. He thought he could catch a breath of the botanical scent he had inhaled so deeply when they were dancing together—like lemons and almond and sweet grass. He blinked, realizing that, in a way, she smelled like home to him.

"I was never exactly unfaithful to Olivia," he said. "But there was something—with Cricket, actually—it was too soon, but after Olivia was already gone in most ways...once we knew she wouldn't be coming back. And I regret that."

Georgia reached out and touched his arm. "I'm sure no one could fault you for that. I'm sure Olivia would have understood."

He shrugged, excruciatingly aware of her fingers on his wrist. "In any case, we were very young when we got married. She was still a teenager, in fact. And we had both been groomed for it, you could say. Her father and my father were good friends. They introduced us and made it very plain what they wanted. And honestly, I couldn't see why not. She was lovely and sweet, and very accomplished, and maybe, you know, a bit rigid—but that was not a reason to say no. And I think, I think she cared for me. So, we did what our families wanted."

Georgia drew her hand away from him. "You loved each other?"

Alejandro nodded. "*Sí*, of course I loved her. I mean, she was the mother of my child, and she was a brilliant homemaker and partner to me, but..."

He shifted uneasily.

"I didn't love her enough. She wasn't happy when she died. She'd been spending more and more time at the ring. There was a flirtation with her trainer. Emotional infidelity. I think immersing herself in the sport was a way to break with me. I don't honestly know that we'd have made it if she lived." He closed his eyes and sighed with the relief of admitting it.

"That has to complicate your grief," Georgia said softly. "I'm so sorry."

He turned and looked at her. "I didn't think I was capable of loving anyone, you know? I mean, not the kind of love she wanted—that all-consuming passion, *la gran pasión*. I just thought, it wasn't how I was built. But now..."

A shadow crossed Georgia's face, and she looked away. "I think," she said hurriedly, "I think we should check on Sugar."

He flinched. And then nodded. "*Sí*, of course."

As they walked back into the barn, he inwardly castigated himself. There, she had done it again—just like when they had danced—she had shut things down just before he'd made a fool of himself. He should be grateful for her sense of decency, for wanting to protect him from his worst impulses.

Sugar was on her side now, breathing heavily. "Ah," whispered Georgia, grabbing his arm, "look!"

The tiny hooves, pointing down toward the floor, had just started to emerge. Alejandro smiled. No matter how many times he saw this—and he had seen dozens of foalings—this never became any less amazing.

The little nose came next, followed by the whole head, and then the shoulders and half the body, slick and wet. Sugar rested for a moment, her baby half in and half out, and then her sides heaved once more and the whole foal slid out and sprawled upon the hay, a tiny miniature of its sire.

Georgia laughed softly and squeezed Alejandro's arm.

"A bay," he said. "A bay. Just like Temper, after all."

Sugar turned her head and calmly sniffed at the little thing and then suddenly struggled to her feet and proceeded to lick it from head to tail with her long, pink tongue. Within moments, the foal was on its own gangly and unsteady legs and nosing at its mother's side, locating her milk.

Sugar turned and stared at them, a disapproving glare.

Georgia chuckled. "Let's go back to the tack room," she said. "Obviously, she wants some privacy."

He nodded, suddenly aware she still stood close enough that they were shoulder to shoulder, and her hand was still on his arm.

Georgia seemed to realize this, too, because she dropped her hand and stepped away.

* * *

They sat together on the couch this time, almost touching, brought closer by the beauty of what they had just witnessed.

"It's amazing," said Georgia, "isn't it?"

He nodded. "I will never tire of seeing that."

Georgia reached her arms up, stretching her back. He tried not to notice the way her breasts strained against the thin layer of her shirt.

"Usually it's over before I even get there," she said, "unless something's gone wrong. It was a treat to see it from start to finish. The first time I saw one was with my friend Sam, when we were young—on his father's farm. That's when I knew I wanted to be a vet."

Alejandro stiffened at the name. "Sam?" he said. "Your visitor?"

Georgia glanced at him. "Your mother mentioned it?"

He nodded, trying to look nonchalant.

"Yes, that was him. We're old friends. Well, high school

sweethearts, really. He came last night to see...if we could maybe start things up again."

Alejandro looked away, aching over how he had so narrowly missed his chance.

"But, you know, sometimes something just doesn't feel right, no matter how much you wish it could. And—"

He crushed her to him, wrapping his hands in her hair and pulling her mouth to his before she could finish, unwilling to miss his chance again. She instantly responded, closing her eyes, kissing him back with a ferocious need that overtook them both.

Suddenly she pulled back, looking up into his face.

"What about Cricket?" she whispered.

He impatiently shook his head. "No, it was just that once. There's nothing between us. *Nada.*" And he greedily pulled her toward him again.

He felt almost frantic after holding himself back for so long, to finally have his hands on her again, his mouth on hers. His fingers tangling through her hair, slipping down her neck, over her shoulders.

She gasped as he grazed her breasts, and he felt her nipples spring up under his palms. He was so hard, he needed her so much...The smell of her, the silk of her skin, he wanted to fall into forever right there.

Georgia slid back and pulled her shirt up over her head, boldly presenting herself to him, meeting his eyes with a challenge. He felt dizzy with lust, as if he might burn to the bone if he didn't take her.

She was so beautiful with her flushed skin and liquid gaze, there was nothing more in the world that he wanted than to pin her down and consume her, body and soul. And yet he knew that if he gave in here, it would be rushed and overheated and frenzied. The tack room was hardly the place, with a sleepy groom likely to stumble in at any moment...

He looked at her tumbled, sun-touched curls, her mouth, swollen and pink with his kisses. No, what he really wanted was to take his time, pour slowly over her, savoring the aching bliss of finally having her back under his hands. With agony, he pulled himself away.

"Not here, *mi amor*," he said hoarsely.

She looked at him and then smiled. "I know a place," she said.

Chapter Sixty

Georgia crept up the ladder with Alejandro at her heels. She pulled herself into the loft, and he rose up behind her and took her back into his arms. The hay loft was lit with pale moonlight; the air smelled heavy and sweet. Alejandro held her close, and she felt tiny shocks of energy pass between them, like fizzing bubbles making tiny explosions snapping against their skin. She gasped, delighted, and tilted back her head for a kiss.

He pressed his lips to hers with a low groan, pulling her closer, so that she could feel the length of him. His hands on her felt so good. His full, firm lips on hers, the heat and height of him. She thrilled all over again at having to reach up to rake her fingers into his soft, thick hair.

He kissed her jaw, her earlobe, the length of her neck, and as he started to pull up her shirt, she almost laughed to think what Billy would say—all those beautiful clothes and now, when it came down to it, she was wearing her scrubs.

"Georgia," he whispered as he ran his hands down her back and then unhooked her bra and dropped it to the ground. "Ah, *mi paraiso*."

She tugged off his shirt, desperate to feel his skin on hers.

She felt as if their cells were melting together, his mouth tasting hers, the incredible strength of his arms wrapped around her, the soft rasp of his chest hair dragging deliciously against her bare breasts, his hands skimming over her body as he slid down her pants and briefs.

She responded in kind, unbuttoning his jeans, and his velvet hardness sprang out between them. She held herself against him for a moment, feeling him throb against her, loving the way the entirety of her body fit just within his. His hands cupped her rear, and his fingers reached into the depths between her legs. She gasped and he groaned, sliding his hands over her, holding her breasts, and greedily taking first one nipple then the other into his mouth. She knelt to take him between her lips, hands on his high, tight rear, as he leaned against the wall of hay bales behind them. He allowed her only a few long, deep draughts before he eased her up and turned her so that she was still facing him, but was cushioned against the hay.

He pinned her arms with gentle strength above her head and held them there. He dipped to kiss her mouth and nibbled the length of her neck, circling her nipples with his tongue. Georgia's back arched but he held her arms in place with his left hand, running his right hand over her belly, her thighs, just brushing the hair between her legs. The shivers triggered by his kisses released an unbelievable feeling of readiness. He let go of her arms and knelt before her. Putting his face between her legs, he teased her, slowly touching his tongue to her most sensitive spot, and then, in response to her urgent whisper, buried his face in her until she shook and cried with wave after wave of pleasure.

Finally, after she was spent, he stood and put a soft, clean horse blanket on the ground, and they lay face-to-face, and

he let her stroke and kiss all of him. Kneeling astride him,
raining kisses up and over his ribs, Georgia wanted to settle the whole of him into memory, imprint the smell of
his skin. He rolled her over, pressing the weight of his
body against hers, and then pulled back again, leaving her
breathless.

She felt her desire surge again as he toyed with her, running his hands over her skin, murmuring over the beauty of
her body in both English and Spanish, telling her that he
never knew it could be this way, that he was, at last, where
he was born to be.

And then finally, when she could stand it no more, she
pushed him back and gasped, "Did Sebastian—" And he
knew exactly what she wanted and, laughing, stood up and
walked over to the windowsill, where he had found the cards
on that long-ago day, and next to the cards—yes, a stash of
condoms.

He lay back down next to her, and she threw her leg over
him, carefully unrolling the condom he offered and placing
it on the straining stiffness of his cock. Then she braced her
hands against his shoulders and dragged the length of him
against her, finally finding purchase and plunging down until she could feel nothing but him filling every millimeter of
her body.

"*Mi amor*," he whispered, and held her still for a moment
as she looked into his eyes, which had gone black with a desire so blunt and powerful that she could only give in with
a wordless moan as he arched up against her and pushed
back into her, again and again, slowly fingering her as they
rocked together, going deeper and deeper until she felt herself dissolving against him just as he exploded into her, a
thousand fragments of light and energy rocketing between

them both, leaving them laughing and marveling it could feel this way.

* * *

They walked back to the pool house after, and Alejandro slept in her bed that night. In her arms. A sleep as deep and sweet as any he could remember.

* * *

Alejandro awoke as the sun rose the next morning and looked over at her, asleep in the rosy morning light. She looked so vulnerable with her mussed curls across the pillow, her pink lips just barely parted. He wanted to trace the soft shadow of her eyelids, touch the coral flush across her cheeks, kiss his way down her long, white neck.

She stirred and made a little sound, moving closer to his warmth. He gathered her into his arms, and when her clear hazel eyes opened and looked into his, the sweetest, dreamiest, just slightly wicked smile drifted across her face.

"Hello," she said softly. "Good morning."

He smiled back at her, running his hand across her hairline and down her cheek, and then he leaned down and kissed her welcoming lips.

He had never felt this way before. Equally inflamed and tender. He felt that no matter how close he was to her, it would never be close enough. He felt he wanted to know everything about her—and not just her beautiful body—but her memories, her opinions, her weaknesses and strengths. He felt—no, he *knew*—that he would never get enough of this woman.

"*Sos la razon de mi existir.* You are the reason for my existence. *Te amo*, Georgia," he said to her.

She gazed up at him, a look of absolute adoration in her eyes. "I love you, too," she whispered back.

Her words fell upon him like soothing rain upon his soul. Tears sprang to his eyes, and he was filled with the most ecstatic desire as he pulled her to him, and pressed himself against her. She arched against him, and he touched her, searching out the silky wetness between her legs. She was ready for him.

She shuddered under his touch. "Please," she said.

All self-restraint vanished as he parted her legs with his thigh and pushed up into her. She was so sweet, so tight, so hot. He pulled back and then plunged in harder as she wrapped her legs around his back and took all of him in. He took her again and again, and as he rode her embrace, he had the distinct sensation of falling—of losing all sense of himself—of not knowing how to be if not together with her. She whispered his name, shivering under him, and then calling out louder, crying his name again and again as she writhed and jerked her hips, and finally he joined her in an explosively sweet release, calling out, "*Mi cielo, mi amor*," as he felt her constrict around him over and over, as she sobbed out her bliss. At last she relaxed under him and unwound her legs, and he shuddered with one last aftershock of pleasure before burying his face into her neck, tasting the salt of her skin, smelling the sweetness of her, and feeling more whole than he had in years.

* * *

They lay entwined together, breathing in tandem, their skin cooling in the sweet morning air. He wanted to tell her a thousand different things, he wanted to make a million plans, but he also wanted to be doing exactly what they were already doing—just holding each other, feeling their hearts beat as one.

"It's getting late," Georgia finally whispered. "And we are in a *pecera*."

Alejandro laughed and looked at her. "Fishbowl? I didn't know your Spanish was so extensive."

She grinned at him. "It's not. Your mother taught me that one."

At the mention of his mother, he groaned. "I should probably get back before they wake up."

She nodded and rolled away from him, but then he pulled her back before she could go too far and kissed her again— soft and deep. He felt himself stir again.

She laughed and pushed him away. "We can't. I mean, I would love to, but we really can't."

He sighed and let her go. "I know."

* * *

Heading back to the house, Alejandro couldn't stop grinning. He'd slept, properly slept, for the first time in years, and that was all because of her. With her, he'd come to rest. He thought of the first time he'd seen her, with her face all but bare of makeup, the premonition he'd had of what it would be like to wake up next to her. He could add to that now, the memory of her damp, tangled hair, flushed cheeks, and the rosy aureoles of her nipples, the dip to her waist and abrupt curve of her hips, the sharp hipbones, heart-shaped ass, and those soft, strong thighs. It was all he could do not to get back in there and start things up all over again...

Chapter Sixty-one

Georgia ate a quick breakfast, dressed, and went to see the foal. She was absurdly elated, veering between all-out bliss and knee-melting desire. She could feel herself grinning like an idiot, but figured hanging around a newborn in the barn that morning was one place she wouldn't need an alibi for the smile.

Enzo and Noni were already there, leaning over the door to the stall with a groom on either side. The foal was adorable, bright as a new penny with her huge eyes and gawky legs. Georgia stood with her as she began to nurse. Sugar, no longer feeling the ferocious need for privacy, now welcomed Georgia into the stall, nuzzling her little foal with glowing pride.

"What time did she arrive?"

"Oh, around four," Georgia said.

"You must be exhausted—" Enzo said.

"She doesn't look it." Noni laughed.

"Alejandro helped," Georgia said.

"Oh, really?" Noni asked with a quick sidelong glance.

"Guess you're still on the adrenaline," Enzo said.

Georgia gave the foal the shots it needed, rubbed some iodine on the umbilical cord, and went off to attend to the other ponies. With the end of the season and Gus gone, there were a million details to attend to in the next few days, blood tests and health papers to clear them all for international travel.

She was with Tango, checking his feet, when Alejandro came in. Her insides melted on sight. Looking up at him in all his ridiculous beauty, standing square before her, she was almost undone by the erotic ownership in his closeness. He kept up professional patter for the benefit of the grooms outside, and Georgia, though she thought it would almost kill her, did her best to answer his questions with appropriate replies. When the grooms' footsteps all finally receded, he pressed her against the side of the stall for a kiss so luscious her knees almost gave out.

He grinned down at her. "We should name the foal."

"She looks so sweet," she said. "Like her mother."

"*Dulce*," he said.

She nodded. "*Dulce* it is."

He kissed her again. "Georgia." The way he said her name now was startling. The way he gazed at her was like sex in itself. She could feel the lids of her eyes dip just looking at him. "I'm not ready to tell anyone about us, to share all this yet. Not for a few more days anyway. Will you go home with me?"

She blinked. "Argentina?"

"Yes, we can be there by morning if we leave tonight. Enzo can cover the barn, and we'll get a temporary vet to finish up things here. I want you to myself, I want you in my bed, I want you to see where I come from."

She stared up into his eyes, her heart throbbing, conscious only of the feeling of surrender. The total certainty she would risk her career, her credibility, her heart, her everything, for another chance at a night in his arms.

Chapter Sixty-two

Georgia threw a few things into a bag—her bikini, a silk slip, jeans, a few T-shirts, a dress from Billy, bless him, and her boots—and waited for the car outside.

The family driver was taking them to the airport, which meant a ride overflowing with unbelievable sexual tension. They kept their distance in the backseat, Georgia gazing out at the passing landscape and trying to ignore the molten heat at the heart of her.

When they reached the airport and settled themselves side by side into the Cessna, Alejandro grinned at her. "I told everyone we were going to Santa Barbara to bid on a pony. Do you think we got away with it?"

"I got a knowing look from Noni maybe, but otherwise all clear," she said.

"We don't have to worry about Antonia," Alejandro said. "She saw this coming a long time ago. And she'll keep our secret as long as we want her to. It's not like she's close to my mother."

"No," Georgia acknowledged and gazed out the window as the plane started to taxi.

Alejandro reached into a bag at his feet and pulled out a small velvet box. "I got you something."

Georgia felt herself flush as she took the gift. It was all so beyond her experience—being whisked abroad, the luxurious private plane, the famous, unbelievably sexy man beside her..."Oh, you really didn't need to do that."

He shrugged. "I wanted to. Go ahead, see what it is."

She opened the box and gasped: a necklace made up of dozens of amethysts and pearls, the bright silver setting etched with an intricate scrolling design of roses and leaves. It was lovely and extravagant, as if from another time, and it took her breath away.

"It was my grandmother's," he said. "My father's mother, Victoria. Our team is named after her. She was wild and sweet and strong, and she never listened to anyone." He reached over and held it up. "She gave it to me before she died, told me to give it to someone who was worth it."

Georgia reached out to touch it. "Will you put it on me?"

He fastened it at the back of her neck. The coolness of the silver and the weight of the stones around her throat made her shiver in delight.

He gave her a piercing stare that sent fire through her veins. "It suits you, *mi reina*," he said.

She leaned into his ear, slid her hand up his thigh, and whispered, "When this plane levels out, we are going back to the bedroom, and I am going to wear nothing but this necklace while I do things to you that prove just how worth it I really am."

* * *

Afterward, they drifted in the soft bed, their limbs a-tangle, and Georgia smiled, sated. She was exhausted. Her muscles were sore in a deep, pleasant way, and she thought about how magical it was to be skimming through the sky, in this man's arms, heading for somewhere beautiful she had never been before.

Her mother flitted into her mind, and for once, Georgia didn't feel pain when she thought of her. For once, she felt that maybe she actually understood something about her.

This is what she wanted for me. Exactly this. "Polo is the passport to the world."

She snuggled closer to Alejandro, laying her head upon his chest. He wrapped his arm around her, and she sighed with contentment as she closed her eyes and they soared together through the night sky.

Chapter Sixty-three

Alejandro actually felt nervous as they turned down the long, meandering drive through his *estancia*. The chalet was much smaller and more modest than the house in Wellington. Olivia had always wanted to upgrade to something grander, more befitting the family status, as she put it, but he had been stubbornly against moving. This was maybe the first place where he had ever felt truly at home, and he'd held on to it despite her insistence that they needed something bigger. He hoped that Georgia wouldn't be disappointed by its rustic simplicity.

He had called ahead and let the caretaker, Manuel, and his wife, Maria, know that he would be there for the next few days. He had asked them to make sure the house was clean and that the kitchen was stocked, but let them know that, other than that, he would like his privacy.

The sun was just coming up as they drove past the barn, and he smiled to see the lights on and his grooms already busying themselves around the yard.

The two-story whitewashed farmhouse was tucked back on the property, between a dense stand of acacia trees that shielded it from the barnyard and a small, glimmering lake behind it. Beyond the lake was open prairie as far as the eye could see. Just seeing this beloved view made Alejandro's heart soar.

He darted a glance at Georgia. Her eyes were round with excitement. "It's even more beautiful than you described," she said. "It's perfect."

As they parked and opened their doors, a huge, white dog came bounding out at them, barking and jumping all over Georgia and practically knocking her over.

"*Hola, Frida, calma,*" said Alejandro. "Sit, *ey*, sit!"

Obediently, the dog, which was almost as big as Georgia, sat, her stubby tail wagging frantically in the dirt.

"This is Frida," said Alejandro. "Frida, this is Georgia. Be nice to her, *perrita*. We do not want you to scare *mi chica* off."

The dog panted happily as Georgia rolled her eyes at Alejandro. "I'm a vet, remember?" she said to him. "You think a dog could freak me out?"

Alejandro shrugged. "She's scared bigger men than you."

Georgia scratched Frida behind the ears and grinned at the big dog. "I'm thoroughly unimpressed with her ferociousness."

"She must like you," said Alejandro. He put his arm around Georgia and steered her toward the house. "She has good taste."

* * *

The house was beautiful, thought Georgia. She could see that it fit Alejandro exactly. For all the impressive formality of the *hacienda* in Wellington, it never felt particularly warm, but this house was the kind of place where you immediately felt at home, as if you could kick off your shoes and curl up in a sun-drenched corner and just be at peace.

It wasn't huge. Only four bedrooms, Alejandro told her, but it was open and bright and airy. The walls were of rough, unpainted plaster that seemed to glow with the light that streamed in through the countless windows. There were bookshelves overflowing with well-worn tomes in both English and Spanish, haphazardly ordered and stacked. There were several large paintings—moody and stark nature studies of horses and trees and one vibrant, gorgeous, nude of a woman's back. The floors were a dark, shiny wood, dotted with colorful woolen rugs. There was a huge kitchen, with a red brick floor and a fireplace so big that Georgia could have stood upright inside it. A long, worn, pine farm table held pride of place. There were amazing views from every room, either of the lake or the trees or the rolling prairie, and the whole place even smelled like Alejandro—bright and spicy and masculine.

Alejandro was a different person here. Showing Georgia round the barns, with his extraordinary stable of three hundred horses, he talked her through his breeding program with excited pride, introducing the fillies, the dams, their newest foals. As he took her hand and led her back to the house, the last traces of worry seemed to slide off his face, his posture relaxed, he smiled and laughed easily, and there was a sparkle in his eye that Georgia had never seen before.

"So, do you like it?" he asked as he showed her his bedroom. He seemed appealingly shy, almost worried that she wouldn't approve.

She took in the stunning view of the lake, and the massive, four-poster bed, heaped with bright pillows and decadent-looking linens, along with the simple, clean lines of the room. She smiled and shook her head. "It's wonderful. The whole place just feels like it's...loved, you know?"

Alejandro took her hand. "I'm glad you see it as I do," he said softly. "I want you to love it, too."

She looked up at him, and she tried to remind herself that it was all going ridiculously fast, that if she had any sense, she would remember that she had really only just met this man and that they were worlds apart in almost every way. But then, he reached down and gathered her to him and kissed her—the kind of kiss that a person might wait an entire lifetime to experience—and she knew that none of it mattered. That what was between them was so rare and miraculous that she would be a fool not to just let herself fall. Fall into his arms, fall into his life, fall into his world...She leaned against him, trying to match every inch of her body to every inch of his. His breath became ragged, and his eyes went dark.

"God. You're a little *bruja*. You make me so crazy. I can't get enough of you. I need you in my bed. Now," he growled, and he wrapped his arms around her and carried her across the room, placing her on her stomach, stretched across the mattress.

She tried to turn over to face him, but he held her in place, kissing and licking down the back of her neck and reaching beneath the little dress she wore. He slid his hands under her bra, grasping her breasts in both of his hands while he rubbed against her from behind.

She felt herself go slick and wet. He kept one hand on her breast, rubbing and teasing her nipple, and used his other hand to pull at her dress, trying to tug it off until he got frustrated and simply ripped it down the back with a snarl of impatience. She could barely contain her excitement.

"I'll buy you another one," he breathed as he pulled the dress away from her body and then stripped off her panties and bra as well. "I'll buy you a dozen."

He grasped her rear and pushed her legs apart, sliding his hand up under her, through her damp curls, and teasing and rubbing her until she thought she'd lose her mind, until she started to beg. "Alejandro, please, please."

"*Mi cielo*," he groaned, "you feel so good. I can't wait any longer."

"Yes," she moaned, and raised herself up against him.

She heard the unzipping of his pants and the rustle of a condom wrapper being ripped open, and then he sank into her hard, taking her until she felt him in every particle of her being. Hot pleasure rippled through her as he pulled back and thrust in again, and again. Finally, the pressure tipped her over the edge, triggering waves of release so intense that she felt as if she might pass out, and he joined her in her climax, calling her name, speaking to her in a jumble of Spanish and English, telling her how much he loved her, how good she felt, how she was *his*, now and forever. Until the both of them collapsed onto the bed, heaving and spent, slick with perspiration, and throbbing with the magic of it.

* * *

Alejandro bathed with her after, both of them climbing into the enormous, free-standing tub and sinking into the hot, steamy water. He soaped a washcloth and tenderly swept it down her neck, over her back, and the length of her thighs. Georgia leaned against his chest, warm and pink, and he wrapped his arms around her and sighed in contentment.

Alejandro loved the freedom he finally had to touch her,

relished the novelty of being able to close the space between them anytime he wanted.

"Tell me about your farm," he said, wanting to lay claim to every hidden part of her.

She shrugged, all at once a little embarrassed and defensive. "It's nothing compared to this place."

"But it's your home," he prompted.

"Yes," she agreed. "It's my home. And it's a little...rundown maybe, but it's beautiful in its own way."

Suddenly she was off and running, describing the stunningly disparate seasons: the almost tropical, deep green summers; the crisp, vivid autumns; the aching, white cold of winter with its glittering ice, fierce winds, and bright blue skies; and the sudden sweet reprieve of spring.

"I think that's what would be hardest about living somewhere like Wellington all the time," she said as they climbed out of the bath and toweled off. "The seasons never really change. In the Hudson Valley, you have to pay attention. Every day is different. I'm not sure I would know how to feel time passing if I didn't have the cues I get from the seasons."

They wrapped themselves in robes and wandered into the kitchen, sitting at the table and making a feast of delicious serrano ham with little hunks of crusty bread and manchego cheese and sipping a rich, red wine while Frida the dog lounged under the table and begged for scraps.

Georgia wiped her lips with a napkin and yawned. "I'm exhausted," she said. "You've worn me out," she teased.

They went back to the bedroom. He watched her crawl across the covers and tug the sheet over herself and then came to lie beside her, pushing the hair away from her face.

"You make love the same way you ride—and swim," she

said, laughing. "I'm not sure I can entirely keep up. I'm not the world-class athlete you are."

"You do just fine keeping up," he said to her.

She gazed up at him, smiling. "I remember the first time I saw you in the tent. Everyone wanted a piece of you."

"I saw you first," he said. "I thought Sebastian and Rory had gotten to you. I'm relieved they didn't."

"And I'm very relieved you're not in love with Cricket," Georgia said.

He laughed. "While we're talking about it, I'm quite pleased you're not about to marry your high school sweetheart."

She cuddled up closer to him and closed her eyes. He continued to stroke her hair until she fell into a deep afternoon sleep.

Chapter Sixty-four

They had a late supper on the balcony adjoining his bedroom, and Georgia had never felt so decadent or so sexy. Alejandro took the wine in his mouth and dribbled it into hers, before they fell back on the bed for more.

In the morning, she awoke to Alejandro's hand trailing down her cheek. She shivered deliciously. "Are you counting my freckles?" she said. "Unfortunate, aren't they?"

"I love your freckles," he said. "*Pecas*, like a trail of cinnamon across your face."

"A trail of cinnamon?" She laughed. "I'm not sure that sounds so appealing. Maybe I'll get rid of them," she said. "Cricket was telling me about a doctor who can help me."

"Don't you dare," Alejandro said, sitting up. "Don't you dare go to one of those doctors who will take everything special about you—your freckles and your laugh lines and your scars. I want your face to move like this when you laugh. Your nose. Your forehead. Your body. I don't want you to change a thing."

"Okay, okay," she said, curling against the broad span of his back, just about ready to die of happiness.

* * *

They rode together that day. Alejandro introduced Georgia to more of his staff, who didn't try too hard to hide their surprise and pleasure at seeing their boss with a woman.

"Apparently, it's been a long time since I have brought a lady friend home," said Alejandro dryly as yet another groom waggled his eyebrows and poked him in the ribs with his elbow.

He chose a couple of mounts, and they tacked up and rode so far out into the prairie that they couldn't see the house anymore.

They tied up the ponies and laid a blanket down on the grass, and he made slow, meticulous love to her under the enormous sky. He stroked her beautiful body as she lay naked in the warm sun, gazing into her dreamy hazel eyes until he made them close in pleasure, kissing her soft lips until they gasped with desire. He drove her to peak after peak, not stopping until she was limp and exhausted, and then he languidly slid himself into her and took his own sweet time, coaxing her to one last heart-stopping climax and finally letting himself let go with her.

They rode back in and skinny-dipped in the lake at dusk, floating hand in hand amid the reflected sunset on the glassy water, watching the sky as it turned red and orange, and then pink and gold, and finally fading into a dusky blue and purple.

He made a fire by the water, and they sat together, wrapped in the same blanket, and when the first star appeared, Georgia said to him, "Make a wish," and he couldn't, because it seemed greedy to ask for anything more than all they had in this perfect moment.

Chapter Sixty-five

The phone rang late that night, and Alejandro was startled awake, his heart pounding. He answered, and it was his sister Noni.

"Jandro? Valentina's been hurt. There was a riding accident."

Antonia didn't know much. She'd only seen the very end of it as Valentina had been taken away in the ambulance. "I'm heading to the hospital now, but you need to call Pilar," she said. "I'm so sorry."

Alejandro hung up the phone. Immediately his mind was working. He called his caretaker and told him he'd need a ride to the airport and to please call ahead and have the Cessna ready. And then he was dialing Pilar and simultaneously pulling on jeans and trying to find his wallet and his keys from the layers of sheets and scattered clothes and mess around the room.

Fuck, fuck, fuck, he thought, sitting on the edge of the bed and pulling on a shirt, his phone tucked under his chin as he waited for Pilar to answer. Why was he nine hours away from his daughter? What madness had convinced him it was safe to leave her without letting anyone but Antonia know where he really was?

Pilar didn't pick up, and he cursed.

It felt to Alejandro that he was seeing the world through cloudy glass. His head was a confusion of terror; a part of him flung back to the first shock of losing Olivia. He had visions of Valentina receding beyond his grasp and felt the full terror of not being able to reach or hear his daughter.

He became aware of someone hugging him from behind, saying soothing things, asking concerned questions. It was Georgia, but he could hardly hear her or register her presence, amid the primal horror of losing his daughter.

He shrugged her off, plucking her hands from his shoulders. He tried Sebastian next and his brother answered.

"Sebastian?" Alejandro cried. "What is it? What happened?"

"Valentina had been night riding. Storm. Something spooked him, or he lost his footing, and he threw her."

"Her neck?"

"Her head and her legs," Sebastian said. "But she's alive, Alejandro. She's in the best hands. And they're fighting for her. We're at the Wellington Regional Medical Center. What time can you get here?"

Alejandro let the phone fall to his lap. He and Georgia hurried to the car in silence. Alejandro couldn't look at her. His eyes couldn't focus at all, really. He slid into the car grateful Manuel would take the wheel and waited for them to drive away, cold sick fear in his heart.

As they were rushed to the airport, he sat with his jaw and fingers clenched, his mind moving from the image of Valentina as a little girl, to Valentina as a teen, to his wife, and the horrible weeks she lingered already half dead in the hospital.

For the entire flight, his mind ran over images of riders

he's known who had been severely injured—lost the use of their legs, broken their necks or backs. He'd known he shouldn't let his daughter ride. He'd known.

Georgia sat beside him all the way in silence, but he scarcely noticed her, brushing her hand away anytime she tried to touch him. The hours dragged by so slowly, time seemed almost at a standstill.

And then, finally, they were landing and getting into the family car, and then pulling up outside the emergency room, and Georgia reached for him again, laying a hand on his sleeve, and he looked at her wildly. Who was this woman? She seemed to him in that moment like some kind of demon. Who was she to have overridden a decision he knew he'd been right to make? What the hell had he been thinking letting his daughter anywhere near a horse again?

"Is there anything? Anything I can do?" she said.

He looked at her, as if it were unthinkable she'd even still be there beside him. "No. No." He was exhausted. "You've done enough. Please. Just go home."

* * *

He strode from the car, and Georgia collapsed back on the seat, reeling from that blow. She found herself in an agony of uncertainty, not knowing whether to deliver his bags home or climb from the car and make her own way.

She caught the steady, kind eyes of the driver in the rearview mirror, and he made a barely perceptible nod of the head, gesturing that she should head inside. As she climbed from the car, he lay his hand on her arm.

"I'll be right here, miss. Long as it takes."

* * *

Alejandro strode through the bright, cold lights of the hospital, eyes scanning for a member of his family. Directed to the fourth floor, he didn't have the patience for the elevator and took the stairs three at a time, bursting into the private waiting room, where his mother sat, her normally straight back slumped over in her chair, while Sebastian paced at the window and Cricket looked at him accusingly.

"Where have you been?" Cricket asked. "It's been hours since it happened."

Pilar looked up at him and murmured that it hardly mattered, he was here now.

Alejandro ignored them both and approached the desk, announcing himself as Valentina's father and demanding to see his daughter—and her doctor.

Minutes later, a tanned and silver-haired doctor came to the door. Taking in the crowd, he insisted on family only. Pilar, Sebastian, and Alejandro followed him.

* * *

The doors closed behind them just as Georgia rushed in, looking around frantically for Alejandro. Cricket looked at her coolly, taking in her unbrushed hair and mascara-smudged eyes.

"How did you hear?"

"Noni called Alejandro—" Georgia said, and the unspoken revelation she'd been with him settled heavily in the room. "How is she?"

"We're still waiting to hear," Cricket said, her voice like ice.

Georgia sat heavily beside her. "He never wanted her to ride. I changed his mind. He thinks it's my fault," she said with absolute certainty.

"Don't make this about you," Cricket said. Her voice sounded both scornful and jealous.

"I love Valentina," Georgia said, realizing as she said it, that it was true.

"You love her?" Cricket sounded outraged. "You don't even know her."

God, she was right, Georgia thought. She was nothing but a temporary employee who'd given what turned out to be catastrophically bad advice to her boss's daughter before going on to sleep with him in clear dereliction of every professional standard.

Cricket glanced from her phone's screen to Georgia's face and seemed to relent a bit. "I'm sure you thought it was the right thing to do."

"I didn't know," Georgia said. "It just seemed like a good way to go, given everything she'd been through. I didn't know this would happen."

"No one ever knows," Cricket snapped. "Some people just do a better job at acting like they know. Some people are better at sneaking into a family and disrupting everything, whether they belong there or not."

Georgia sat, feeling sickened. It was true, when she thought about the enormity of Valentina's grief and Alejandro's loss and responsibility. She'd been playing God, as if she, with her stupid, broken home life and stunted childhood, had any idea how to fix anyone else. If Valentina would just be okay, she prayed, if she'd just make it through, she swore never to meddle in the family again.

Pilar came out and looked at Georgia in confusion before

settling her gaze on familiar Cricket with an expression of relief. Cricket stood to put a hand on Pilar's arm, and her delicate frame started shaking with tears.

"*Lo siento. Lo siento.* It's okay. The scans are good news. There's no brain damage. She'll need time for her legs to heal, but she's all right, *todo va a estar bien.*"

Cricket took her in her arms and murmured soothingly, "Thank God. Thank God. I'll let everyone know. Corinne and Molly will be so relieved, and Xanthe, and Elizabeth."

She rattled off names that meant nothing to Georgia and looked at her levelly over Pilar's shoulder. The message was clear: *I've got this. Why are you still here?* Georgia took her cue. The circle was closing. She wasn't needed.

Chapter Sixty-six

Georgia took the stairs back outside, relieved to see the driver still waiting. He jumped from the car, eyes all questions, and Georgia let him know that the prognosis for Valentina was good, thank God.

In the backseat, where only the day before yesterday she'd been full of such delicious anticipation, the gratitude she felt about Valentina was battered by the impossible sadness of saying good-bye to so much hope with Alejandro. She pulled on sunglasses so the tears could flow.

The driver was discreetly silent until they reached the barn, where Enzo was just getting started, working with the new temporary vet to load the horses for shipment to Argentina.

Enzo was grateful for Georgia's reassuring report from the hospital and as he asked after each of the family in turn, she realized how devoted he was to Valentina, and to Noni and all the Del Campos—and how fond she had become of him. When Enzo heard she and Alejandro had flown out of Argentina at four that morning, he insisted that Georgia head back to bed.

"Honestly, Georgia. You've worked like a trouper all season. We can take it from here. The only remaining obligation for you would be an appearance at the end-of-season party, but given what the family's been through, I'm guessing that's not happening. So you can really go home at any time now. You've earned it."

Georgia couldn't bring herself to go back to the pool house just yet so she drifted into the barn, where she lingered with Sugar and her pretty foal. Along with Tango, they were the hardest for her to leave. That figured, she thought wryly, it was only the half-breeds with whom she really ever fit in. Everything she heard that morning seemed to confirm her sense of herself as a meddling interloper. She heard grooms discussing the cost of the season and the fact that the Del Campos had rented out their yacht to Kuwaitis for $250,000 a week. Another talking about the family place in St. Moritz, which was covered by the stud fees on Tango alone. How in God's name could she ever have begun to think she might belong?

Saying good-bye to Valentina's horse, mercifully uninjured by the girl's fall, she felt a fresh wave of shame at how selfish and reckless it had been to encourage her riding, given the legacy of grief over Olivia. God, how could she have invited loss right back into Alejandro's life like that?

She felt close to a state of total collapse. This was why her mother had left her behind. She knew—she knew that Georgia would never fit into this world. That she would make a mess of things here.

Her eyes were starting to swim with exhaustion. Enzo came back, insisting she would get sick and must give herself a break. She hadn't taken a clear day off since she was hired, and truly she could go home now, as far as he was concerned. They had everything covered.

She didn't trust herself to speak beyond a thank-you before making her way back to the pool house.

She was revolted by all the pathetic self-pity kicking in as she packed her bags and sent a text to her father, letting him know that she'd be home early. She kept telling herself to be glad about Valentina. That was the only thing that truly mattered.

Chapter Sixty seven

Alejandro kept a constant vigil at the hospital. As Valentina's room filled up with flowers, the array changing every day as friends sent their tributes, it was as if his body wouldn't let his eyes or mind rest. His whole system was on high alert. Even when he left his daughter's bedside and tried to catch a few hours' rest on a cot, his eyes were pinned awake, his mind tortured by replays of what might have been.

He couldn't believe all season he'd been worrying about the team's performance when he should have been thinking about his daughter. Nothing and nobody mattered like she did.

* * *

Georgia decided she'd take the train home. She wasn't ready to be back at the farm as fast as a flight would take her. She felt almost crazy with grief at leaving Alejandro, and her shoulders were shuddering with tears as the shuttle bus left Wellington.

Her mind kept replaying those days and nights—the

warm sun on her skin, the searching look on Alejandro's face just before he kissed her, the feeling of him pressed up against her as they lay under the infinitely blue sky—over and over. It was torture.

Gradually, she found the motion meditative, and her sobs had receded by the time she left the bus at Miami and boarded the Silver Bullet.

She ate dinner in the dining car, avoiding any attempts at conversation by fellow passengers, and swayed back along the aisle to her cabin for bed.

She slept through, soothed by the homeward motion, and by the time she changed trains in New York City, she felt she'd achieved a new clarity.

Billy had warned her up front. This whole thing with Alejandro had been a lovely fantasy, a big, beautiful, massively flattering diversion from reality, but of course their worlds were poles apart and they'd never had any real future together. She'd been a fool. Good sex didn't equal destiny.

Pulling out of Penn Station on the last stretch of her journey, she had a nice e-mail from Pilar, thanking her for everything and apologizing for being so dreadfully unavailable at the hospital. The key thing was that Valentina was out of danger. *Thank God*, Georgia thought, for Valentina, for Alejandro, and for her own sense of relief.

Heading out past the beautiful, low-slung Tappan Zee Bridge, Georgia felt her spirits lift a tiny bit. It was a relief to see the familiar Hudson River and the majestic scenery. The air was warm, and the sky was blue. It was finally spring in upstate New York.

Slowing in the approach to Rhinecliff, she watched a heron on the water's edge, a flag, a church spire, the clifftops beyond, and through it all, her own reflection, where she was surprised to find herself almost wanting to smile.

* * *

Her dad was there to greet her at the station, waiting at the waterside platform. She saw his eyes worriedly scanning the train cars as they slowed to a halt and light up when he found her familiar face.

He wrapped her in an extra scarf as she laughingly protested. "You're not used to these temperatures anymore, and I don't want you getting sick."

"New car?" Georgia asked as he flipped the trunk on a red Subaru.

"Laurie's," he said, coloring slightly.

"Laurie?" Georgia asked.

"The lady I was helping with the renovation... Very nice lady, it turns out."

"Oh." Georgia smiled. "Okay."

It was a cozy thing driving with him again, side by side, and rediscovering the feeling of easy repartee. And Georgia hadn't realized she needed any kind of apology, but then her dad coughed and said, "Honey, I was wrong to put all that guilt on you about staying down there. I feel like I've been angry and bitter forever. You're not your mother. I know that. Did you see her down there, by the way?"

Georgia shook her head.

"I was hurt when she left," he continued, "but more than that, I think I was embarrassed. I'd overreached—so publicly—in marrying her, and when she left us both, the failure... I don't know. It seemed like it just proved what everyone had always said—she was too good for the likes of me."

"Dad, stop," Georgia said. "Maybe you were too good for her."

"Well, I certainly don't know about that. But you're right, I'll stop. It's never helpful to complain."

"Whatever else happened," she reassured him, smiling, "if you hadn't married her, you wouldn't have me, right?"

"You're right," he said, and laughed. "Thank God. You're right. Regrets unnecessary."

Her dad looked at her worriedly, a world of unasked questions between them. "You okay?"

She closed her eyes for a moment, but then opened them again. "I'm okay," she said softly. "No regrets."

"Hell then," he said, "we're both good to move on."

* * *

Georgia felt a moment's dismay on arriving home, seeing just how much still needed to be done, but it was quickly displaced by gratitude that the animals and the old house had made it through the winter. She would work her way through all of this.

Her dad's friend Laurie was busy in the farmhouse kitchen, a lasagna in the oven, a bottle of red and a crisp green salad waiting, and though she tactfully offered to leave father and daughter to their reunion that first evening, both Georgia and her dad said they were happy to have her there.

A pretty, blond woman in her fifties who had a bit of money but liked to keep busy with her own marketing agency, Laurie was warm and unaffected and won Georgia over with her clear and complete certainty that her dad was the best thing ever.

Georgia insisted on washing up while Laurie and her dad

said good night. As she meditatively scrubbed the lasagna pan, she felt a moment of grief for Alejandro strong enough to make her want to lay the dishes aside and weep. But instead of giving in to the tears, she took a ragged breath and shook them off. She was fit, healthy, qualified to help in the field she most enjoyed. And for the first time in her life, her bank balance wasn't actually a worry. She certainly had no business with self-pity.

When she awoke the next morning in her own bed, she was struck by the feeling that Wellington had never happened. After all, here she was, back in her old bedroom, animals needing to be fed. Alone again. She was tempted for a second to pull the quilt over her head and give up.

No, she thought. No one she admired did that. She would rise. Work. And shine.

She'd been lucky to get to go to Wellington and have the professional bar raised. And there were plenty of ways she could raise her game here at home. Saratoga was only an hour away and boasted a racing season to give Wellington a run for its money. Between Saratoga Polo and the international show-jumping scene in the village of Saugerties, she could still do world-class work right here.

With her dad spending more and more of his time with Laurie, she quickly settled into a routine: rising early, thankful to note each new hint of returning green to the landscape, seeing to the animals' immediate needs with the new efficiency she had learned from working the precise routines of Wellington, and then spending the afternoon mapping out the business and lifestyle she wanted to make a reality.

The nights were a bit harder. With not so much to keep her busy, it was difficult to keep things at bay. The memories and loss came back strong and clear. But she learned to stay still in her bed, to breathe slowly, to withstand the way the feelings battered at her, until she could reach the merciful oblivion of sleep.

* * *

It was torture for Alejandro. If he'd had insomnia before, it was only worse now. He was able to feel righteous in his fear and anger—to push any thoughts of Georgia away—until Valentina's eyes fluttered open and the first thing she did was beg him to let her keep riding.

Nothing helped now. Not his ponies, not the game, not the team. The world had gone flat and colorless.

And now that his daughter was walking again—taking her first tentative steps—he couldn't help constantly reliving the look on Georgia's face when he'd dismissed her that night at the hospital, the way the light had died in her eyes. Every time he saw Sugar and Dulce, he thought of her, every time he tried to sleep, every time he rode, every time he was alone, every time he closed his eyes.

* * *

A couple of weeks after her return home, Georgia received a letter from Lord Henderson with a generous reference and an end-of-season bonus, which meant the barn could be re-painted and the fences mended right away. It was a lovely thing, waking to the sound of happy collaborative building, hammering, and tapping that meant things were beginning to be shipshape.

Her dad told her Sam had found an aesthetician to rent the space above his office that might have been Georgia's practice. Georgia might have been happy to leave that there, but at her father's urging, she went by for a visit, to see that there were no bad feelings.

Sam, bless him, was excited for her new business and offered her a loan. Georgia shook her head, knowing that she'd socked away enough in Florida to make it through. But she was pleased that he had that much confidence in her, and even more pleased not to need his help.

When the place was painted and repaired and the potholes in the road filled, Laurie presented her with a set of photographs, which she used to advertise in all the equestrian magazines: "FELLOWES FARM: Short- and Long-Term Boarding with Resident Vet."

Her tag line was: *Wellington-Level Equestrian Services in the Hudson Valley.*

After all the worry about money, suddenly there was plenty. Georgia hired a few locals she knew from town and found herself managing a team with an ease she'd never have anticipated before being part of the Del Campo operation. It was genuinely fun, getting ready for the summer influx of horses who'd need stabling. Maybe, she thought, there was something a bit contagious about prosperity after all.

* * *

One afternoon, she got a text from Billy. He and Beau were visiting the city and were getting on the train upstate at that very moment. They were dying to see their Peaches and told her to drop everything so they could spend the afternoon catching up.

Georgia smiled when she saw them getting off the train a couple of hours later. They were as gorgeous as ever, holding hands and looking blissfully in love. After hugging hello, they all ducked into the bar at the Rhinecliff Hotel and ordered a bottle of wine.

"So," said Billy after they'd each thrown back a couple of glasses of red and Georgia had caught them up on all her business doings, "yes, yes, you're a mini-mogul now, business is booming, your dad's got a nice girlfriend, your ex is probably minutes from marriage to a manicurist, and all is well and good, but"—he put his hand on top of hers and peered searchingly into her face—"how are you?"

Georgia looked at him for a moment, and the smile stretched thin across her face. "I'm fine," she said with a false note of brightness in her voice.

"No," said Beau, "he means, how are you, *really*?"

The mask she had been working so hard to keep in place for all these months slid down off her face. "I—" she said. Her breath caught in her throat, and tears welled in her eyes. "I—" She gasped as the tears fell. "I miss him," she finally managed to choke out. "I miss him horribly," and she buried her face in Billy's shoulder and shuddered with sobs. "It hurts so much, you guys."

Billy pulled her into a hug. "Oh, Peaches," he said, "I'm so, so sorry."

"Well, of course you miss him," said Beau, patting her back. "He was like Billy is to me—the love of your goddamned life."

Georgia raised her head just in time to see Beau exchange a sweet look with Billy.

"I don't think you're helping her much, babe," Billy said to Beau.

"Well, maybe not. But I'll tell you what, I'd rather have just a little bit of time with you," said Beau, "than a hundred years with someone else. I mean, at least you had a little bit of time with him, right, Georgia?"

Georgia sniffed, trying to get a hold of herself. "Yes," she finally said. "Yes, it was worth it."

Beau raised his glass to her. "Here's to true love, honey. Even just a little bit of it."

Georgia smiled through her tears and clinked her glass to his.

Chapter Sixty-eight

It was a soft and gorgeous dusk in late spring. The wild roses were blooming and their sweet scent drenched the air. The first fireflies were making their appearance, blinking their message of unmistakable longing. New fences enclosed the rolling meadows; beyond those the wooded hills offered an endless variety of green as far as the eye could see. Georgia was just finishing up a training session with a new horse on the lunge line—a horse she was beginning to think she should show or even breed—when the low rumbling of vehicles stopped her in her tracks.

There was a bright red horse trailer coming up the drive in the evening light. Georgia stood, frozen, watching the vehicle make its way slowly toward her.

* * *

There she was, Alejandro thought. In her element. Exactly as beautiful as he remembered her. Especially with that look of absolute surprise on her face.

His heart started to pound.

Valentina squeezed his hand, grinning. "Go get her, *Papá*."

He stopped the truck and watched Georgia for a moment longer as she tethered her horse and walked out to meet them. He opened the truck door and took a deep breath.

"That's quite an entrance," she said.

Alejandro opened his mouth to speak but found that his voice caught in his throat. It was almost too much, having her in front of him again. What a fucking fool he'd been. He swallowed. "*Hola*," he finally said.

She didn't smile. "Hello."

"So this is your home."

She nodded, her eyes wary.

He looked at her. "Beautiful," he said.

"It's insanely pretty!" Valentina cried. "No wonder you abandoned us!" She took Melvin the sheepdog's head in her hands, rubbing vigorously behind his ears and sending him to heaven. "Come on, boy, show me the barn!" she cried, and ran happily behind the dog to see the fresh stalls.

Georgia's face softened as she watched Valentina's easy run. "All better?" she said.

"Better than ever," he said. "Thank God."

A familiar whinny came from the trailers. Georgia cocked her head questioningly.

"So, I heard you were taking boarders. I thought maybe, if you had room for a few more," he said. "No obligation..." He unbolted the box. "For your consideration..."

It was Sugar, and Temper, and their foal, Dulce. Sugar gave an excited whinny to see Georgia again. Georgia smiled as she caught the little pony's head in her arms and kissed her nose. She led mare and foal down the ramp and turned them out in the field, where Sugar and Dulce bolted for the far side and stood back and attentively watched Alejandro and Georgia as if they were expecting some spectacle. Temper came to the foot of the ramp and stood stubbornly at their side.

Alejandro was painfully conscious of Georgia beside him. He wanted to touch her so badly, but hardly daring to hope she'd reciprocate, he stroked Temper instead. The evening shift of stable hands looked at the pair in frank curiosity. Alejandro found it excruciating, the scrutiny, when all he wanted was to talk to Georgia.

"Ride with me?" he said roughly.

She hesitated, but seeing Valentina chatting happily with one of Georgia's grooms, a girl about her age, she gave a little nod.

He mounted Temper and reached a hand for her. Georgia gave herself a leg up from the fence.

"Surprisingly comfortable," she said, slotting close behind him on the stallion's bare back.

"When you are on a great horse, you have the best seat you'll ever have."

"Churchill?" She laughed.

"Churchill," he confirmed.

She pointed out where to take the mossy trail to the top field and they climbed in silence awhile, shy to be alone, feeling each other's heat, Temper strong and steady beneath them. "So," she said, once she could trust her voice to stay steady, "how are you?"

He paused. "I can't sleep," he said hoarsely.

"You can't . . ."

"Sleep," he said. "I haven't for months. Not really. Not since you left."

"Oh," she said, and a blush spread over her face. It was all she could do not to rest her hot cheek against the broad span of his back.

"I was so wrong, *mi cielo*," he said huskily. "I was so wrong to hurt you. I was so wrong to drive you away."

"You were scared," she said softly.

He reached back to take her hand in his. "I was blind," he said. "I was a fool. And I am so, so sorry."

She looked up at the sky, where Venus had risen beside a delicate crescent moon. "It's all right," she said and gave a little shrug. "Doesn't matter."

But she didn't take her hand away.

When they reached the top field, he brought Temper to a halt and helped her down, feeling the relief that finally they were alone and in private again. "No," he said, "it's not past. I still need you. I still love you. Every time I close my eyes, you're the only thing I see."

She was still for a moment, her eyes glinting with unshed tears. Then she slowly stepped closer to him, turned her face up to his, and finally met his gaze. He exhaled. He realized it felt as if he'd been holding his breath, his hands clenched, for months now.

His fingers trembled as he touched her cheek, stroked his thumb along her jaw, but instead of kissing her, he pressed her against his chest.

"I thought I'd lost you for good," he said. "And I don't know how to live without you."

She started to cry and pulled back to see him. "Would you mind kissing me now, please?" She smiled through her streaming tears.

He bent to kiss her, tasting the bitterness of saltwater on her lips, then the sweetness underneath. He kissed her, and it was as if the blood had rushed back into his veins and the color had blossomed back into his world. He kissed her and felt his life returning to him. She sighed, and he caught her in his arms as she melted against him, and there, on that warm, sweet spring night, they found each other again.

WHEN HER FATHER'S HEALTH BRINGS KAT
HOME TO WELLINGTON, THE LAST THING ON
HER MIND IS ROMANCE. BUT NOW SHE'S
FORCED TO WORK WITH SEBASTIAN DEL
CAMPO, A DEVASTATINGLY HANDSOME
TABLOID GOD AS WELL-KNOWN FOR HIS POLO
PLAYING AS HE IS FOR BREAKING HEARTS.

PLEASE SEE THE NEXT PAGE FOR A
PREVIEW OF

Nacho Figueras Presents:
Wild One

Chapter Four

Her husband is in the hospital, *pobrecita*," said Sebastian's mother, Pilar, as she poured him a cup of morning coffee. "A stroke, apparently."

Sebastian accepted the cup gratefully, rubbing his temple. The bright morning light pouring in through the kitchen windows made him wince. The girls had finally left just before dawn. "I'm sorry," he said, "but which maid? Surely not the blond one—I didn't even know she was married."

Alejandro snorted as he leaned over to his baby son and spooned some cereal into his mouth. "Not that it would make any difference to you if she was."

Pilar tsk'd, distracted. "Ay, don't say such things, Jandro. Your brother would never be involved with a married *doña*."

Alejandro nodded. "*Sí, Mamá*. I know."

"Well, I suppose it depends on just how big her husband might be," Seb joked.

Pilar gave him a little punch in the arm. "*Basta ya, hijo.* Anyway, I am not talking about a maid. I'm talking about Corinne. The housekeeper. Really, Sebastian, she's worked for us for years."

"Oh, poor Corinne! When did this happen?" asked Alejandro's wife, Georgia.

Unlike her husband and mother-in-law, who were both immaculately dressed and groomed, Georgia was still in her pajamas, her caramel-colored hair in casual disarray. Sebastian glanced at her and smiled, glad to have a *compañera* in his dislike for early mornings.

Pilar spooned some sugar into her tea. "Two days ago. It was a small stroke, but still, he will need time and rehabilitation. I only just found out now. Corinne called to let me know she wouldn't be in this week. I told her not to worry, *por supuesto*, we would be fine, but she's insisting that she'll bring in some help. She has a daughter who used to work for her, apparently."

Georgia put down her fork. "Well, I'm going to call and see if there's anything we can do. Surely a meal or two at least?"

Alejandro smiled at his wife and reached out to touch her arm. "That is very sweet of you, *querida*."

They gazed at each other for a moment, exchanging a glance so private and charged that it made Sebastian look away, embarrassed.

He smiled ruefully. If he didn't see proof of it on a daily basis, he never would have believed that his brother could fall so hard and so deep for a woman.

Having grown up under the shadow of a father who regularly and openly strayed from their mother, the two brothers had each struggled to find their own ways of coping with their paternal legacy.

But as much as he admired his brother's marriage, Sebastian couldn't see himself taking the same path. He'd figured out quite young that no one could get hurt the way his mother had been if no one ever got attached. So he flitted from one woman to the next, having his fun along the way, and being certain that he never paused long enough to form any real connection.

Pilar cleared her throat, and Alejandro and Georgia

jumped, suddenly seeming to remember that they were not actually alone. "Yes, well," said Pilar, "let me know what Corinne says. And I'll order flowers. But I'll need one of you to deliver them to her house. You know *el hospital* cannot be trusted."

Sebastian snorted. Ever since his mother had once sent flowers to an ailing friend that had been misdirected to the maternity ward, she refused to believe that anything would be delivered properly. "Send Jandro, *Mamá*. Old ladies like him better than me."

Georgia giggled and then quickly covered up with a cough when her husband shot her a look.

Pilar frowned at Sebastian. "Between the game and the award he is getting tonight for mentoring those barrio children, your brother has enough to do." She smiled at her elder son and patted him on the arm.

Alejandro smirked at Seb as if he were nine years old again and had just been given the last piece of cake.

Sebastian rolled his eyes. "Fine, then, wouldn't want to interrupt Saint Alejandro's quest for a Nobel Prize." He turned to his brother. "Pity I won't make it to practice this morning, though, but obviously, this is much more important."

Pilar shook her head. "No, no, the flowers won't be delivered until later today. You can do both, *no problemo*."

Alejandro smiled smugly at Seb. "*Sí, hermano*, you can do both, *no problemo*."

* * *

Sebastian headed for the barn, annoyed. He was hungover and exhausted, and the last thing he wanted to do was ride, but it wasn't worth seeing the pissed-off look on his brother's face if he insisted on taking the morning off.

He sighed as he brushed out his pony. When did things get so bad between him and Jandro? Of course, Alejandro had always been more responsible, more conservative. He'd had to be. He was the older brother, the head of the family since their father had died. But Sebastian's lifestyle—his drinking, his partying, the women—had never seemed to bother his brother before. In fact, Jandro had always seemed amused by it all, if anything, enjoying his younger brother's sense of humor and lust for life.

The pony snorted her protest at Seb's heavy hand with the currycomb. Seb instinctively lightened his touch.

He knew that Alejandro had gone through a lot. His brother had been unhappily married, and then widowed, very young. For years he'd raised his daughter, Valentina, on his own while he also led the polo team and managed the family dynasty. He'd definitely carried the weight of the world on his shoulders. But things were different now. Georgia was more than his match in every way. Valentina was safely off to college in New York City. They had little Tomás, who was a bright and easy baby. The team was winning again. The Del Campos were respected and admired just as much, if not more, than they had been when their father was still alive.

Really, in most ways, Alejandro was happier than Seb had ever seen him.

And yet, his relationship with Sebastian was worse than it had ever been. Whenever Jandro turned to his little brother, it seemed that the happiness simply slid off his face. He was brusque, sharp, and disappointed. It was almost as if, once Alejandro had managed to get his own affairs in order, his focus had simply shifted onto Sebastian's life. And, thought Sebastian ruefully, his brother had obviously found it to be greatly wanting.

Seb put down the currycomb, annoyed. Why should he try to please Alejandro when his brother treated him with so little respect? Why should he practice when he was exhausted? If he was going to play at all decently this afternoon, what he really needed was a nap.

He patted his pony as he led her back into her stall. "Sorry, *chiquita*. I'll make it up to you later."

He passed his mother behind the wheel of her Mercedes as he made his way back to the *hacienda*. She stopped her car and rolled down her window. "*Bueno*, Sebastian. I'm glad you're back. The flowers should be delivered within the hour. I left Corinne's address on the kitchen table. Run them over with our regards as soon as they arrive, okay?"

Seb reluctantly nodded. So much for his nap.

Instead of going back to bed, he made his way down to the home theater in the basement, yawning as he sank into the butter-soft leather sofa. He'd have time to watch a movie at least, he thought as his eyes slowly closed.

Chapter Five

It never failed to amaze Kat how her parents managed to keep every last detail of their home exactly as it had always been. It was as if the cottage were encased in amber. The worn, indescribably comfortable, red sofa in the living room; the cheerful grass green tile on the kitchen floor; the round, pine table in the dining room, crowned with a vase of her mother's prize tea roses. Even the succession of identical, slightly mangy black cats who all seemed to enjoy the same sunny spot in the living room window. Kat's father was an animal lover and he always said that no one ever wanted black cats— so he made it a special point to give them a home.

She had not seen her father yet. Her mother had picked her up from the airport, and they had gone straight to the hospital, but her father had just been whisked away for tests, and the doctors said it might be a few hours before he could receive visitors. Her mother had insisted that Kat go home so she could unpack and rest a little before coming back to the hospital. She assured Kat that her father was not bad at all. "Just a little stroke," she'd said. "A teeny, tiny one. He'll be absolutely fine." And Kat desperately wanted to believe her.

Kat drifted into her old bedroom, which was also untouched but strikingly different from the rest of the cottage. Instead of perfect cleanliness and order, here were messy clues to her past, and a chaotic map of her future. The walls were papered with movie posters and pictures torn from magazines: Susan Sarandon and Geena Davis grinning out from *Thelma and Louise*, Holly Hunter from Jane Campion's *The Piano*, stills from *Clueless*, *9 to 5*, *Bull Durham*, *Breakfast Club*, *She's Gotta Have It*...a whole collection of Katharine Hepburn, Bette Davis, and Marlene Dietrich. On one wall, she had pinned up her tickets from every movie she had seen from the time she was ten years old.

She smiled as she touched the overlapping collage of film stubs and memories—she had seen some great films, but a lot of terrible ones as well. She hadn't known how to differentiate yet. All she knew was that there was no place she was happier than the air-conditioned multiplex on a Sunday afternoon.

On another wall were pictures of her favorite film couples—Bogie and Bacall, Liz and Dick, Maria and Tony, Richard and Julia, Rose and Jack, Harry and Sally, Satine and Christian, Buttercup and Westley...These made her feel wistful, remembering the girl she had been—endlessly lying in bed, staring up at these images of true love, feverishly spinning her own romantic future...God, that's probably why she'd never found the right guy. All these expectations. There was no way real-life romance could hold a candle to the glories of the silver screen.

She sighed and sank down onto her narrow bed. Her body fit into the mattress as if she were sixteen all over again. She turned her head on the pillow and took a deep breath. She could almost smell the Anaïs Anaïs perfume, Noxzema face wash, and Mane 'n Tail shampoo.

Oh, if she could only go back to that girl and give her some advice—let her know that the braces would come off, her skin would clear up, that being tall and smart were not such bad things after all. She would tell her what mistakes to avoid, what men to stay away from, not to spend so much time worrying that she'd be stuck in Wellington forever.

Except, of course, here she was, home again.

She tried to tell herself she'd come home for her parents' sake, but deeper down she couldn't ignore the niggling suspicion that she would have ended up back here anyway. There had been simply nowhere else to go. And prospects seemed dim that she'd make it back out this time. Unless she could finally find the way back to her work.

The buzz of the doorbell startled her. She groaned and buried her head in her pillow. Her first instinct was to ignore it—hoping that whoever it was would go away—but then, she reprimanded herself, she had come here to help, not hide in her room like a recalcitrant teen.

* * *

Sebastian felt foolish. A gigantic bouquet of purple, hot pink, and orange blooms—wisteria, peonies, and birds of paradise—blocked his view. The florist must have made a mistake. There was no way his mother would have ordered something so ostentatious. But he'd overslept and the flowers had been delivered before he had woken from his nap. He knew that if he bothered to take the time to return them and negotiate the exchange, he'd never get them dropped off and still make it to the club for the opening chukka.

The door swung open, and instead of the motherly-looking maid he was expecting, a tall woman with tan skin, high cheekbones, riotous black curls, and cool gray eyes looked back at him.

"Uh," he said, "Mrs. Parker?"

The woman shook her head. "She's out. Can I help you?"

Her voice was low and husky.

He blinked, momentarily forgetting why he was even there. There was something about her steady gaze that unnerved him. That, and the little beauty mark just above her upper lip. It looked like a tiny smudge of chocolate. "I uh—Mrs. Parker—"

"My mother," she prompted.

He nodded. Right. He'd forgotten that her daughter was in town. He looked at the flowers in his hands. "Ah, oh yes, these are for your *papá*. Your father." He thrust the enormous bouquet into her arms. "Courtesy of the Del Campo family."

The woman raised her brows, looking amused. "Wow. Well, I'm pretty sure this is the biggest bouquet my daddy's ever received." She ducked her head and smelled a peony, looking up at him through the fringe of her long, dark lashes. "Actually they're probably the only flowers he's ever received." She smiled.

Sebastian's heart constricted. Her smile was slow and sweet and absolutely dazzling. He felt breathless.

She looked at him expectantly for a moment longer, and then said, "Oh! Sorry! Wait. Hang on," and left him standing in the doorway.

He blinked, confused, and then she was back with her purse in her hand. She dug out a five-dollar bill and tried to hand it to him.

He stared at her bewildered.

She wrinkled her nose. "Is it—is it not enough?"

"What?"

"The tip?"

He almost laughed. She thought he was the delivery boy. She waited earnestly for his answer.

He smiled, mischievous. "Oh, well, normally it would be

fine, but you know, for around here..." He shrugged.

She flushed and pulled out another ten and offered it to him. He grinned and took the money from her.

A tingling bolt of electricity passed through his body as his fingers brushed hers.

Her eyes widened. She obviously felt it, too. He gazed at her for a moment—noticing the tight curves of her body beneath the simple jeans and tank top she was wearing, her shapely legs that seemed to go on forever. Suddenly, he felt a little less playful.

"I'm sorry," he said, "I didn't catch your name."

She frowned. "I didn't give it."

He took a step toward her. She didn't move. He smelled something sweet and dark—like caramel. He wondered if it was her or the flowers. "Maybe you should," he said.

She looked at him, her cheeks flushing an even deeper pink. "I—I don't think so."

She took a step back.

"Wait..." he said.

But she had already shut the door in his face.

Appendix

THE GAME OF POLO

Each TEAM is made up of 4 PLAYERS. The players are designated positions from 1 to 4 and wear the corresponding number on their team shirts. Player 1 is primarily offensive; Player 4 primarily defensive. Normally, the most experienced and highest handicap players play Positions 2 and 3, with Position 3 being akin to the captain or quarterback of the team.

Each player is given a HANDICAP from −2 (the worst) up to 10 goals (the best). Only a handful of the greatest professional players achieve the prestigious handicap of 10.

Polo is played on a large grass field—or PITCH—3,000 yards long and 160 yards wide. There are GOALPOSTS at either end, placed 8 yards apart.

THE GAME begins with players lined up in the center of the field. One of the 2 UMPIRES bowls the ball between the teams. The players then use a combination of speed, skill, and teamwork to mark each other—and to score.

Players SCORE by hitting the ball between the goalposts. A pony can score a goal for its team if it knocks the ball across the line between posts. After each goal, and at the end of each chukker, the teams change playing directions. Play resumes with another throw-in.

CHUKKA: The number of periods in which a game of polo is divided. Players change out their ponies between chukkas. There are generally six chukkas in a game (in Argentina there are eight and each chukka lasts approximately seven minutes.)

At HALFTIME, which is typically 5 minutes, the custom is for spectators to walk onto the polo field to tread in the clumps of turf—or DIVOTS—kicked up by ponies.

The horses ridden in polo are known as POLO PONIES, whatever their height. Originally, no horse taller than thirteen hands and two inches (54 inches) was allowed to play the game. Though the restriction was removed early in the twentieth century, the terminology has remained.

Polo ponies can be thoroughbred or mixed breed. What matters is that they are fit (they might run a couple of miles during each chukker), strong, disciplined, intelligent, and love to play. Some of the finest ponies are bred in Argentina. Most ponies begin their training at the age of five, and this can last from six months to two years. As with their riders, it takes many years to master the game, and most ponies reach their peak age around nine or ten. Barring accidents, a pony can continue to play until eighteen or twenty.

During a game, a player will use as many as eight ponies—known as a STRING OF PONIES. The higher the level of competition, the more ponies in a player's string.

ABOUT THE AUTHOR

Argentine polo player **Ignacio "Nacho" Figueras** has become one of the most recognizable and talented polo players in the world. He is currently the captain and co-owner of the Black Watch polo team.

In addition to playing polo, Nacho has been featured as a face of Ralph Lauren and its Black Watch clothing and watch collection since 2000. In June 2009, he was voted the second handsomest man in the world by the readers of *Vanity Fair* and has appeared on numerous television shows, such as *Oprah* and *Chelsea Lately*. Nacho currently splits his time between Miami and Argentina with his wife, Delfina, and their four children, Hilario, Aurora, Artemio, and Alba. Learn more at:

Facebook.com/NachoFigueras

Twitter @NachoFigueras

Jessica Whitman lives and writes in the Hudson Valley, New York.

Fall in Love with Forever Romance

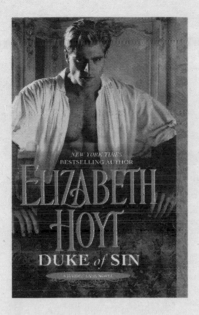

DUKE OF SIN
By Elizabeth Hoyt

Valentine Napier, the Duke of Montgomery, is the man London whispers about in boudoirs and back alleys. A notorious rake and blackmailer, Montgomery has returned from exile, intent on seeking revenge on those who have wronged him. But what he finds in his own bedroom may lay waste to all his plans.

Fall in Love with Forever Romance

NACHO FIGUERAS PRESENTS: HIGH SEASON
By Jessica Whitman

World-renowned polo player and global face of Ralph Lauren, Nacho Figueras dives into the world of scandal and seduction with the first book in the Polo Season series, all set in the glamorous, treacherous world of high-stakes polo competition. It's the perfect beach-reading for fans of Susan Elizabeth Phillips and Jill Shalvis.

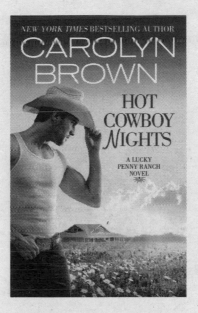

HOT COWBOY NIGHTS
By Carolyn Brown

New York Times and *USA Today* bestselling author Carolyn Brown brings us back to the Lucky Penny Ranch for some HOT COWBOY NIGHTS. Toby Dawson never was and never will be the settling-down type. But what harm could there be in agreeing to be Lizzy Logan's pretend boyfriend? They'll put on a show so all of Dry Creek knows Lizzy's over her ex, then be done. Yet the more Toby gets to know Lizzy—really know her—the harder it is for him to keep his hands off her in private.

Fall in Love with Forever Romance

PRIMAL INSTINCT
By Tara Wyatt

When Taylor's record label hires a bodyguard for her, she's less than thrilled to find it's her one-night stand, ex-army ranger Colt, who shows up for the job. But as danger from an obsessed stalker mounts, crossing the line between business and pleasure could get them both killed. Perfect for fans of Suzanne Brockmann, Pamela Clare, and Julie Ann Walker.